Breaking Clear

MJ SUMMERS

piatkus

PIATKUS

First published in the US in 2015 by HarperCollins Publishers Ltd
First published in Great Britain in 2015 by Piatkus

1 3 5 7 9 10 8 6 4 2

A CIP catalogue record for this book
is available from the British Library.

ISBN 978-0-349-40710-4

Printed and bound in Great Britain by CPI Group (UK) Ltd, Croydon, CRO 4YY

Papers used by Piatkus are from well-managed forests
and other responsible sources.

MIX
Paper from
responsible sources
FSC® C104740

Piatkus

For my beautiful children, O, E and A.
You've shown me just how full one's heart can be,
you remind me every single day that the world is full of
infinite possibilities, and you force me to continue
to grow and learn, whether I like it or not.
As with Grandma and Grandpa,
you three are never, ever to read my books.

Dear Reader,

Well, here it is—my third novel. If you had asked me two years ago if I would ever write a book, I would have looked behind me to see who you were talking to. And now, as I sit at my desk, hours away from completing my third novel, I find myself with a wonderful career that I can take anywhere and work on anywhere, creating stories that you can enjoy anywhere. Well, except the naughty scenes. There is a time and a place to enjoy them and most certainly a time and a place to write them.

Breaking Clear (Book 3 of the Full Hearts Series) is the story of old friends and new love. It is the story of a family trying to heal from a painful past and trying to make room for one another once again. It is the story of Harper Young, who I hope you met and loved in *Breaking Love* (Book 2 of the Full Hearts Series). She may be the life of the party, the strong, feisty best friend everyone wants to have, but she's also had her share of heartache that she does her very best to forget. She is about to become reacquainted with Evan Donovan, the super-hot boy next door who grew up to become a super-hot man. Their love story, like so many in real life, is full of ups and downs, tender moments and terrible arguments. They've both been hurt badly and need to help each other find their way home.

Unlike real life, their love story is a work of fantasy and as such, Evan and Harper do not have to practise safe sex. Were they real, they most certainly would.

Before we begin, I want to pass along my heartfelt gratitude for honouring me with your time as you start this story. It is because of you that I have a wonderful new life in which I can spend hours every day lost in worlds of my own creation, which, as far as I'm concerned, is the very best job on the planet. My sincerest hope is that you, too, will find your escape in these pages.

Happy reading,

MJ

Breaking Clear Playlist

"Sometime Around Midnight" by The Airborne Toxic Event
"Give Me Love" by Ed Sheeran
"Break Your Plans" by The Fray
"Foolish Games" by Jewel
"Detlef Schrempf" by Band of Horses
"Hold Fire" by Delays
"Let Your Hair Down" by Magic!
"Rotten Love" by Levy
"One More Night" by Stars
"Not a Bad Thing" by Justin Timberlake

Breaking Clear

ONE

The call came on a Thursday afternoon. It was an early summer day not unlike many Harper Young had spent as art director at *Style* magazine. She silenced the ringer on her cellphone without looking to see who it was. It would be several hours before she would check her messages and hear the news. It would be many months before she would realize that this was the call that had caused her carefully carved-out life to veer sharply in a direction she never could have anticipated. Sliding her phone back into the pocket of her trousers she continued to work, forgetting about the call completely.

"Stop, Assaf. Wait. The balance in this shot is off. We have one too many to the left." Harper strode quickly across the set and motioned to a tall, slim girl wrapped in a leather-belted trench coat.

Assaf, the photographer, nodded and a stylist whisked the girl away. Harper stepped over to one of the models to quickly adjust the collar on his jacket. She glanced at his face, her hands never stopping. "Dylan, was it? Your first day?"

The young man nodded.

"You're adorable. But you need to stop giving me the blue-steel look or you'll be fired." Turning back to the rest of the waiting team, she clapped her hands together. "Okay, everyone! Let's get moving. Music up. Models, eyes forward. Think cold winter streets, think frostbite—but sexy frostbite." This caused some people to laugh, and Harper smiled too. "That's it, people. Let's have some fun!" she called out, giving Assaf a wink.

Even though it was an unseasonably hot day in New York City, Harper's mind was on the November issue of the magazine, full of luxurious cashmeres, tall leather boots and the darker makeup trends that come with the winter season. Sia sang over the speakers as the camera snapped and the models pouted and turned under Assaf's direction. In her twelve years at the world's premier fashion magazine, Harper had spent the last four as art director, overseeing hundreds of shoots like this one. She controlled every detail, managed every crisis, commanded respect from everyone around her. She had made her way up the ladder and knew what it took to stay there. Decisiveness and confidence were every bit as important as knowledge of fashion.

This moment was her favourite—the thrilling culmination of weeks of planning and dozens of choices. This was when she felt most alive. The buzz of activity around her, the art and beauty she had envisioned being captured so it could be shared with the world. This was why she had gotten into fashion all those years ago. This made wading through all the challenges of tempers, prima donnas and nervous advertisers worth it. Tomorrow, in the quiet of her office, she would examine the contact sheets and see the fruits of her hard work; she would have that familiar sense of satisfaction in knowing she had done what she set out to do. Another moment she savoured.

Glancing at the door, she noticed her immediate boss, Blaire Jones, watching the shoot's progress. At forty-eight, Blaire looked closer to forty than fifty. Her petite frame did little to stop her from intimidating others wherever she went. Blaire gave Harper a quick nod before exiting the studio. After so many years working together, Harper was trusted to handle even the most important shoots and today's was no exception.

Harper eyed the lighting and was about to call out to Assaf when her cellphone buzzed in her pocket again. Taking the phone out, she saw it was her brother Craig calling. Putting her cell on silent mode, she made a mental note to call him back when the shoot was finished. Right now, she had to keep her eye on the room.

Boulder, Colorado

The sun ducked behind a fluffy white cloud, offering Evan Donovan a temporary respite from the heat as he reached into the chalk bag strapped to his waist with one hand, the other clinging to the tiny hold above his head. Glancing down, he could see the ground was at least a hundred feet away now, and a satisfied smile crossed his face as he reached his chalked fingers up to find the next hold. Climbing gave Evan a thrill that was beyond compare—the solitude, the freedom, the knowledge that he had both the determination and the staying power it took to make it to the top. Climbing wasn't just a sport for him. It was a reminder of how he wanted to live his life—taking smart risks that would lead to success. Taking risks required confidence, focus and drive, all of which he felt as intensely as the granite his body was pressed against. Here, he was unstoppable. Here, he would dominate. And there was nothing in the world like it.

Glancing down again, he called, "Hey, dog! You coming or what?" His dog, Boots, ignored him and continued sniffing around at the bottom of the cliff, searching for butterflies to chase. What he would do if he ever caught one, Evan didn't know. Boots, a massive grey pit bull, was probably the most gentle animal he'd ever come across. The dog had found Evan, not the other way around, six months ago when he had appeared late one evening at a new house Evan was building. He had been close to starving and bore both fresh wounds and old scars. Even now that his wounds had healed and he was healthy, Boots was a terrifying animal to look at, but he was quick to offer a big dog-smile, and his exuberant tail wagged his entire body whenever he greeted someone. "I'm going to beat you to the top!" Evan warned, chuckling to himself as he watched Boots peer up and then race to the trail that led around the side of the cliff and to the top of the ridge.

The cloud passed by, giving way to the sun again. Fresh beads of sweat formed on Evan's face. The heat didn't bother him, though. In fact, today, nothing could bother him. He'd finally gotten the approvals for all of the utilities on the largest land-development project of his career. He'd put in the bid over a year ago, knowing it was a long shot. But he had won it and now was back on top, putting a long distance between himself and the hardship the recession had caused. With all the permits in place, he could get his crews to work first thing Monday. And once everything got started, it would be a long time before he would find himself climbing again.

But this wasn't the moment to think about all of that. He needed to clear his mind of both his success and his responsibilities so he could stay focused on what his body was doing. Each muscle needed to work in unison to avoid a fall. Even though he was harnessed into safety gear, he knew from experience how painful it was to slam against the rock if he slipped.

Ten minutes later, with the last of his strength, he pulled his muscular body up over the side of the cliff, then stood and turned to take in the view. Boots, who had made it to the top already, hurried over to join him.

"Let's have some water and relax a while." Reaching into his pack for a bowl and a water bottle, he filled the dog's dish before plunking himself next to the animal. Evan endured Boots's customary face licks before wiping his cheek and sucking back a long, refreshing drink. Taking off his shirt, he used it to wipe the sweat from his face and chest before tossing it into his pack.

"We'd better enjoy this. As of Monday, we're going to be at work nearly every day for the next three years," he said, rubbing his hand over Boots's large, flat forehead.

As Evan's mind wandered back to his work, a mixture of pride and anxiety filled his belly. He knew what it was like to rise to the top and lose it all. But he would never fall like that again. The first time around, he had been young and reckless, spending money as quickly as it came in. And he had a wife with expensive tastes who liked to help rid him of his cash. This time would be different. Life had taught him to be smarter than that and to live modestly. If another recession hit, he would be ready. At thirty-eight, he was on his way again and this time nothing was going to stop him.

TWO

Manhattan, New York

Seven hours later, Harper stood in front of the door to her tiny apartment, digging around in her Balenciaga bag, frantically searching for her keys. She squirmed from side to side, wishing she had visited the ladies' before leaving the club, where she had been celebrating her assistant, Jasmine's, birthday. Four glasses of wine and a long cab ride were not a good combination.

"Should have gone at the club . . ." she sang urgently as her fingers finally grasped the keys.

Letting herself into the apartment, she locked the deadbolt, tossed her bag onto the counter, kicked off her heels and scurried to the bathroom, making a wide turn around one of the racks of clothes and accessories that lined the wall. The racks gave the room an unfinished look, but it was something she had learned to live with. Her need for an extensive wardrobe far outweighed her desire to live in a beautiful space. Besides, she was rarely home other than to sleep. Returning a few minutes later to the cramped space that doubled as kitchen and living room, Harper brushed her teeth with one hand while she searched her purse for her cell-phone, hazily remembering there was something she had forgotten to do.

"Uh-oh," she muttered when she realized that her brother Craig had called three more times.

She dialed her voice mail, putting her cell on speaker to listen to her messages.

"Harper, it's Craig. Call me back as soon as you get this. It's about Dad."

She deleted the message and spit the toothpaste into the kitchen sink, her heart quickening in her chest as the next message began.

"Harper, where are you? Call me." Click.

"Harper, it's Craig. I wish you would call me back. I don't want to leave this on your voice mail but this is the third time I've tried you. Dad's been in an accident at work. I don't know exactly what happened. He's been rushed to the hospital. They don't know if he's going to make it . . ." Craig's voice trailed off, followed by a long pause. "I'm waiting for a call to find out more. I'm off the coast of Texas right now and I can't get home for at least a couple of days."

Harper's hands shook as she forced herself to listen to his next message. "I don't know where the hell you are. He's still in surgery. Can you please call me back as soon as you get this?"

Dialing her brother's number, Harper slid to the floor, waiting to hear the worst.

"There you are. What the fuck, Harper?" Craig answered.

"I'm so sorry . . . Is he . . . ?"

"He made it out of surgery. He's in intensive care."

Harper took a gulp of air. "Oh God. What happened?"

"A part of the building they were working on collapsed. The guys on his crew said the beam that landed on his back weighs at least five hundred pounds. It took four of them to lift it off Dad." Craig's voice cracked. He cleared his throat before going on. "If he makes it, they think he's going to be paralyzed."

"Shit," Harper whispered, tears streaming down her cheeks as she leaned her head on the cupboard door.

"How fast can you get home?" Craig asked.

Harper's breath caught as she tried to stifle a sob. "I'll start looking for a flight now. Maybe I can get on a red-eye or something." Standing, Harper wiped her face as she hurried over to her laptop. "Does Wes know?"

"Not yet. I can't reach him. I think they're doing some night raids right now. I left a message with his staff sergeant."

"Okay. Okay, Craig. I'll get there as soon as I can. I promise."

"Thanks, Harper." Craig let out a long puff of air. "I just don't want him to be alone, you know?"

"I won't let that happen, Craig. I promise, I'll get there."

* * *

Twenty minutes later, Harper sat in the back of a cab watching the buildings whiz by, her knees shaking. Though she was freezing, she could feel hot tears streaming down her face. She needed to get to her dad. She needed to see him. She couldn't let Roy be alone in the face of death or his now-uncertain future. He had been there for Harper her entire life. And for most of her life, he was the only one who had been there. Her mother had left them when Harper was fifteen years old. They had heard from her only a handful of times since then, each call reopening the wound she had inflicted.

When his wife left, she took Roy's heart with her. He shut down for several months, barely speaking other than to give one-word answers. When he finally emerged from the darkness, a quieter, slower-to-smile man remained. He finished the job of raising his children, doing his level best to help all three of them as they suffered through their teenage years without a mother.

It had been especially hard on Harper, the only female in the house, without a mom to guide her. Roy, a tough-as-nails construction foreman, struggled to understand his youngest child, a creative and fiery girl who seemed to want to run free in a way that terrified him. Looking back, Harper could see how he had pushed through his own discomfort to help her when she was going through the inevitable high school drama, or to awkwardly answer questions she had about boys, his usual response being, "They're all idiots; stay away from them." He'd focused on ensuring that she would grow into a strong woman who could handle whatever life threw at her. And in this endeavour he had been a tremendous success, something Harper now wished she had told him. Why hadn't she taken the time to thank him properly for everything he had done and given up for her? He hated overt displays of emotion, but surely she could have found a way to let him know what he meant to her.

The guilt she felt at not picking up Craig's calls squeezed at her chest. Why hadn't she answered the damn phone? She could be in Boulder by now, already at her dad's side. Please let him live, she prayed silently. If she could just get there by the time he woke up, she would say everything she had neglected to tell him.

Boulder, Colorado

Harper sat listening to the incessant beeps of the machines hooked up to her father, her eyes refusing to stay open. Head bobbing down to her chin, she jerked herself awake for the hundredth time. She had flown through the night, with two stopovers between New York and Boulder. Checking her watch, she saw it was evening already. She'd been sitting by her dad's bed for ten hours now but he hadn't stirred since the surgery. Harper was starting to worry, having been told that he should be awake by now. Instead, he lay there, a halo brace attached to his head and shoulders. The only signs of life were in the low rise and fall of his chest and the bright green lines on the display that served to represent his vital signs. Getting to her feet, Harper stretched her back and walked over to the window to take in the last of the sunset over the mountains in the distance. Her silent prayers continued as darkness blanketed the world. *Let him live. Let him be okay.*

"Petra?" a voice croaked behind her.

Harper turned, relief hitting her first before the horror registered. Her dad was awake. And he'd just called her Petra. Pushing that aside, she rushed to him and grabbed his hand. She could feel his fingers faintly squeezing hers. Or had she just imagined it?

His eyes were full of emotion as he stared at her, seeing someone else. "Petra . . . You're back. Missed you"—he pressed his fingers to her palm again, this time she was sure—"so much."

"No, Dad. It's me. Harper." But he had already slid back into unconsciousness.

Her dad had spoken. And his fingers had moved. She *felt* them move. The fracture to the top of his spine must not have robbed him of the ability to use his upper body. And if they were really lucky, when he woke again, he would have feeling in his legs. Then everything would be alright.

Harper was suddenly fully awake. A jolt of adrenalin at hearing her dad's voice and seeing his eyes open had given her renewed energy. She rubbed her hand over his gently. "I'm right here, Dad. I'm not going anywhere."

She pushed the call button to summon a nurse before grabbing her phone and dialing Craig's number. Swallowing the lump in her throat when she heard her brother's voice, she gave him the news he'd been waiting for. "Craig, he woke up for a second and said a few words!"

"Seriously? So, that must be a good sign, right?"

"I'd say so. He squeezed my hand! It was almost nothing, but he did it twice!" Harper could hardly keep her voice steady.

"Yes! What a relief! What about his legs? Has he moved them yet?"

"Nothing yet," Harper answered.

"Let's hope for the best. I'll get word to Wes."

"Thanks, Craig. I'll let you go."

"Sure . . . And, Harper, thank you for getting there so fast. I'm glad you're with him."

"Me too. I feel like the lucky one to be able to be here."

"Hey, what did he say," Craig asked.

"Oh, that. It wasn't really coherent. I think he must have been dreaming."

When Harper got off the phone, she sat back down in the chair next to Roy's bed. Tucking her knees into her chest, she hugged her arms around them and stared at her dad's hand, a nagging feeling coming over her. She had lied to Craig. She had heard exactly what he'd said. But there was no point in bringing up Petra's name with Craig. That would only leave him with the same pain she felt. Roy had mistaken her for their mother. A woman who was nothing but a painful memory. A woman who'd turned their lives into the most sordid of scandals, a topic for gossip in their not-so-small town. A woman Harper pretended she didn't see when she looked in the mirror. Most days, a woman Harper could successfully forget had ever existed. But being mistaken for Petra by her father made that impossible right now. Did her dad really still miss her after more than twenty years? After what she'd put him through? He couldn't. He must have been dreaming.

THREE

Manhattan, New York

The following Tuesday, Harper was back at work after spending three emotional days at her father's bedside. Blaire sat propped on the edge of Harper's desk, listening as Harper recounted her trip home.

"I promised I'd go back to take care of him when he gets out of the hospital."

"Really?" Blaire's eyes grew wide.

"It's something I have to do. The man basically raised us on his own. He did everything he could to hold things together after my mom walked out. I can't leave him on his own now, when he needs me most."

"What about your brothers? Couldn't one of them look after him?" Blaire asked.

Harper shook her head. "Wes won't be home from his tour for another year, and Craig can't exactly drill for oil from home, whereas I could probably do a lot of my work from there. Craig's home a month then gone for a month, so I could alternate living there and here for a little while. It could work, couldn't it?"

"Hmm. Well, maybe. You wouldn't be able to oversee the photo shoots, but you could plan them and do edits from there. I can direct the shoots you can't be here for, or the ones where we're on location. It wouldn't be ideal but I'm sure we could make it work."

"Thanks, Blaire. I was hoping you'd say that."

"It's not me you have to worry about," Blaire said as she sipped her coffee.

Wincing, Harper gave Blaire a tentative look. "I know. I also need your help to convince Hartless to let me go."

"That might be a bit harder, but I'll speak up for you. You are the best in the business, so that's got to count for something."

Harper's assistant, Jasmine, knocked on the open door of the office. "Hartless wants to see you right away."

"Super," Harper groaned sarcastically as she stood, picking up her notebook. "Wish me luck."

"Luck," Blaire replied, plucking her coffee off the desk and walking out the door.

* * *

Cybill Hart, or Hartless, as the staff called her behind her back, had been the editor-in-chief of *Style* since the magazine's inception. She had clawed her way to the top, not caring whose back she scarred, until she sat as one of the most powerful figures in the fashion industry.

Harper rapped on Cybill's door as she entered, then adjusted the cuffs on her royal-blue silk shirt and smoothed her wide-leg grey trousers. She seated herself in the chair opposite Cybill's desk without a word. Waiting for Cybill to acknowledge her presence, Harper sat wishing she had taken time for full makeup instead of a hurried dusting of bronzer and a single swipe of mascara as she dashed out the door. She knew the dark circles under her eyes would not go unnoticed by Cybill, who insisted that her staff look polished at all times.

"Ah, Harper. There you are. How was your vacation?" she asked distractedly as she looked over a set of layouts.

"I wasn't on vacation. You'll recall my email in which I explained that my father was in the hospital in critical condition?" Harper's voice was dripping with a sweetness as fake as a box of Splenda.

"Right. Of course. How did that turn out?" Cybill asked impassively, without looking up.

"Fine, Cybill. He made it."

"I'm sure that's a relief for you. Now, what are you going to do to get caught up for those days you missed?"

"Work faster."

"Well, if that's possible, why don't you do it all the time?" Her eyes flicked up to Harper before returning to the layouts in front of her.

"Everyone on the team has had four extra days to get ahead of me. Normally I have to wait for them."

Cybill's gaze finally settled on Harper. She stared her down for a moment before answering. "I see. So everyone else here is just too slow for the great Harper Young."

"That's not what I meant. Everyone here works hard, Cybill. We get the job done."

Cybill shrugged. "I suppose. I don't know. I'm getting bored with your work lately."

Harper stared at her, feeling confused. Though she hadn't seen the spreads, she knew the shoot had been perfect. Then she realized what this was about. The month before, at a departmental meeting, she and Cybill had had a very public disagreement about which mood to set for a fall casual-wear shoot. Harper had let her temper get the better of her, and instead of holding her tongue, she had told Cybill she was way off base on this one. The room had fallen silent, everyone waiting to see how Cybill would react. She had smirked, asking "Am I, now? Well, as long as my nameplate says editor-in-chief under it, I'd like you to remember that I am the base."

They'd gone ahead with Cybill's plans for the shoot, only to have to redo it once Hartless had seen the results. She had stormed into Harper's office to yell at her, accusing her of screwing it up on purpose. The episode had cost the magazine thousands of dollars that it couldn't afford to spend. Harper now realized that Cybill had been waiting for the perfect moment to pounce on her about it, and the moment had arrived.

She sat quietly, hating the fact that she needed to ask for time off to care for her dad. She knew that Cybill could very well refuse, forcing her to make a very difficult decision.

Trying to remove any hint of anger from her voice, Harper replied, "Well, if you're finding my work boring, maybe what I'm about to ask you for will actually be to your liking." She paused, seeing she had Cybill's undivided attention now. "I need to take some time off to look after my father while he recovers. He has no one else, and my brothers and I can't afford full-time care for him without wiping out our savings. I wouldn't have to leave until he's let out of the hospital, which is a couple of months away. I have five weeks of unused vacation time, and I can work from there so you won't have to do without me entirely. I'd be back every other month when my brother is home from his job. Blaire said she can direct any photo shoots I miss."

Cybill's right eyebrow shot up, never a good sign. She leaned back in her seat with the tiniest trace of a smirk on her lips. The look in her eyes was that of a cat with one claw dug so deep into its prey that there would be no escape. "You want to take a few months off? Why, of course, Harper. It's no problem, really. I'll just call an emergency board meeting and let them know we won't be putting out any issues this winter. Then I'll order Accounting to give back all the money we've gotten from our advertisers. I'm sure no one will mind."

She sat up, smoothing back her perfectly coiffed blond hair with one hand before pressing the intercom button on her phone. "Victoria, grab your notebook and come in. Harper has decided we don't need to put out the magazine for a few months. I'll need you to notify everyone immediately."

"Um, okay, ma'am. I'll be right in," Victoria responded quickly.

Harper glared at her boss now, finding it impossible to hide her loathing for another second. "People have family emergencies, Cybill. It happens. They need time off at some point in their lives, and then they return. It's part of life. It's unrealistic to think this kind of thing will never happen."

Victoria hurried into the room, flashing a look of concern in Harper's direction. She stood silently, waiting to be addressed by her boss, pen at the ready.

"Victoria, apparently I'm unrealistic. Can you pencil in some time for a reality check for me?"

Victoria nodded, writing and muttering, "Schedule reality check."

Harper dug her nails into her palms. She hadn't realized her career had been circling the bowl, but she knew now that Cybill's bony finger had been firmly positioned on the handle and she was about to flush.

"I've been here for over twelve years, Cybill. All-nighters, week-ends, cancelled vacations, whatever you needed, whenever you needed it. Twelve years. Now I'm asking you to let me work from Colorado for a few months, using my vacation time and getting some-one to cover for me. You won't notice that I'm gone. I promise."

"Victoria, schedule Harper into that same reality check as me. I think we're suffering from the same illness."

FOUR

The sun beat down on the cab of the Rent-Haul truck as Harper drove west for the third straight day. She slammed her fist on the dash, hoping that the air conditioning would magically start working. Of course it didn't. Taking a swig of her now sickeningly warm water, she glanced down at the navigation screen on her cellphone. It showed that she still had four hundred miles of driving ahead of her. But that was without any delays. At the moment, she was stuck in a line of fed-up motorists that was so long she couldn't see the front of it. Construction had the traffic moving slower than she could walk.

Her phone rang. It was Megan Sullivan, her best friend in the world.

Harper pressed the hands-free icon on her cell phone. "Hey, Megs."

"Hey, you. Where are you at?"

"Still in Nebraska. Fucking construction everywhere. It's going to be at least six hours before I'm home. Maybe ten, for all I know."

"Well, come here first when you get to town. Luc's just at the market with Elliott and he plans to spend the afternoon in the kitchen, so there will be one amazing welcome-home dinner waiting for you."

"Thanks, hon. If I'm there even close to supper, I'll come by. But I'm warning you, I'm a revolting, sweaty mess. I'm going to have to throw out this D&G T-shirt I wore today. It's about two hundred degrees in this truck right now, and there is no way I can salvage this thing."

"Oh God, the air conditioning broke?"

"Of course it did. Somewhere in the middle of Ohio. Right when we're at the end of the hottest June on record. But it's fine. I need to lose ten pounds, so I'm trying to pretend I'm in a steam room at some swanky country club."

Megan laughed. "Ten pounds? More like ten ounces, tops. How are you doing?"

Harper sighed heavily. "I'm at about a level eight on the 'my life is poo' chart. I think I'm still in shock. I can't seem to wrap my head around the fact that I'm unemployed. I did not see that coming. *Style* is my whole life."

"I can't believe it either. It's insane. You'll land on your feet, though. You're so connected in the industry, you'll find something even better when you're able to go back to work."

"I wish I was as sure of that as you are. Cybill is probably doing a lot of damage to my reputation as I sweat. She can make it very difficult for anyone to ever want to be seen with me again, let alone hire me. Fucking witch."

"She is a witch. I'm just glad you managed to get in a few shots before you left."

"It did feel good at the time, but now I'm thinking I probably shouldn't have asked if she'd had Botox injected into her heart to stop her from having feelings or if she'd just had her face frozen into place so no one would know she was having an emotion. That may not have been the smartest choice."

Megan burst into laughter. "I'm sorry, I know I shouldn't laugh, but she so badly deserved it. I hope she falls off the earth and is never heard from again." Harper could hear a little cooing sound in the background. "Amelie agrees. Cybill's a total shit."

Harper laughed. "Tell her thank you from Auntie Harper. I'm glad she knows a shit when she hears about one. Smart little monkey. What's she doing?"

"Having lunch."

"How's that going, by the way?"

"Good. She's nursing a lot better now and she's not as fussy as she was for a while there."

"I'm glad."

"Us, too. It's getting much easier. It was a rough couple of months at the beginning. Part of me was expecting Luc to get on a plane and head back to France for good once he realized how tough it is with a newborn in the house."

"No chance. Luc's not going anywhere, Megan. In all the years I've known him, he's never sounded happier."

Just as she finished her sentence, Amelie started making some fussing sounds. "Oh good Lord, you should smell what just erupted from my daughter's bottom. I think I'm going to puke."

"Eeew, I'm going to puke just hearing about it," Harper replied. "I'll let you go deal with that."

"I better. My eyes are watering. Sorry, Harper. Call me later to let me know if you aren't coming. Otherwise, just show up."

"Sounds good. Thanks, Megs. Tell Luc thank you from me."

As Harper hung up, traffic started moving again and a hot breeze blew through the truck's cab. It didn't so much cool her down as relieve her from the suffocating heat she had been sitting in for the past twenty minutes. She groaned loudly to herself. Each mile was bringing her closer to a past she had left behind, one she'd been running from her entire adult life. She was about to come face to face with all of it, with all those people who knew about her mother and the shame she'd brought on their family. Each time Harper had gone home before, the glamour of her career had allowed her to hold her head high, to brush off those old feelings of humiliation. But now she had no career to hold up as a shield. And she wasn't going to be able to make her usual quick appearance, then dash off. She would be there for the long haul.

FIVE

Boulder, Colorado

Nine hours later, Harper pulled up in front of her childhood home, turning off the engine with a sense of doom. "I don't want to do this," she told herself as she rubbed her burning eyes, then searched through her purse for her house keys. It was late in the evening and she had missed dinner at Luc and Megan's, stopping for a deeply unsatisfying chicken burger and fries along the way. She could still taste the grease coating the inside of her mouth as she collected the garbage scattered around the seat and scrunched up the bag that had held her supper.

Sitting in front of her old house, reality started to set in. She was here to stay as her father made his painful recovery. The three days she had spent in the truck were nothing compared to what was coming. Opening her door, she slid down, dragging her bag along with her as she exited the truck. She would leave unpacking for tomorrow. Right now all she wanted was a cold beer, a long shower and to drop into bed for about twenty hours straight.

After letting herself into the house, Harper undressed and turned the tap to full to heat the water for her shower. Nothing happened. Not one drop of water came out. "What the . . ." she muttered to herself, walking over to the sink and trying it, only to get the same result.

"Are you fucking kidding me?" she inquired of the sink.

Hurrying to the kitchen in the nude, she grabbed her cell and dialed her brother's number. He would know what was wrong. No answer.

She texted him.

Craig. I'm at Dad's and the effing water isn't working. I smell worse than Wes after he plays hockey. I NEED a shower. Do you know how to get the water working?

Looking out the kitchen window, she glanced at the Morleys' house across the street. "Never."

She noticed the light of the TV in the living room of the bungalow next to theirs. Mr. Patterson was home. He would know what to do! He had been a plumber before he retired. In Harper's mind, he was also one of the few people in the world who wouldn't be horrified by her current disgusting state. Donning her dad's old blue bathrobe and his flip-flops, she scurried across the street, hoping the dark sky would cloak her. The door opened after her first knock and a teenage girl gave her a surprised look. "Yes?"

"Oh, sorry. Does Mr. Patterson not live here anymore?"

"No. I think he went to Florida, maybe? We moved in a couple of months ago," she responded, looking Harper up and down with wide eyes. "Can I help you with something?"

"Not unless you're a plumber, by chance. My dad lives across the street." She pointed at the house. "I just got to town and the water's not working. I've been driving all day and I'm desperate for a shower."

"Um, well, I don't think my parents would want me to let a strange lady in to use our shower. Sorry," she answered, starting to close the door.

"No, no. That's not what I meant. Sorry to have bothered you—" she said as the door shut. "Please forget this ever happened," Harper said as she turned to leave, her cheeks flushed with embarrassment.

She crossed the street, only to discover that she had locked herself out of the house. "Oh yeah, this might as well happen," she snarled. She would have to climb the fence. The spare key was hidden near the back door and the gate latch was inaccessible from outside the fence. Her father had a lot of expensive equipment in his workshop and was careful about securing it. Finding a break in the shrubs along the wooden fence, she put one foot on a low branch to steady herself as she hoisted herself up with both hands. Managing to boost herself to the top of the fence, she got one leg over, praying no one would see her. Her robe was doing little now to hide the fact that she was nude under it. Once on top of the wood, she realized what a long drop it was to the other side. Jumping down had suddenly become a frightening proposition.

"Oh, Harper, why did you do this?" she groaned, as the old fence teetered under her weight.

"I was just wondering the same thing," came a voice from behind her.

The voice was low and amused and it was one she would recognize anywhere. It made her heart skip a beat, just like it had done since she was fourteen years old. It was the voice of Evan Donovan, the one she had secretly lusted after almost her whole life, the one all the girls lusted after. He had played football and hockey, and was gorgeous and cocky as hell, but with the game to back up his attitude. He had been three years ahead of her in school, a classmate and close friend of her brother Wes. Even though they'd lived next door to each other until Evan went off to college, he had never noticed her. Until now. When she was perched on top of a fence. In nothing but a ratty bathrobe. And was all sweaty, with smudged makeup and her hair piled on top of her head with a metal clip.

Please have a comb-over and a huge paunch, she begged silently, turned her head, her face and neck now burning with humiliation. Harper reluctantly took in the sight of the muscular frame his blue T-shirt and jeans were displaying on his behalf. As her eyes travelled up his body, a sexy grin spread across his face, causing those dimples in his cheeks to pop. Nope. Still insanely hot.

Clearing her throat, she tried her best to sound casual about her current circumstances. "I seem to have locked myself out. And now I'm a little bit stuck up here."

"You always were a little bit stuck-up, so this seems about right," he teased, moving closer to her.

"Stuck-up?" she asked with righteous indignation. "That's not . . ." Turning back to him again, she saw him step toward her, which reminded her of how naked she was. "Stay back!" she ordered. She could not let him see her like this. She was going to look her best when she ran into him again. Hair and makeup perfect, wearing just the right outfit. It was not going to happen this way.

He stopped on the spot. "How am I supposed to help you from back here?"

"You won't. The thing is, I am fairly naked under this robe, and if you come any closer, you might . . . see things," Harper explained.

"I'm pretty sure I've seen those things before. It won't exactly ruin me for life," Evan replied.

"Well, you haven't seen my things before, and I think we should keep it that way. Besides, I really don't need any help. I've got it."

"Okay. But I'm guessing that leg you've swung up on the fence is starting to hurt. You sure you don't need a hand?"

"Nope. I'm good," Harper answered, trying to shift her weight to relieve some of the pressure of the wood cutting into her thigh. Damn him for being right!

Her movement caused the fence to start teetering even more than when she first climbed it, which in turn made her lose her balance and fall backwards. "Oh shit!" she cried in a tiny, high-pitched voice.

She didn't land in the pokey branches of the shrub below as she had feared might happen. She landed somewhere much more comfortable for her body but much more uncomfortable for her sense of decency. She landed in Evan's strong arms, her robe now fully open, the sash hanging uselessly from a nail on the fence.

"Gotcha!" he said as he caught her. His eyes grew wide as he caught sight of her full breasts so close to his face. Quickly setting her down on her feet, he glued his gaze to the grass as she closed the robe tightly around her body. Reaching for the sash, he plucked it off the fence and handed it to her before turning away to let her finish securing it around her waist.

"You all set?" he asked over his shoulder.

"Yes. Thank you for catching me," she answered, her voice businesslike.

Evan turned and smiled at her, a hint of laughter in his eyes. "No problem. Really. I didn't mind as much as you might think."

Harper shut her eyes tight, knowing he was referring to having seen her breasts. Her embarrassment was being edged out by excitement that he seemed so impressed.

"So, we need to figure out how to get you into the house, and then get your water on."

"Yes. Do you have a ladder or something?" She tapped her chin with a finger. "Wait. What are you even doing here? And how do you know about the water?"

"I live next door. I bought my parents' house from them a couple of years ago," Evan answered, pointing to the house beside them with his thumb. "Craig texted me to turn the water back on for you." Pulling a key out of his pocket, he held it up to her. "I watch your dad's place for him when he goes to Mexico in the winter."

Harper's face brightened as he dropped the key into her hand. The luxury of soap and water was in her near future. Now if only she could erase his memory of having seen her all sweaty and horribly dressed. And maybe her breasts too. No, that part she could live with.

"Who shut off the water?" she asked as they crossed the lawn together and walked up the steps to the small bungalow.

"I did. You're supposed to turn off the main waterline if you're going to be away for more than a few days. I can show you how to do it," he answered, following her into the house.

"Can we do the tutorial another time? I'm beat. I've been driving with no air conditioning for three days straight."

"You drove that rig across the country yourself?" Evan asked. "I gotta say, Harper, I'm impressed." He gave her a nod of approval.

"This might come as a surprise to you, but I didn't do it to impress you. Unlike most females in Colorado, I don't make every move with you in mind."

He chuckled a little. "You might be giving me too much credit, but either way, it's my loss. Be right back," he said, jogging down the stairs to the utility room.

Harper's heart pounded as she searched through her purse and was rewarded by a package of blotting papers. Furiously dabbing at her face, she hoped the effort would help at least a little. A moment later, the pipes groaned loudly and a sputtering sound erupted from the bathroom as water started to gush from the taps. She rushed to turn off both faucets before walking back to the hall in time to see Evan ascending the stairs.

"There you go," he announced. "It's going to be about twenty minutes before the hot water is ready, though."

"Can I offer you a beer while I wait?" Harper asked, not wanting him to leave just yet. He'd already seen her looking like hell, so she might as well drink in a little more time with him. "It's the least I can do to thank you."

"That would be nice. I think I'll take you up on that." He stared at her a second longer than he should have before settling himself at the small kitchen table. Harper tried not to notice how the muscles in his arms rippled as he leaned back in his chair and rested his hands behind his head. A flash of him running those strong hands all over her body pierced her mind, and she quickly looked away before those sexy, ice-blue eyes of his read her thoughts.

Harper opened the fridge, knowing it would be stocked with Budweiser. Not disappointed, she pulled two cans out and seated herself in the chair opposite his, sliding a can across the table to Evan's waiting hand before cracking hers open and taking a long swig.

"If I were stuck-up, would I be in my dad's ancient bathrobe, drinking beer out of a can?" she asked as she rested the beer on the table.

Evan smirked as though satisfied that his joke when she was up on the fence had finally landed. "Sure, you'll do that when you're back in Colorado, but I bet your high-class fashionista friends in Manhattan and Paris have never seen you with a can of Bud in your hand. I'm sure it's either wine or dry martinis."

"You know the word fashionista? That surprises me somehow."

"I'm a man of the world now." He grinned at her playfully. "There are all sorts of things I know that would surprise you."

"Really?" Harper tried to sound unimpressed, then took a long sip of cold beer to stop herself from asking him to describe those things in detail. "So, how come I've never seen you here if you've been living next door for two years?"

"I've been wondering the same thing. We must keep missing each other. I go visit my parents and Karen's family down in Arizona for most holidays. When I'm in town, I'm not home much."

"Why not?"

"I've been accused of being a workaholic, and when I'm not at work I'm usually hanging from a cliff somewhere."

"Hanging from a cliff? Like Tom Cruise in *Mission Impossible*."

Evan laughed. "Something like that. Except I actually do all my own stunts."

"So does he, apparently."

"Nah, he pays people to say that."

"Still cocky, I see . . ." She pressed her lips into a fine line.

"You mean charmingly confident. But yes. Anyway, I should let you hit the shower. Thanks for the beer."

"Any time," Harper answered, her voice verging on a purr. Disgusted with herself, she straightened up. "Thanks for saving me."

"My pleasure," he replied, his amused expression returning as he stood and started for the front door. "Just don't tell your brothers I saw your tatas. They'd try to kick my ass even though it wasn't in any way my fault."

Harper's face scrunched in embarrassment at the memory. "Deal. How about neither of us ever mentions it or thinks about it again."

A slow smile spread across his face. "I might be able to stop myself from talking about it, but I can't promise I won't think about it."

"Well, in that case, you should probably let me see what's under your clothes so we'll be even," she proposed, planting a fist on her hip.

He gave her a flirty grin, his dimples making an encore appearance. "Better not. If I show you what's under here, it would ruin you for other men for the rest of your life."

Before shutting the door, Harper watched him stride across the grass to his house. She didn't need him to take his clothes off. She was imagining what was under them all on her own, and just the thought of it had ruined her for other men a long time ago.

* * *

Evan got into bed that night with a lighter feeling than he had most nights, and it had everything to do with Harper Young. She'd always been a cute, feisty teenager, with that lanky body of hers. Back then, she had barely spoken two words to him, not that he had ever really tried to get her talking. He could tell she was a real handful, watching her with her dad and her brothers. Smart. Fiery temper. Determined. Even at fifteen, she was going places.

He hadn't seen her since he'd left to play hockey for Montana State. Time had clearly been kind to her, though, adding all those curves to that slight frame. Now, twenty years later, as Evan lay in bed staring up at the ceiling, he couldn't get her out of his mind. Or rather, he couldn't get those gorgeous breasts of hers out of his mind. Those were breasts a guy could lose himself in for a good long while. It had been far too long since he'd been able to lose himself like that, and he knew he was going to struggle not to think about her, knowing she was just next door.

SIX

Harper woke to the sound of the birds outside her window, feeling refreshed. It was a sunny, beautiful day and she had slept hard, dropping off as soon as her head hit the pillow. Looking at the clock, she saw that it was a quarter to eight. She hopped out of bed and went to brush her teeth and wash her face. She was going straight to the hospital to see her dad. Unpacking could wait.

Her face warmed when she thought of Evan and the feeling of his strong arms catching her as she fell. He had put her down quickly but not before she got a whiff of his aftershave. She could picture the lust in his eyes when her robe came open and his sideways grin as he teased her. And those dimples she wanted to lick. Splashing water onto her face, she saw the colour returning to her cheeks as decades of desire for him rekindled. It was like the flame on one of those trick candles that, no matter how hard you blow, won't go out.

An image of him looking up at her as she teetered on the fence flashed before her: his gorgeous face, wearing an expression of surprise and amusement that softened his chiselled features; his broad shoulders and powerful torso that narrowed at the waist; his dark brown hair, a thick mass of waves cut shorter now than when they were teens. After all these years, this man still affected her like no other. He was rugged and rough around the edges, and he stirred feelings that made her blush—first crush–type feelings, with all the excitement and novelty that comes with them. Feelings that caused her to memorize his every word, every look, every tone of voice. Now that life had deposited her next door to him, she wasn't sure how she was going to handle being so near a man no one could even begin to compare to. He wasn't just a man. He was *the* man. And she knew without a doubt that she would be utterly unable to resist shamelessly throwing herself at him if he paid her even the slightest bit more interest.

She pulled out the last set of clothes in her overnight bag—black slim-fit cropped pants and a light-knit white boat neck sweater for a classic summer look. Tying her auburn hair back in a ponytail and quickly applying her makeup, she stood for a moment, satisfied with what she had accomplished. She looked natural enough that it wouldn't seem like she was trying, but she had still managed to raise her cheekbones a little and make her eyes that much bigger and her lips that much fuller. She found herself wishing she'd run into Evan today, when she looked put together.

Three hours later, she was back at the house, having visited her dad and picked up some groceries. She made her way out to the Rent-Haul with a groan, not wanting to face the job ahead of her. Lifting the rolling door on the back of the truck, she noticed that everything had shifted during the trip. Several boxes had spilled their contents, leaving magazines and books scattered. "Crap," she said to herself, climbing up into the back.

Just as she had finished returning the contents to their boxes, she heard a truck pull up behind her. Risking a glance, she saw it was Evan. She watched as he got out, tossing his keys in the air and catching them as he approached. He was dressed in a white tank top and dark grey shorts, an outfit she would have hated if it hadn't been displaying his considerable muscles. He took off his aviators when he reached the shade of the rental. A stout grey dog with white paws stood next to him, wagging his body enthusiastically at Harper.

"If it isn't the girl next door!" Evan announced. "Can I give you a hand?"

"I could use both, actually," she answered.

"Then you can have 'em both. You pass things down and I'll haul them to the house."

"Perfect." As she turned to select a couple of boxes, Harper could feel Evan's eyes on her as she bent down. Or maybe that was just wishful thinking on her part. He had been flirty the night before but, of course, he would be. She'd flashed her breasts at him. "I didn't know you had a dog."

"It's more like he has me," Evan replied. "This is Boots. He's a little hard to look at but he more than makes up for it with personality."

"I can see that," Harper said, looking over at the dog, who was panting happily at her.

"So, what were you up to this morning?" she asked, hoping this casual question would provide an answer to whether or not he was with anyone.

"I met a few friends to do some climbing out at the Flatirons. Perfect day for it."

"Sounds fun. I'll come with you so I can show you where I'm putting everything." She slid a few boxes to the back edge of the truck, then started to climb down. Evan moved in to help her, taking her by the waist and gently lowering her to the ground in front of him.

Their eyes locked. "Thank you," she said, annoyed at how breathy her words sounded.

"Anytime," he answered, picking up two large boxes and carrying them toward the house.

Boots gave Harper's leg a nudge, clearly hoping for some pats.

Harper smiled down at him, her hands too full to give in to his request. She gave him an inquisitive look. "Why Boots?"

Evan winced, then laughed. "I let my niece and nephew name him. When I agreed to Boots, I thought it was because of his white paws, but later I found out I had named my dog after the monkey on that *Dora* cartoon."

Harper laughed with him. "Why didn't you change it?"

"Ah, it suits him. Plus, I gave them my word they could pick his name. I couldn't go back on that."

"Makes sense." She gazed at him for a minute, taking in what he'd just said. A hotter-than-hell man who kept his promises. But that must just be talk meant to impress her. No one really kept their promises.

Just as she was starting to feel excited about an afternoon alone with Evan, she heard another truck pull up and suddenly there stood Craig. Harper felt a mix of happiness at seeing her brother and disappointment that she'd now be relegated to third-wheel status as sports talk took over. She brushed off her momentary self-pity, realizing it was ridiculous, and dropped the box, hurrying to greet her big brother. "Craig!"

"Hey, Harper!" He looked worn out to her. He was only two years older, but a hard life working on rigs around the world made him look like he was on the wrong side of forty. He lowered his tall, lanky frame to hug his little sister before pulling back and ruffling her hair in the way that had always driven her nuts. His hair was much lighter than hers, and his eyes were a brilliant shade of green to her blue. There was little about them physically that marked them as siblings, other than their tall frames.

"I thought you couldn't make it until Monday?" Harper asked, swatting his hand away and smoothing her hair.

"Managed to get off a little early. Dad said I just missed you at the hospital." Craig stopped when he saw Evan, his face spreading into a wide grin. "Hey, man, how the hell are you?"

"Can't complain. Great to see you!" Evan said. "I thought I'd come help unload all the shoes and purses."

"Me too. I was planning to tally them all up and see if Harper might hold a world record in useless accessories." Craig laughed, lifting a box down.

"Are we taking off the gloves already, Craig?" Harper asked, crossing her arms at her brother.

"Oh yeah, we are!"

An hour later, most of Harper's things had been unloaded from the back of the truck. As they worked, Harper suffered through dozens of cracks about how many boxes of clothes and shoes she had. She was glad they'd never know she'd given more than half of her clothes and accessories to Jasmine and a couple of the other assistants who had come to her apartment to help her pack.

"Evan, do you have an empty room? Because pretty soon we're going to run out of space at my dad's," Craig teased.

"My basement is pretty empty, but that won't be enough. I was just thinking maybe I could build on to the back of the house. Another two thousand square feet ought to do it."

"Ha ha. You two are hilarious," Harper cut in with a deadpan expression. "You should take that act on the road. It would kill among people who love really obvious jokes."

"Evan, have you noticed that she doesn't have even one piece of furniture?" Craig asked.

"Look, Plague, the clothes and accessories are part of my job," Harper interjected. "I sublet my apartment, so I took all my personal items and left the furniture. If you'll notice, there are also plenty of books and magazines."

Evan burst out laughing. "Plague! I forgot all about that nickname."

Craig levelled his sister with a dirty look for a second, then suddenly a twinkle appeared in his eye. "So, Evan, did you know Harper had a thing for you in high school?"

"Shut up, Plague," Harper hissed.

Craig, ignoring his sister, turned to Evan. "Yeah, I'm pretty sure we'd find her old diary in one of these boxes if we looked long enough. Harper Donovan is written on almost every page!" Craig laughed as though he were a comic genius instead of the village idiot.

Harper's face turned bright red as she stepped up into the back of the truck to retrieve some of the last boxes. She briefly considered crawling into one of them but her plotting was interrupted by Evan's voice.

"Is that so, Craig? How do you know I don't have a diary where I wrote Harper Donovan on every page?"

Turning quickly, Harper saw the shocked look on her brother's face as Evan shut him down hard. She picked up a box and handed it down to Evan with an expression of pure gratitude. He gave her a little wink, then strolled back to the house with the box in his arms.

* * *

The next morning, Harper went to the hospital just after breakfast. She brought two coffees in travel mugs, knowing how much her dad hated the idea of spending four dollars at a coffee house for something you could brew at home for a few pennies. Gratitude rushed over her when she saw him. He was alive. And she was there to be with him.

"Good morning!" she said, giving him a quick peck on the cheek. She placed a bendy straw in the hole at the top of the mug and carefully handed it to him. "Coffee from home. It's cooled enough by now for you to use the straw."

He offered her a small smile that looked as though it took more than a little effort. "Thank you. You finish getting all moved in yesterday?"

She gave him a confident look, settling herself at the foot of his bed where he could see her. "I did. After I visited you, I actually finished putting everything away. I hope you won't mind that the basement is kind of full of boxes right now."

"Doesn't matter. I may never see the basement again, anyway." Roy's voice was quiet.

"You will, Dad . . ." Harper started but stopped when she saw her dad wave off her pep talk.

"I heard you lost your job."

Harper stiffened up at his words. "Yes, I did. I'm sure you're not too impressed with that."

"On the contrary. Craig told me how it happened. That took some balls, kid."

Harper looked at him in disbelief. That was not what she was expecting to hear from her father after her temper had basically cost her her job.

He continued, "Shows me maybe I've misjudged you a little. I figured you for the type who wouldn't let anything get in the way of your career, but it sounds to me like you took a stand when your old man needed you."

Tears sprang to Harper's eyes against her best efforts to stop them. Quickly standing, she picked up a bouquet of flowers that needed water, taking it into the tiny bathroom attached to his room.

His voice followed her. "Now, don't go getting all soppy on me or you'll make me wish I hadn't said anything."

She filled the vase with some water, checking to see that she didn't look blotchy before returning to the room. She cleared her throat loudly. "No, of course not," she said, turning to him with an incredulous look. "The coffee went down the wrong way," she lied. "What? You thought I was . . . Pfft . . . No."

"Anyway. Thanks, kid."

* * *

"Evan? Evan-from-Heaven Evan?" Megan asked as she stopped herself next to a lounge chair in her backyard. She stared at Harper in disbelief as she handed her a glass of iced tea. Harper, who was relaxing in a chair near the pool, nodded excitedly.

"You better dish fast before Luc gets Elliott to bed and comes to join us!"

"Yes!" she whisper-yelled, trying to be careful not to wake the baby asleep on her shoulder. "Can you friggin' believe it? He bought his parents' house."

"Rigghhtt. Now I remember hearing that. I completely forgot to tell you. Is he still the hottest guy on the planet, other than Luc, of course?" Megan asked excitedly.

Harper was giddy. "Oh. My. God. He's seriously gotten hotter than he was in high school. Remember how he had that athletic build when we were teenagers? Well, he's all muscly now in that really manly way. How is that even possible, Megs?"

"I don't know, but it happens. I saw pictures of Luc as a teenager and although he was cute, I definitely met him in his prime. Okay, but back to Evan. Single?"

"I think so. He hasn't mentioned anyone and I have to say, he was a little bit flirty with me."

"Of course he was. You're gorgeous! He could use a good woman after what his awful ex-wife did to him."

"Yeah, what happened there? Craig told me they broke up, but you know him, as far as getting the gossip, he's not worth a shit."

"Well, I did hear a little from one of the moms at Elliott's school who grew up with Avery. Apparently, she left him during the recession. As soon as he told her they had to sell their massive house to keep his crews employed, she was gone. I guess she told him that it was them or her."

"Seriously? That is so awful."

"Yeah, well, he's the one laughing now. He landed the bid for the Pine Crest subdivision. It's a new neighbourhood going in next to Boulder Mountain Park. He's developing the entire thing, and from what I hear, he's going to make millions."

"Wow. He never said a word about it yesterday. Good for him." Harper shifted a little in her chair to pick up her drink. "I can't believe she walked out on him just when he was losing everything. What kind of person does that? But more importantly, why would he be attracted to someone like that?"

"Good question. I think she did a very convincing nice-girl act until things started going downhill. You don't really know someone until you've been through a crisis with them."

"You mean like being woken up every hour for two months straight?" Luc interjected. His interruption was a welcome one but mainly for the fact that it was accompanied by a tray of cheese and crackers. He bent down and gave Megan a kiss on her forehead before setting the dish between the ladies. "That would definitely qualify as a crisis in my books. How did I do?"

Megan beamed up at him. "I have to say, you did very well."

Luc carefully lifted his daughter from Harper, settling her against his chest before relaxing into a chair beside his old friend. He pressed his lips to his little girl's head gently before inhaling her new-baby smell. "I did do well, didn't I? I had very good advice from Megan's mom, who told me to forgive anything your wife says before five in the morning."

Megan laughed, her eyes shining with love as she stared at their little girl in Luc's arms.

"How is your dad?" Luc asked Harper.

"Oh, you missed all my fretting earlier. I was just filling Megan in on all the details. Still no sign of feeling in his legs. He was so quiet when I went to see him this morning, which is understandable, but I'm a little worried he's starting to get depressed."

"I'm sorry to hear that. This must be very difficult for you as well," Luc replied. "You will let us know if there's anything at all we can do, yes? If you hear of a hospital or a doctor that can do more for him, we'll gladly take care of sending him wherever he needs to be."

Harper felt that annoying lump in her throat again. "Thanks, Luc. I know you would, but I can handle it."

Megan gave Harper a stern look. "Listen, lady, you don't have to be a rock all the time. You need to know when to ask for help. Doesn't make you weak, it makes you human."

Harper wrinkled up her nose. "Yuck. I've never liked the thought of being human. As a species you all are too vulnerable."

The three sat for another hour, catching up and enjoying the last of the pinks and purples disappearing behind the mountains. Harper shared her horribly embarrassing story of getting locked out of the house the night before and they all laughed as quietly as they could until their stomachs hurt.

When Amelie woke, Harper decided it was time to make her exit. "I better go. Thank you for supper. It was delicious. And thanks for letting me have some Amelie time, Megan. But not you, Luc, you baby hog."

"I can't be blamed. I am too much in love with her to let any-one else hold her. She has me under her spell, like her mother," Luc replied, his French accent making his words sound all the more romantic.

"That may be the case, but I'm only going to be in town for a few months. It's only fair that I should get a lot of cuddle time in now."

"Sorry, mon amie," Luc answered. "I'll try to keep that in mind."

"You better. If it weren't for me, you wouldn't even have that little bundle of joy," Harper replied, running her finger along Amelie's chubby cheek. "You let your mom and dad get some sleep, little monkey, or Auntie Harper isn't going to teach you how to apply makeup when you're older."

"My Amelie won't need makeup. Look how beautiful she is," Luc stated defensively.

"Easy there, buddy. No one is saying she isn't beautiful." With that, Harper gave Megan the "call me" sign on her way out.

* * *

As she drove across town, Harper thought about Megan's life, feeling happy that things had worked out between her two friends. Harper had introduced them, hoping only that Megan would have a little fun with Luc. Megan had been a single mom for over five years and had been working so hard to build her photography business and take care of her son, Elliott, that she hadn't bothered to give herself a break. No one could have predicted that they would fall in love and become a family. Amelie had been a surprise that came along only a few months after they met, but she was obviously a welcome one at that.

Luc, a highly successful nightclub owner and real-estate investor, had never seemed more content in all the years Harper had known him. He was absolutely overflowing with love for Megan and both of the kids. And Megan had come to life again as well. She wasn't as serious as she had been after her marriage to Ian had ended in tragedy. He had developed a devastating drug problem shortly after

Elliott was born. Now Megan seemed more like the girl Harper had grown up with. Confident, fun, lighthearted. Elliott, too, had bene-fited from Luc's presence in his life. He finally had a full-time dad who cared for him, took him to Little League games and played with him. He seemed more carefree now. Instead of being like a miniature man who was always worried about his mom, he seemed more like a young boy now. Harper was grateful that things had worked out so beautifully for them, and as she drove along, she even felt a hint of pride at the part she had played in it all.

But as she neared her new old home, a small seed of loneliness took root. She was going back to her dad's house on its quiet street, a place full of memories, both happy and horrible. Somewhere she'd avoided as much as possible for over half of her life. The thought made her ache for her apartment in Manhattan, right in the centre of the universe. There, she could find ways to distract herself twenty-four hours a day.

But it wasn't just a hideout for Harper. New York was her home. She missed her friends and the feeling of excitement in the air, but she missed her work most of all. She loved being on the cutting edge of the fashion industry, seeing the incredible artistry of the biggest designers and knowing who was going to set the trends long before the rest of the world found out how it would be dressing a year from now. It was like being in on an incredible secret. She would need to put that part of her life on hold, knowing she would have her chance again. For now, she would be here for her dad, and as soon as he was strong enough, she would go back to her real life in Manhattan.

* * *

A loud bark caused Evan to lose his place filling in a spreadsheet on his laptop. It was late in the evening and he was trying to finish up so he could get some sleep. Tomorrow would be another long day at the site. He heard the squeak of Roy's truck door through the open window in the bedroom that served as his office. Boots sounded the happy alarm again, compelling Evan to get up and walk down the hall to the living room. There he found the dog, paws on the windowsill, looking back and forth from him to Harper as she came up her dad's front walk.

"Yeah, I see her," Evan told the dog. "And no, we're not going over there right now. We're playing it cool, remember?"

Boots lowered his head as if he were disappointed.

"I don't have time for a woman right now, no matter how much you like the way she scratches behind your ears."

SEVEN

The next morning, Harper woke early. She got ready for the day as though she had a job to go to, dressing professionally even though she was only going to visit her dad and get groceries. Climbing into her father's big truck, she drove to the hospital, praying that his legs had shown some sign of regaining feeling since the day before.

Her mind wandered to the moment he had mistaken her for her mom. She wanted to find a way to ask him about it. She had almost managed to convince herself that he must have been dreaming, but what if he really did miss Petra? Was that why he'd never really moved on or gotten remarried? If that was the case, she should bring it up when the opportunity presented itself. Maybe he didn't consciously realize it.

She found Roy picking at what looked like a very unappetizing breakfast. He looked up at her, his eyes reflecting the same weary expression they'd had the day before. That expression signalled to Harper that today was not going to be the day to bring up Petra. She'd need to wait until he was stronger, if at all.

"Hey, Dad," she said, crossing the room to give him a peck on the cheek. "What is that god-awful food they've given you?"

Looking down at the tray before him, he shook his head. "I think these runny things are supposed to be eggs. I'm guessing that the soggy squares were toast at one time."

Harper laughed at his observation, glad to find that he hadn't completely lost his sense of humour after everything he'd been through. "I'm going to start bringing you breakfast every day, okay?"

"I'll take you up on that. I may not be the brightest bulb in the room, but I'm smart enough to know not to turn down a good offer." Roy picked up a slice of the toast, letting it hang limply from his fingertips.

"Do you want me to run out and get you something now?" Harper offered, scrunching up her nose.

"Nah. I'll make do with this shit for today. They're taking me for more tests in a bit so I wouldn't even be here when you got back anyway."

"If you're sure." Her tone was skeptical but she knew better than to push him on any point. Once Roy made up his mind, he never changed it. "I was wondering if you'd mind if I give the house a good spring cleaning. You know me, I can't stand sitting around doing nothing all day."

"You're preaching to the choir, kid," Roy said, glancing at his legs.

"Shit. Sorry, Dad. That was insensitive of me . . ." She paused for a moment, trying to think of what to say. "But if you think about it, you're not doing nothing. You're recovering. That's a big job in itself. You had a building collapse and literally land on your back. It's incredible that you even survived. Cut yourself some slack."

"Yeah, I'm a regular superhero." He sounded sarcastic as he lifted the toast above his nose so he could lower it into his mouth.

"I would say that's actually a very accurate description."

She sat with her dad for another hour, chatting about the headlines in the paper one of the nurses had left for him. Looking down at her purse, Harper remembered that she had brought a couple of books for him to read. Pulling them out, she held them up to him. "Tom Clancy? I found them on your shelf so I know you must have read them already, but I thought I'd bring them just in case."

"Thanks. I will read them again. That's the nice part of getting old. You can read the same books over and over because you forget what happened."

Chuckling, Harper shook her head. "You're not old. You just need a new haircut and a shave."

"Oh, not this again." Roy rolled his eyes. "Say, don't you need to get home and start cleaning? It's been years since those walls have seen a wet rag."

"Right. I almost forgot. I better get at it."

"You better. I'll be really disappointed if that place isn't sparkling when I get back," he said with a twinkle in his eye.

Standing, Harper touched her hand to her dad's grey hair. "See you tomorrow for breakfast. Unless, can I bring you some dinner?"

"No, Craig said he'll come by. Maybe he could bring me a burger or something."

"I'll text him your order."

* * *

Over the next week Harper fell into a routine. Each morning she brought her dad breakfast and visited with him while he ate, struggling to hide her increasing concern that he still showed no sign of having any feeling in his legs. She spent the rest of the day cleaning one or two rooms in the house, organizing closets and cupboards as she went.

Thoughts of Evan flowed freely through her mind as she sang along to the radio. Every song reminded her of him—the romantic ones, the ones about longing, the ones about sex. She hadn't seen him since the weekend. It hadn't escaped her attention that his truck was gone early each morning and wasn't parked in front of his house again until late in the evening. *Okay, Harper, you're becoming a stalker.*

He probably hasn't given you a second thought since he left here on Saturday. Her thoughts were interrupted by a call from Blaire.

"How are things in the Big Apple?"

"Ugh. Not great. I need to ask you something every hour or so. It sucks here without you."

"Is it bad that I feel a little bit happy to hear that?" Harper asked.

"Yes, but you always were a bit of a bitch, so I'd expect nothing less," Blaire answered wryly. "How's your dad?"

"Not good. So far, he has no feeling in his legs. He doesn't say anything but I know he must be scared. Not to mention that his back must be very painful."

"That's terrible. How are you doing with all of this?" Blaire's voice was full of concern.

"I'm alright. It's really hard to see him like this." Harper felt a sob rising in her throat but she managed to push it back down. "Most of the time, I'm just happy he's alive. And I'm keeping busy. When I'm not at the hospital, I'm spring cleaning his house. Top to bottom, every room."

"That's my version of hell on earth."

"Mine too. That's how desperate I am for something to do. How do people live like this on a regular basis?" Harper asked. "Alone with your own thoughts? It's been only a few days and I feel like my skin is crawling."

"I seriously don't know. Just keep reminding yourself it's only temporary. You'll be back here in no time," Blaire said, as though it were a fact.

"I wish I was there right now. If only I could just wave a magic wand and have my dad back to normal and have my old life again." Harper sighed. "I shouldn't be complaining, though. What I'm facing is nothing compared to what my dad's facing. I definitely shouldn't be a baby about it."

"Oh yes. Please don't do that. You know how I hate babies."

Harper laughed, knowing Blaire was more serious than joking. "Today, I realized this is the first time in my life that I don't have a plan. What the hell am I going to do when my dad doesn't need me anymore?"

"You'll be back here before you know it. We'll figure out a way, I promise."

"If that happens, I'll be the happiest woman on the planet," Harper said.

"If that happens, you'll have to fight me for the title. I have to run. We have a planning meeting in five."

"I have to go too. I have an important conference call with a mop and bucket that I can't get out of."

"Take care, my dear. Chin up. Keep in touch."

"You too."

As she got back to work, Harper groaned loudly. She should be on her way to that planning meeting right now. They would be working on the December issue and she desperately wished she were a part of it. December was one of her favourites—all those jackets and boots and warm, cozy sweaters to offset the glamorous cocktail dresses. She loved fall and winter fashion. It offered women who weren't in perfect physical shape the chance to look amazing in the latest trends. Summer clothing was often too short, too tight and just didn't fit right on any-one with flaws to hide. So when the cold-weather clothes came out, she could imagine women feeling fabulous as they adorned themselves with the perfect pair of wool slacks or a cashmere top that fell just right. And a few months after she had carefully attended to every detail of the fall and winter issues, she would see those looks on the streets of Manhattan. And it was wonderful. Gratifying in a way that few things had ever been. But she wasn't there to be a part of it this time. And she had no idea if or when she ever would be again. Could that chapter of her life really be over? Was the career that she had given her life to, and that in return had given her so much, really finished?

* * *

That evening, Harper made several trips to the curb, dragging many bags and boxes for the next day's garbage pickup, feeling very satisfied. As she stood on the driveway, she realized that she would have to find another way to spend her free time. But now she needed to channel her artistic side. It would be the best way for her to keep her sanity. Staring back at the yard, she decided that she should revitalize the tired flower beds in front of the house. That would allow her to bring something beautiful to her dad's little corner of the world. Tomorrow, she would stop at a nursery on the way home from the hospital and pick up some plants. She put a little skip in her step as she made her way into the empty house to plan her next project.

* * *

Morning found Harper outside with a measuring tape and a pad of paper. The birds serenaded her as she drew sketches of the front yard, measuring the beds as she went. They were, for the most part, very bare, with the exception of the weeds that had taken over. A few overgrown evergreen shrubs stood as though randomly plunked into the ground. They were spaced too far apart, with nothing tying them together.

Harper sat on the front step, sipping her coffee and planning what would go in each spot. The warmth of the sun on her face brought a new sense of contentment with it. Maybe for now she needed to just go where her life was taking her, instead of trying to control everything.

Looking over at Evan's house, she noticed that his truck was gone. She hadn't seen him leave that morning and she found herself hoping that he had left for work early and not slept at someone else's house. "Speaking of things you can't control . . ." she said to herself.

By afternoon Harper was covered with sweat and dirt, which had stuck to the sunscreen on her arms as well as, somehow, to her neck and face. Glancing down at her jean shorts, she was glad she had dug around to find some old clothes for the job. It was a hot day and she was grateful the sun had already gone around the side of the house, so that she could continue pulling out weeds, working in the shade now. Stopping to take a long drink of cold water, she looked down at the pots of plants waiting to go into their new home. The muscles in her hands and back ached.

"Okay, Harper," she told herself. "Let's get this done."

She thought of her dad lying in bed, staring out the window when she had arrived that morning. He was lonely. He had been lonely for many years, but now he was really alone. Until now he'd been able to hide from that feeling from sun-up to sundown at a construction site. Harper knew it was killing him to lie there, unable to do anything for himself. Her dad was a man who despised weakness so vehemently that she knew a part of him would have preferred that the accident had ended it all right then. But it hadn't. He had lived, and Harper was going to do whatever she could to make sure his homecoming and recovery were as smooth as possible. Maybe this could be a fresh start for them as a family. Maybe almost losing him would remind them all of how much they still had, in spite of the void her mother had left.

Her pondering was interrupted by the all-too familiar sound of Mrs. Morley from across the street calling her name. "Haarrrpppper! Helllooo!" she called as she bustled over on her short legs. She wore a pastel track suit and running shoes, as she did every day. The neighbours believed that her attire was chosen for the sole purpose of making it easier for her to keep tabs on everyone in the vicinity. She was a little wider now than when Harper had last seen her, and her short hair was salt-and-pepper, but she still moved with the agility of a cat when there was a story to be uncovered.

"Oh, hi, Mrs. Morley. How are you?" Harper asked, feeling her heart sink as the neighbourhood gossip closed in on her. She rose to her feet and gave her a tight smile.

"Excellent and improving. Things were a little rough there for a while. Neil needed a hip replacement in February, so that wasn't easy going, let me tell you. But he's doing much better now. Even started golfing again."

"Oh, I didn't know Mr. Morley needed surgery. I'm glad to hear he's doing well," Harper answered politely, wondering how long it would take for Mrs. Morley to leave her alone.

"How's your poor father doing?" she inquired, her face pulling into a pout.

"He's coming along, thank you. And thank you for sending him those cookies. He really appreciated it."

"Well, it's the least I could do. He's been through so much. So, so much . . ." She let her words hang there as though tallying up all the horrible events of Roy Young's life. "Such a shame that he never met a nice woman after your mother left with that boy. You and your brothers certainly could have used a motherly figure in the house. But maybe he'll fall for one of the nurses. You know, a Florence Nightingale thing? Wouldn't that be wonderful?" She nattered on as Harper turned and began arranging the plants in the flower bed. There really wasn't much need for her to answer. "It's not like you or your brothers are ever here, anyway. You all take after your mother, never wanting to stay in one place too long." Mrs. Morley put a hand on her generously sized hip and gave Harper a knowing look.

Harper stiffened at her words. "I've been in the same place in New York for eight years, actually." She didn't know whether to be more annoyed with Mrs. Morley or herself for feeling obliged to answer at all. "I should get back to work." She crouched down to yank out a weed she'd missed, wishing that something—anything—would just get this woman the hell away from her.

"I really like what you're doing out here. It's about time someone fixed it up. I've been staring out at this mess for years now. Pretty much since your family moved in." Mrs. Morley laughed to soften her comment, though they both knew she meant it. She walked over and picked up one of the pots. "I see you picked up a few bleeding hearts. They'll do nicely on this side of the house. This one's a bit spindly, though. You should put it at the back." She switched the plant with a large one that Harper had set closer to the house.

"Actually, I'm going to stick it right out front and centre to give it more sun," Harper answered, switching the pots back to where they had been.

"Oh. Well, I suppose that might work too . . . I noticed you cleared out quite a few things yesterday. I bet it was just a mess in there. One man alone in that house all those years." Mrs. Morley clucked her tongue in disapproval.

"He's pretty good at keeping things neat."

"Oh. If you say so," Mrs. Morley went on. "I saw Evan Donovan helping you unload your things the other day."

"Mmhmm."

"That Donovan boy is quite the looker. Always was. What that awful wife of his did to him! He never should have married that one. Should have stuck with a nice girl from this side of town. Someone he had more in common with." Mrs. Morley sighed heavily, as though the drama was her own. "I told his mother to warn him, but you know how men are about taking advice. Now, he just goes to work and comes home to his empty house. I still keep in touch with Nancy down in Tucson. She says he's fine, but I don't think she really knows. I think he's hiding it from her. Such a waste for a man like that to be alone."

Now Mrs. Morley had Harper's full attention. She stopped pondering the placement of the plants long enough to risk a glance at her neighbour. "Hopefully he'll find someone."

Mrs. Morley's stare hardened, indicating that she hadn't missed that flash of hope in Harper's eyes. "I've been telling my niece to come by so I can introduce them. She'd be perfect for him. She's a medical receptionist now but she'd give it all up for the right man. Nice girl. He needs someone like her, not some busy career woman or someone who needs a lot of fancy clothes or closets full of designer purses, like that ex of his. A man like that needs a good wife to take care of things at home while he's at work."

The sound of Mr. Morley's voice saved his wife from the retort on the tip of Harper's tongue. "Delores! What are we doing for supper? I'm getting hungry!" he called.

"Just a g.d. minute!" she hollered back. "At least say hello to Harper! You haven't seen her in ages!"

The man gave Harper a sympathetic nod and a wave. "Hi, Harper. How's your dad?"

"Hi, Mr. Morley. He's doing much better, thanks!" Harper called back.

"Tell him I say hi!"

"Will do."

The screen door slammed, indicating that he had gone back inside to wait for his dinner. Lowering her voice, Mrs. Morley said, "Well, I better get back in there. If I leave him too long, he's likely to start messing around in my kitchen, thinking he can cook. I'll be days cleaning up the mess." She shook her head at the thought.

"Now, you're going to want to put some bone meal in the holes before you add the plants, a little extra for that spindly one. Makes a huge difference in how quickly they'll take root. I'll send Neil over with a bag."

"I have some already," Harper answered, neglecting to mention that it was only because the man at the nursery had thrown it in for free.

"Good. A handful in each hole. And plenty of water for the rest of the season so they'll—"

"Delores?" her husband's voice called. "Should I start browning this hamburger meat? Are we having spaghetti?"

"Don't touch it!" she yelled back, rushing across the street. "You come by for coffee, Harper!" She waved over her shoulder as she scuttled home to prevent the impending culinary crisis.

Harper swore under her breath as she got back to work, digging holes and planting the smaller perennials. Their conversation swirled around in her brain, creating a ball of righteous indignation in her chest. Mrs. Morley and others like her, who felt it necessary to assert themselves in matters that were none of their business and who judged her motherless family, were near the top of her list of good reasons she had left Boulder. In New York, no one knew that her mother had had an affair and abandoned them, and if they did find out, they wouldn't bat an eyelash.

How could a woman—in a lavender track suit of all things— make her feel less than? It was ridiculous. Harper thought of Mrs. Morley's not-so-subtle way of telling her she was all wrong for Evan. "Screw her."

EIGHT

The heat of the day clung to the air as the sun began to disappear behind the mountains in the distance. The sound of Evan's truck prompted Harper to quickly dab at the sweat on her face with the edge of her T-shirt. *Of course. I don't see him for days and then he appears when I'm a sweaty mess again.*

"Evening," he called, strolling over to her with Boots bounding ahead of him. As she took in Evan's appearance, she realized she needn't have worried about being sweaty or covered in dirt. He looked very much the same, although she was sure it suited him more than it did her. His dusty old jeans and work boots, along with two-day-old stubble, just added to his rugged sexiness.

Harper looked up at Evan from her position on her knees, arching her back to relieve some of her sore muscles. Suddenly realizing how that must have looked, she straightened up. "Hi," she replied, hoping he couldn't hear her heart as it pounded in her chest. She reached out and gave Boots a vigorous rub behind his ears to stop him from licking her face. In response, the dog flopped down to the grass and rolled over onto his back, clearly hoping for a belly rub. Harper gave in. "You know how to wrap us humans around your paw, don't you, Boots?"

"He certainly does. I never wanted a dog and yet, here he is."

Evan dropped down beside her on the lawn, stretching out his long legs and leaning back on his elbows as he admired her handiwork.

"How come you never wanted a dog?"

"Too much commitment. I realized a while ago that the simpler I keep things, the happier I am. He's working out okay, though." Evan nodded toward the nearly completed flower bed. "Did you do all that today?"

Her mouth curved up slightly as she looked over her latest artistic endeavour. "I did indeed." She tried to renew her enthusiasm for her accomplishment but it had faded with the heat and her irritation.

"Good for you. It's hard to believe it's the same yard that was here this morning. Seriously impressive," he replied, taking his eyes off the plants to stare at her. He cocked his head to the side, frowning a little. "You okay? You don't seem like your normal, bubbly self."

"It's nothing worth talking about."

"If it's bugging you, it's worth talking about."

Harper rolled her eyes. "Mrs. Morley came by to remind me of her opinion of my family, including my horrible mother, in case I had forgotten."

"I'm sorry to hear that. Why the hell can't people mind their own business?"

"Gossip is like a pastime around here. And my mother gave them the story of the century." Harper plucked a blade of grass and tied it in a tiny knot.

Evan watched her fingers for a moment before answering. "Anyone who'd bring that up has got to be a pretty small person to begin with. Still hurts, though, doesn't it?"

"No, it's just irritating," Harper answered. "Actually, I'm more annoyed with myself for letting her bother me."

"Well, it's hard not to. She's got an ill-informed and unwanted opinion on everything. And unfortunately, she loves sharing those opinions," Evan commiserated. "She's always trying to set me up with her niece." He shuddered, pretending to be disgusted.

Harper laughed. "Oh, I know. She practically claimed you as family territory already. I think she's worried I'm going to move in on you now that I'm home for a while. She made sure to tell me how wrong I'd be for you." The words were out of her mouth before her common sense could tell her to swallow them. Shit, that could make things a little awkward. But it didn't.

"Like I said—ill-informed," he replied in a low tone, his eyes locked on hers.

Swallowing hard, Harper stood and grabbed the shovel before she acted on her impulse to straddle his lap right there on the lawn and have her way with him. She stepped back into the flower bed, then gave the earth under her a stab with the shovel. She had left the two largest shrubs for last, a mistake now that her muscles were all begging her to stop.

She struggled to force the blade into the hard ground, finally resorting to standing on it with both feet. But the shovel wouldn't move more than a few inches into the surface, even when Harper held the handle and hopped up and down on the shoulder of the blade.

"I'm torn. I know I should dig that hole for you but it's just so fun watching you jump up and down on that shovel in those little shorts of yours," he said, finally getting up.

Harper could feel her face heating up and she tried to calm herself before she turned to him from her perch. "And they say chivalry is dead," she remarked.

"In that case, I better help. Hand it over, lightweight," he ordered, standing and taking the tool from her. His fingers brushed against hers as he did, causing a surge of sexual tension. He took a step forward, closing the space between them. "But I need a favour from you in return. I need some help getting Mrs. Morley off my back about her niece."

Harper glanced at their neighbour's house and saw her through the front room window, misting a large fern. "That plant must be soaked by now. What's the favour?"

"Make this look good," he murmured as he leaned down, letting his lips hover over hers. He reached one hand up to her cheek, tilting her head back just enough.

Without a moment's hesitation, his lips were on hers. Harper's eyelids lowered as she felt herself disappearing into an entirely new world. His kiss was so much more than she had dreamed it would be. It started out gentle, careful even, with an undercurrent of passion that soon overtook them both. Her response was full of yearning, decades of pent-up desire and curiosity. She reached out and balled up the bottom of his T-shirt in her fist, pulling him closer. Wrapping his arm behind her, he dipped her back, his tongue finding its way between her lips, searching her mouth for more. She felt her body awaken as the most delicious aching pulsed through her. And then as suddenly as he had begun, he lifted her back upright and stopped.

Harper's eyes opened slowly when she realized he wasn't coming back for more.

"There. That ought to do it," he said, glancing across the street. "I just saw her close the curtains."

"Oh, great," was all Harper could think to say. Her mind was completely scrambled, her body quaking with an urgent lust.

"Thanks for helping me with that. Now, your turn."

Harper watched as he easily cut through the ground with the shovel, his powerful body making short work of what would have been a monumental task for her. Surely he must be tired and sore from such a long day on the construction site. But he moved with ease. And there she stood, weak in the knees from one kiss. She had to quell an overwhelming desire to step up behind him and wrap her arms around him and under his shirt. Dear Lord, what would he look like without that annoying piece of fabric covering his body?

She had a very good idea that he would look amazing. And feel amazing. If his body moved anything like his lips and tongue, she would be putty in his hands.

* * *

Evan stood under the spray of the hot water, unable to get his mind off Harper. How her bottom curved perfectly in those shorts she was wearing and how her legs seemed to go on for miles, her beautiful reddish-brown hair pulled up in a messy bun, those incredible blue eyes, that ivory skin that was flawless in spite of the smudges of dirt.

It wasn't just her body, though. It was the way she spoke, her strength, her determination. When he really thought about it, he realized she'd always been like that, but now she had the confidence of a woman who'd accomplished a lot in life. And success suited Harper.

He thought of how Mrs. Morley had managed to hurt her, slinging her poison-tipped arrows, managing to pierce old wounds that would never fully heal. There was a trace of vulnerability residing in Harper and he was surprised by how fiercely it made him want to protect her. In that moment, he would have done just about anything to make her feel better. So he made an excuse to kiss her. But it wasn't solely for her sake—it was also because he needed to. Even though it was against his better judgment, he just couldn't help himself.

He wanted her to know he saw her for who she was, not for what her mother had done. He wanted her to know that, for the first time, he was really seeing her. But now that he really saw her and had really kissed her, his eyes couldn't unsee her and his tongue couldn't forget the taste of her.

He knew that she was probably in the shower just then too, and found himself wishing he had seen her let her hair down and rub soap all over that gorgeous body of hers, instead of just imagining it. His hands wanted to feel her soft skin against them, his body wanted to feel her curves against him, his cock wanted to bury itself inside her in the worst way. He hadn't wanted a woman in this way for a long time, not since Avery. He had slept with a few women in the two years since their divorce, and had gotten a lot of offers, but he hadn't needed them like he needed Harper. This was a completely new type of desire. It was the type that could cause a man a lot of trouble. It could ruin lifelong friendships. It could make hamburger out of his heart. His brain was telling him to leave her alone, but the rest of his body was telling his brain to shut the hell up.

* * *

Harper tossed and turned half the night, overtaken by a wild restlessness as her brain tortured her with Evan's kiss. The scene played on a loop, arousing every part of her until she ached for him. There was only one thing that would satisfy this insatiable craving and he was next door, probably sleeping like a log. She could imagine him there, under the covers. Did he sleep in the nude? That would be quite the sight—his hard body all tangled up in his sheets. Thoughts of sliding into bed with him and running her hands everywhere came into her mind. Letting out a loud groan, she threw the sheets off and stalked down the hall to get a glass of water from the kitchen.

Frustration wasn't a big enough word for what she was feeling. This was pure agony. His smile, his concern for her feelings, his kiss. Dear God, that kiss. It was so much more than she had imagined it would be. And his reason for kissing her so much more than simply wanting to. He had pretended it was for his own sake, but he'd also managed to show their nasty neighbour that he thought Harper was every bit good enough for him. And that alone filled her with a need that wasn't going to quietly slink away.

NINE

"Hey, my friend, you all ready for tonight?" Harper had her phone on hands-free while she brushed bright pink polish onto her toenails.

"There's been a shitty change of plans," Megan answered, her voice weak.

"What's wrong, Megs? You sound awful!"

"I am. Elliott brought home a horrible flu bug and now I have it. I was up all night either puking or looking after a puking child. Luc's not home from Paris until late this afternoon, so it's been really friggin' awful."

"Oh God, that sounds like an absolute nightmare. Can I come by and help?" Harper's voice was full of concern.

"My mom just got here. She's going to watch the kids so I can sleep for a while. But I do need to ask you something. You know how I was going to be taking pictures while you got drunk at the Band on the Bricks event tonight?"

"Mmhmm. You're going to need to find someone to cover for you for . . ." Harper stopped mid-sentence. She suddenly had an idea of where this was going, and the thought had butterflies fluttering in her stomach.

"Yeah. I definitely have to have pictures of tonight's show for the contract. No way I can miss Hazel Brown. Which brings me to the part where I beg my very best friend in the whole world to go for me."

"Oh, Meg, I don't know. What if I totally fuck it up? Why don't I call around and find a professional to take them for you? I don't even mind paying for it."

"Honestly, I don't want to ask anyone else. Some of the photographers in town are like vultures. If I give them the chance, they'll be snacking on my corpse before sundown. That city gig is sweet—I get to attend everything for free and I've made some really great connections. Besides, you'll do a terrific job. You know how to work a camera, for God's sake." Megan paused for a moment.

"I do, but what if I screw it up?"

"Not a chance. Seriously, I wouldn't ask if I thought you couldn't handle it and if I wasn't dying."

"Okay, since you're on your deathbed. I'll swing by in a bit to get your equipment so I can practise for a while first. I'll call and you just put it out front and shut the door. I don't want to catch what you've got there."

Megan let out a sigh, sounding relieved. "Thank you, Harper. Best. Friend. Ever."

"What time should I be at the show?"

"I'm supposed to be there for five o'clock, in time for the beer garden. Head to Pearl Street, the thirteen hundred block. You'll see the stage; go there and ask for a guy named Guy. He'll give you all the instructions, the volunteer pass and drink vouchers."

"A guy named Guy?"

"I know. I'd like to think I would have some witty comment about that, but right now I've got nothing."

"It's okay, sweetie. You don't have to entertain me when you're sick. See you in a couple of hours."

* * *

When she pulled up to the house, Harper saw Megan standing in the living room window in her bathrobe. She got out of the car, carrying a grocery bag. Megan opened the door and put the camera bags on the front step before walking back inside, leaving the door open so they could speak from a distance.

"Thanks, Harper. I owe you one. I'll add it to the list."

"No problem, my friend." Harper held up the bag. "Chicken noodle soup, saltines, ginger ale, Dramamine, and Freezies. The barfer's buffet."

Megan managed a weak grin, which only made her slightly green face appear even more sickly. "You're the best. I'm so glad you're living here now."

"I'm glad I can be here to help. I just hope I don't mess up your contract."

"You won't. Say hi to Hazel for me."

"Sure thing." Harper gave her friend a sympathetic smile. "Feel better, you."

* * *

As Harper parked near Pearl Street, she reflected on how nice it was to live close enough to help Megan out. She had been so far away for so many years that she had completely missed out on the opportunity to really be there for her best friend, her brothers and her dad, for that matter. She had offered support over the phone but it wasn't at all the same as being with them through life's ups and downs. It felt good to be needed and to be able to take care of those she loved the most, even if it was just for a little while.

Getting out of the car, she heaved the camera bag over her shoulder and inhaled the clear summer air. A midday downpour had swept through town, leaving behind a sweet smell and darkened pavement.

The whole world felt fresh to Harper as she crossed the street to the municipal building. She had knots in her stomach about doing this work for Megan, but deep down she knew she could do a good job. A great job, if she could just relax a little and try to enjoy the moment. The best photo shoots she had worked on all had the same elements of joy and confidence that fed into any artistic endeavour. She could get some great pictures—it would be a matter of quantity tonight. The more shots she took, the better the chance she would get the ones Megan needed.

Half an hour later as the beer garden opened, Harper was ready. She felt somehow important with the camera in her hands and the press pass around her neck. There was already a good-sized crowd out for the event; some were dressed casually and some appeared to have come straight from work, still in their suits but with ties off and collars loosened. The atmosphere was one of anticipation, hundreds of people determined not to miss this moment. As the sun lowered, Harper made several adjustments to the camera's settings and continued shooting candids of the crowd and volunteers. Just after 7 p.m., the band took to the stage, welcomed by thunderous applause for the legendary Ms. Brown. Lifting the camera, Harper zoomed in on Hazel's face in time to catch a joyful expression as she laughed and got the audience to its feet. Harper tapped her foot to the beat as she worked.

"Harper?" A male voice sounded from behind her.

Turning, Harper broke into a smile as she saw Brent Yearwood standing there, red Solo cup in hand. Brent had been a friend of Harper's throughout high school. He moved in for a hug. What he lacked in height, he more than made up for in muscle. He resembled a bouncer, complete with the shaved head and crooked nose. "Damn, you're looking good these days. It took me a minute to recognize you." His words brought a strong waft of beer with them.

Harper pursed her lips, letting the corners turn up. "Oh, thanks. God, it's been a long time. You look great too. How are you?"

"Terrific. Even better now that I see you. What are you doing here?" He pointed to her camera.

"Oh, I'm filling in for Megan Sullivan. She's at home with the flu."

"You two are still friends? That's a dangerous combination."

"It would be if we were both here, so everyone's safe for tonight," she returned.

He grabbed her hand. "Come over here. There are a lot of people who'll want to see you."

Plucking the equipment bag off the ground, Harper let him lead her over to a crowded table.

"Look who's back in town!" Brent called, slinging an arm around her shoulder. The group turned to him, their eyes falling on Harper.

She stared into several faces from her past along with some who were new to her, feeling a nervous excitement as she greeted everyone. Smiling, she gave the table a wave. "Hi."

Hugs were given and introductions made. Brent sat down, but not before stealing a chair from the next table and squeezing in a spot for Harper next to him. They fell into familiar banter as though no time had passed. After a bit Harper stood up, announcing that she had to get back to work.

Brent lifted his arm, placing his fingers lightly on her lower back. "Come back over here when you're done. We're going over to O'Neill's after we get kicked out of here. You have to come."

Harper's answer was cut short as her gaze fell on Evan, who was making his way through the tables toward her. They hadn't seen each other since he'd kissed her, and warmth spread through her body as she watched him. Their eyes met and she could feel her heart pounding beneath her ribs as he neared. She saw him glance at Brent's hand, his eyes narrowing. Turning back to Brent, she gave him the killer smile she meant for Evan. "Love to. Mind if I leave my bag here while I go do another round of pictures?"

"Sure thing, darling. I'll take good care of it," he called as he watched her walk away.

* * *

Evan watched Brent's eyes track Harper's ass as she manoeuvred around the table, his blood heating up to a simmer. Although he knew he had no business thinking it, he didn't want *anyone* looking at her that way. Before he had time to understand just exactly why this bothered him in the first place, she was heading straight for him, in a low-cut black shirt and dark jeans that curved around her hips exactly the way his hands were itching to. Her red heels brought her big blue eyes four inches closer to his. How the hell could she walk in those things without toppling over? Instead of falling, she was moving like she was on a runway and she owned it.

She slipped through the crowded space and came face to face with Evan. He gave her a little nod. "Hey, didn't expect to see you here."

"I'm filling in for Megan. She was supposed to cover the event for the city," she said, moving closer to speak into his ear. Her proximity to his neck allowed her perfume to reach his nose, then travel directly to his cock. "Are you going over to O'Neill's after this?"

"Yeah. You coming?" he asked.

"I just received an invite. I thought it might be fun," she answered, just as one of the other patrons knocked her forward into Evan's chest. He grabbed her waist with one hand to steady her.

"I'll make sure it's fun. Save me a dance," he said into her ear, leaving his hand on her.

Harper gave him a sultry look. "In that case, I might stop by," she answered before turning and cutting through the crowd toward the front.

Now Evan's eyes were the ones doing the tracking. He blew out a long breath at the sight of her walking away. She did not have that ass when they were in high school. That he would have remembered.

* * *

Harper worked until the show ended, then made her way back to the table to put away the equipment. The partygoers started to disperse, some singing to themselves, others searching for the next venue to keep the good times going. Their group followed the crowd through the gates, Brent walking beside her. "You ready for some fun?"

"I am. It's been a while since I cut loose. I'm just going to drop off Megan's equipment in the truck," Harper answered, glancing behind her and seeing Evan walking with a couple of his old hockey teammates. His eyes were set on her intently.

Harper veered off the sidewalk toward the parking lot on the opposite side of the street.

"Harper, hang on a second," Evan called, jogging after her. "You change your mind?"

"No, I just thought I'd drop off Meg's stuff in the truck." She paused so he could catch up.

Evan took the bag from her, slinging it over his shoulder. "Why don't you put it in mine? I needed the Fort Knox security system, so you might as well use it too."

"That would be nice. Thank you."

Once everything was locked up, Evan turned to her. "Shall we go?" he asked, holding his arm out.

Harper looped her hand under his considerable forearm, wrapping her fingers around his skin. They walked in silence, the tension rising between them. Once inside the pub, Evan leaned in. "What are you drinking?"

"Surprise me," she answered, heading over to the bar table where their friends were standing.

Harper smiled to herself. Maybe Boulder wasn't so bad after all. So far tonight had been wonderful. She'd been welcomed with open arms by her old friends, and there was one in particular from whom she was pleased to be receiving such a warm reception. A martini glass was lowered onto the table in front of Harper. And there he was.

"Figured you for a cosmo girl," Evan said.

Turning her head to thank him, Harper was surprised by how close he was to her. She could feel the heat off his body as she glanced up at him. His arm brushed against her shoulder as he took a drag of his beer. If he kept this up, people were going to get the wrong impression. Or maybe it was the right impression.

A few minutes later, an old Destiny's Child hit rang out. Harper downed the rest of her drink and yelled, "Let's go, girls! We need to show these guys just how bootylicious we are!"

They laughed and weaved through the crowd to the dance floor, then gave their best moves, hips swaying, arms in the air, shoulders shimmying, knowing that the guys were watching. After a few songs, they went to the bar to replenish their fluids. Brent teetered over to the group, ordering shots for everyone and snugging up to Harper with a sloppy grin. "You are nothing like the Harper I knew in high school. When did you get so hot?"

"Right around the time I left Boulder." She laughed, turning to face him.

"So you got bolder when you left Boulder," he remarked, earning him a light chuckle from Harper.

"You know," he said moving in, "you look exactly like your mom.

She was smokin' hot." He planted his hands on her hips, tugging her to him. "Are you wild like her, too?"

Harper's face turned to ice. She pushed his hands off her and tried to sidestep him but he was too fast, pinning her against the bar with his arms on either side of her. "Hey now, don't be like that. I'm trying to compliment your hot ass. You should say thank you."

"Fuck off, Brent," she spat out, pushing at him without any success. He was the human equivalent of a bulldog—short, stocky, solid muscle.

"Don't be like that, baby. I know you want it. You come from a line of women who like to get nasty." The stench of his breath and his words made Harper's stomach lurch as she arched her back over the bar to get away from him.

"Get the hell off—" Harper's words were cut short as she witnessed Brent's arms suddenly being lifted and pinned straight above his head.

Evan was standing behind the bulldog and had looped his arms in front of Brent's, then pulled up while grabbing the back of Brent's head. The effect was immediate, leaving Brent flailing and immobilizing his upper body. Evan tugged him away from Harper. "You're way out of line, Brent. Go sleep it off."

Brent struggled a minute before giving up. When he finally relaxed, Evan let him go. Instead of walking away, Brent rounded on Evan and tried to punch him in the jaw. Evan grabbed his fist and held it, squeezing his knuckles as he gave Brent a sharp jab to the gut. "I said go sleep it off. I'm not going to tell you again."

Four bouncers descended, grabbing both men and dragging them out of the bar. Harper was quickly surrounded by her old friends. They were all talking at once, and a mixture of indignant rage and sympathy on her behalf flooded over her. She pushed past them, offering a distracted reassurance that she was fine. She needed to get out of there. The hot air felt like it might choke her, and she wanted to get to Evan before he left.

She hurried to the door, a chill running down her spine as Brent's words played over in her mind. Once outside, she stayed behind the bouncers in case Brent was still there. Evan stood dead still while Brent took off down the sidewalk, turning back with his eye already beginning to swell shut. Evan's bottom lip was bleeding and starting to puff up.

Harper rushed over to him. "Oh my God, Evan. Are you alright?"

"Fine. He just wouldn't let it go." Evan looked down at her, his expression changing from rage to concern in an instant. "You okay? I caught the tail end of what he said to you. Fucking asshole."

"I'm fine," Harper answered, reaching into her purse to get a tissue. She held it up to Evan's lip, gently dabbing the blood. "Don't worry about it. I'd never let someone like him bother me," she scoffed, ignoring the lump now taking hold in her throat.

Evan's voice came out gentle as he lifted his hand to hers. "You don't have to pretend you're okay when you aren't, Harper."

Something about his words and the concern in his eyes caused Harper's shield to dissolve. She blinked quickly at the dark sky, wrestling with the tears that now demanded to fall.

Evan wrapped his arms around her, pulling her in. "He shouldn't have said that to you. No way should you have to account for what your mother did twenty years ago. It's no reflection on you or the rest of your family."

Harper nodded into his thick chest, feeling safe. "It just took me by surprise. I was having so much fun that I guess I let my guard down. Anywhere but here, nobody knows, so I can pretend it never happened. I should know better than to hope people around here would have forgotten."

"Most people have, Harper. When they talk about you, it's

because you're a high-powered fashion executive in New York. Don't let him get to you. He was just pissed because he knows you're too good for him." Evan pressed his cheek to her hair, holding her close.

Torn between wanting to stay locked in the warmth of his arms and feeling angry at herself for letting Brent get the best of her, she drew in a deep breath. "Thank you, Evan," she whispered into his shoulder. "I should go," she said, pulling away.

"Let me drive you home. I'll bring you back for your truck tomorrow. I don't want you to be alone right now."

* * *

Evan stepped into the shower, finally noticing the tightly wound balls of tension that had fixed themselves in his neck and shoulders. He cranked the temperature up as high as it would go, hoping it would relax him. Harper's face planted itself in his brain. She had looked so sad, so hurt, so beautiful. Rage coursed through him when he thought of that fuck, Brent. Evan knew he had a mean streak in him and had considered warning her but decided to keep an eye on them instead, not wanting to sound jealous. Now he was wishing he'd let himself look like a fool rather than let her be taken by surprise. "Goddammit!" he let out.

At least he'd managed to put a halt to things when he did. But he hated like hell that she'd been humiliated by the past yet again. No wonder she stayed away. Tonight he'd seen a glimpse of the pain she held onto, but as quickly as it had reared its head, she'd cut it off, throwing up that wall of sarcasm and sass she shielded herself with. He wanted her to let him behind that wall. He understood what it was like to feel the sting of public humiliation, and he could help her heal if she'd only let him.

* * *

Harper lay in bed that night unable to sleep. The events of the day and evening swirled around her, bringing a wave of emotions so strong she felt as though she were being dragged under. She tried to focus on the excitement of the day, the success of helping Megan, but the smell of Brent and the sound of his words kept creeping back in, crowding out anything good. She'd taken a long, hot bath, hoping to unwind and forget about him, but it hadn't worked. As long as she was in Boulder, she was going to have to keep her guard up. She'd need to be ready for people like him who took pleasure in her family's misery. It was entertainment of the lowest form, but for some reason, many people seemed to revel in it.

And then Evan's face popped into her mind. His ice-blue eyes shining with warmth for her. His strong arms wrapped around her, his delicious smell as he held her near. His gentle words. Somehow this was the image that brought her to the surface again. Now she could breathe. Because of him. Her mind drifted to that moment at her front door when he'd said good night.

She'd smiled at him, hoping to seem completely confident. "Go put some ice on that lip, Donovan, or you won't be in any shape to kiss that long line of ladies waiting for you."

"You sure you're going to be okay?" Evan's eyes bored into hers.

"Are you still talking about that? That is long over." She gave him a wink.

"I'll come get you tomorrow morning."

"Only if you have time. I can always take a cab."

"I'll have time." He started to leave, then turned back. "Harper, about that kiss the other night . . ."

"Oh, that. I know you were just trying to make me feel better." She shrugged. "You're going to have to stop rescuing me like this.

You'll turn me into a damsel in distress, and there's nothing I hate more."

He planted his hand on her cheek, carefully placing his thumb over her lips to stop her from talking. "I was going to say I can't stop thinking about it. As soon as my lip heals, I'm hoping we can do that again."

He turned and strode away as her knees turned to jelly.

TEN

Harper walked into her dad's hospital room after knocking lightly on his door. The room was darkened by drawn curtains for the fifth day in a row. She tried to hide the dread she was feeling as her eyes adjusted to the dimness.

"Dad, you up?" she whispered.

"Yes."

Harper crossed the room to the window. "It's a beautiful day. Let's let some light in here." She reached for the window but his voice stopped her.

"Just leave it. I don't feel like looking outside." He spoke quietly, never taking his eyes off the blankets covering his legs. His gaze held such intensity it was as though he could force his lower limbs to work just by staring at them long enough.

"Alright. I brought you coffee and oatmeal." She walked over to his bed and flipped on a low light.

"No, thanks. I'm not hungry this morning." His voice was a monotone, as though speaking had become too much effort.

A knock at the door was quickly followed by the entrance of a doctor. "Good morning, Roy. I'm Dr. Smyth. I'll be taking over your care," he said with a confident smile. He appeared to be in his late thirties and was tall and handsome, with boyish good looks and an athletic build. He was the type of man she would have given a second look if Evan hadn't been in her brain, blocking her vision.

Roy gave him a little nod. "Okay."

"Hi, Dr. Smyth. I'm Harper, Roy's daughter." She held out her hand to him.

"Nice to meet you." He reached out to shake her hand, his eyes staying on her a beat longer than they should have.

Dr. Smyth glanced down at his clipboard. "So, Roy, I've been reading over your file. Says here that you have full use of your upper body but we're still waiting for your lower body to come around."

"Yup."

"Well, it's still early but I imagine this must be tough on you. The waiting. How's the pain management going?"

"Fine."

"Good. Well, that's something." Dr. Smyth made a note on the chart. "Should we open the curtains? It's a bit gloomy in here."

"Nope. Suits me just fine."

Dr. Smyth tilted his head toward Harper, giving her a concerned look. "Roy, I'd like to bring someone in to talk with you about how you're feeling. A psychologist. It's very common for people to start feeling depressed in your situation."

"No, thanks. Not interested."

"That's the thing about depression. It makes it hard to be interested in anything. Her name is Dr. Chan. She can help."

"No. Thank. You," Roy barked, glaring at the doctor.

"Take some time to think about it. You can let me know tomorrow."

"Already did."

"I have to finish my rounds but we're going to take you downstairs for a few tests later."

Roy nodded and Dr. Smyth turned to Harper. "Could I see you outside for a moment? I need to go over some forms with you."

The bright light of the hallway streamed into the room as they walked out, leaving Roy alone again.

Dr. Smyth turned to her. "I've been talking with Sadie, the head nurse. We have concerns about your father's mental condition."

Harper nodded, unable to speak without her voice breaking.

"We can't force him to talk to a psychologist but I think we should try to get someone in there as soon as possible. I can prescribe anti-depressants, but of course he'd have to agree to that."

"Alright."

"I just want to reassure you that this is completely expected in his situation. At the same time, we don't want to let him slip too far, so if you know of a way to convince him to get help, please do so."

"I will."

Harper walked back into her dad's room. Through the darkness, she could see that his eyes were now closed. "Go away."

"It's me, Dad."

"I know that. It's better if you just go. I'm not fit to be around anyone. I'm in a shitty mood and I'm just going to say something I don't mean."

Harper sat in the chair next to him. "Then we don't have to say anything. I'll just sit here with you and we can feel shitty together." She took his hand and held it until the orderly came in to get him.

"I'll be back tomorrow. We can talk or we can just sit. But I'll be here." She gave him a kiss on the forehead.

* * *

Late that afternoon, Harper sat out on the small deck in her dad's backyard. Closing her eyes, she tried to drink in the warmth of the Colorado sun and breathe in the fresh air and quiet. But instead of finding the escape she sought, she felt miserable. She thought of her dad, lying in the hospital bed, unable to move. Her heart dropped at the thought of what his life would become if he ended up confined to a wheelchair. The man who could never sit still for long, who always had some ongoing wood-working project in his shop. She thought of how quiet he'd grown in the days since his accident. And there was nothing she could do for him. She couldn't fix it. So far she could only bring him oatmeal and try to cheer him up. And what would the future bring him? Or her, for that matter? She'd lost her job, the one thing that made her who she was.

Tears of frustration and fear streamed down her cheeks and for once, she didn't stop them. Tears for her dad eventually turned into tears for herself. She shouldn't be here. She didn't belong in Boulder and hadn't for many years. Her entire adult life she had been Harper Young, fashion insider, and she couldn't be that here. She finally straightened her slumped shoulders, resolving to keep her chin up, help her dad and then get the hell back to Manhattan the moment he was well again.

Going back inside, Harper was determined to feel better. She took a long shower then made herself up, complete with smoky eyes and light pink high-gloss lips. She swept her hair into a messy updo and stood staring at the clothes in her closet. Her eyes fell on the two ball gowns she'd allowed herself to keep. Reaching out, her fingers grazed the black, strapless Carolina Herrera gown with delicate embroidered daisies and full skirt. Why not? No one was here and it would make her feel better to completely glam it up. She made herself a small fruit plate, carefully arranging grapes, melon and strawberries in a pleasing way before grabbing a bottle of wine, a glass, a napkin and her tablet. Checking the time, she realized it would be hours before Evan was home from work. She could sit outside and no one would see her. Making her way out to the deck, she seated herself carefully so as not to crease her dress. She was going to eat and drink and pretend she was anywhere but here. Somewhere glamorous and happy.

She popped a grape into her mouth. The sound of Evan's screen door slamming shut startled her, causing her to choke on the grape. She spit it discreetly into the napkin, praying he hadn't seen what had just happened, then chanced peeking over the low fence and spotted him standing on his raised deck. Of course. He was going to see her playing dress-up. Maybe he wouldn't look over. She sat frozen in place, watching as he stretched his arms over his head and rolled his neck to each side, as though he were trying to loosen sore muscles.

A wide grin spread across his face as soon as he caught her looking at him. "Well, if it isn't the girl next door!"

Harper gave him a sheepish wave.

It seemed to take a moment for him to register her attire. His mouth fell open for a second. "You look gorgeous. Where are you off to?"

"Um, thank you." Unable to think of a good reason to be dressed in a ball gown, she decided to ignore his question. "You're home early," she answered without thinking. Shit, why did I say that? Now he'll think I'm keeping track of him. How to terrify a man in one easy step.

If he had noticed her stalker-like observation, he pretended he hadn't. "I like to get everyone out a little early on payday. Seriously, where are you going that you need a ball gown?"

Closing her eyes, she could feel the heat in her face. "Once in a while, I do this as a pick-me-up."

He gave her an appreciative look. "That's . . . um . . . You're the only person I know who does that."

"Yes, well, frankly I have no idea why more people don't do this. It really is a fast way to feel happy." She spoke matter-of-factly, hoping to regain her composure.

"So, you're not going anywhere? No plans? Other than . . ." He pointed at the tray of fruit and the bottle of wine.

Shrugging, she replied, "This is my plan. It's sort of an escape, really."

"Oh, so it's an escape she needs," he answered lightly. "Your wish is my command. Give me ten minutes."

Harper sat, picking at the honeydew melon, wondering what had just happened and why the hell he always managed to catch her in life's most embarrassing moments. After a few minutes, she started to think he had gone inside to get away from her. She must have finally managed to scare him off. But then she heard her doorbell ring.

She walked through the house to the front door and pulled it open. A small gasp escaped her lips. There he stood in a black tuxedo, looking as if he'd stepped out of a Hugo Boss ad. He held out his hand to take hers, delivering a soft kiss to the top of her knuckles. His dark hair was a bit damp, she assumed from a shower, and she could smell his aftershave, which caused an instant war between her dignity and her lust. Much to her relief, she was able to keep still instead of burying her face in his neck. "Your lip looks much better."

"It was nothing. So, where to? While I was getting ready, I had a few ideas. An elegant dinner somewhere? Dancing? Maybe we could crash a wedding and do both?"

Harper laughed and shook her head. "I can't believe you put on a tuxedo for me."

"Why not? You said it's a fast way to feel happy. I like happy. So, where to?"

"I have no idea."

"Sounds terrific," he held out his arm for her. "Let's go."

In her hurry to leave, she decided to forgo the search for the perfect heels and slid her feet into a pair of jewelled flip-flops sitting next to the front entry.

* * *

"You hungry?" he asked as he started his truck.

"A little." She grinned at him.

"Upscale restaurant?"

Harper thought of the possibility of running into someone like Brent. "I actually don't feel like being around other people right now."

He glanced over at her, a knowing look in his eyes. "In that case, I know just the spot."

Forty-five minutes later, they were a few miles outside of Boulder. They pulled off onto a gravel driveway that led to a treed property set into the side of a hill.

"Where are we exactly?"

"This is my secret hideaway. Wait here," he said, getting out and walking around to open her door. He helped her down, his eyes locking on hers. "Let me grab the food."

Tucking a plaid blanket under his arm, he picked up the pizza box and six-pack of cider she'd decided on, then led her to a gate. Unhooking the wire holding the gate shut, he pushed it open and started along a narrow path through the trees. When they reached a clearing, Harper sucked in some air. "Wow. This is beautiful."

"Glad you like it." He looked back at her. "I bought the place earlier this year. I'm going to build on it someday."

The sun was just starting to go down, turning the grass and the trees that brilliant shade of green that happens only late in the day. The sky was pink and purple and orange, as though it had been painted just for them. For this one moment. Harper let out a long breath as she admired her surroundings. They had a perfect vantage point overlooking the rolling hills and a babbling creek below. In the distance, the city lights were becoming visible.

Fanning out the blanket with a snap, Evan let it drop to the grass, then arranged the pizza box and drinks. Offering his hand, he helped Harper as she carefully seated herself on the blanket.

She smoothed out her skirt. "This is not how I was expecting today to turn out."

Evan laughed. "Me neither, but I'm glad we're doing this." He flipped open the box lid and served Harper a slice on a paper napkin. "How'd the pictures turn out?" he asked as he twisted the top off her bottle of cider.

"Pretty good, I think. Megan said they were perfect, but I think she was probably just being kind."

"I don't know. I was watching you and it seemed like you knew what you were doing."

"I bet you say that to all the girls," Harper answered.

His eyes rested on her lips for a moment. Then he cleared his throat to break the spell. "So, how's Wes doing? I haven't heard from him in a while."

"He's doing well. He might get leave soon to come and see our dad."

"That would be nice." He paused. "I can't stop thinking about the other night. At the bar. I've been wondering how you're doing."

"Never better." Harper gave him a smile that all but killed the comforting sentiment that was no doubt perched on the tip of his tongue. "Mmm, this is delicious. Very decadent meal, Mr. Donovan. And you somehow got the best table in the house."

"I know the maître d'."

"I'm sorry, but I still can't believe you just threw on a tux and brought me here to eat pizza. You didn't even seem embarrassed when we went into the restaurant, or the supermarket, for that matter."

"Why would I be? We're the best-dressed people in town," he replied as he raised his slice of pizza to his mouth.

"It's just . . . I didn't know you had this side to you. That you would join me in my little fantasy world. I think most men would be worried about how it would look to everyone else."

"You know something? I used to waste a lot of time caring about what other people thought. Somehow, losing everything put things into perspective for me. Now I go after what I want without caring about other people's opinions. And look where it's gotten me. I'm sitting here with the most beautiful girl I know, watching the sunset."

Harper gave him a long smile. "Thank you."

"Thank you." His gaze was intense, his voice thick with emotion. There was a whole other conversation going on between them that had nothing to do with words and everything to do with wanting each other.

Harper broke her gaze to take in the view of the property again. "So, how much of what we're looking at is yours?"

Evan pointed, drawing the borders for her with his finger. "Right down past the creek to the edge of the forest. And about a hundred feet into the trees on either side."

"Wow. This is going to be quite a change from Maplewood Drive."

"Yeah. I'm looking forward to it."

"I hope you don't mind me asking, but I've been wondering how you ended up buying your parents' place."

"Oh, my dad was just set to retire and they were going to move to Tucson to help Karen out with her kids. About ten minutes after they put their house up for sale, the market crashed." He paused, wiping his mouth with a napkin. "I needed to unload my monster of a house, so it worked out pretty nicely."

"That must have been a huge relief to your parents," Harper answered. She knew he was leaving out a lot of the story, the part about downsizing so he could keep his crews employed. But she wasn't going to push him on the topic.

He shrugged off her compliment. "It worked out well for me too." Taking a sip of his cider, he gave her a curious look. "What about you? Where are you planning to set down roots when your dad is recovered?"

"I'll be on the next flight to New York as soon as humanly possible."

"I guess that makes sense. You haven't necessarily received the best welcome home."

"I don't care about that," she replied quickly. "My whole life is there. I can't leave it all behind." Harper looked over at him and saw a serious expression on his face. If she didn't know better, she'd think he was disappointed.

They finished their meal in a charged silence. "What would you say to another cider?"

"I'd say sure, I'm not driving." She took the bottle from him, feeling a little dizzy as his hand brushed hers, more from having just eaten a meal with Evan-from-Heaven than from the drink. The teenage girl inside her wanted to scream and jump up and down with excitement. The woman in her wanted to scream, jump up and down, then rip his clothes off.

A quiet fell over them as they sipped their drinks and stared out at the remains of the sunset. Soon, the only light would be from the moon. It was that do-or-die moment and they both knew it. They had reached the fork in the road where they either went for it or forgot the whole thing. And now that she'd told him she was leaving town as soon as possible, maybe he'd decide to forget the whole thing.

Clearing off the blanket, Evan lay down on his back. "Let's do some stargazing."

"Sure. We are in formal wear, after all, so we should surround ourselves with stars." Harper lay beside him, resting her hands on her tummy and watching as the tiny lights appeared in the sky above.

"What would you do if you could do anything or go any place in the world right now?" Harper asked suddenly, glancing over at him.

Evan turned his head, his expression one of surprise. "That depends. Would there be consequences to my actions or would I just get a free pass?"

"Free pass all the way. Time stops until you say so. No one but you would remember."

"Hmm. In that case, I'd do a lot of things. I'd want to empty out a bank vault, of course."

Harper nodded. "Of course."

Evan looked up, considering his answer. "Then there's riding down a long stretch of highway on a motorbike, full throttle. Guys always wish they could do that."

"Really? Me too."

"Really?"

With a straight face, she said, "No. Not really. That would be a ridiculous waste of time."

Evan chuckled at her before continuing. "Drink a six-pack on the pitcher's mound at Yankee Stadium."

"That I understand, except I'd go with chocolate cake and the Queen's throne at Buckingham Palace."

He gave her an impressed nod. "Oh, break the sound barrier in an F-22 Raptor," he continued.

"I'm assuming that's some type of airplane?"

"Uh, yeah."

Even though this was fun, it wasn't going the way Harper had hoped. Maybe they were heading down the "forget the whole thing" road. Damn it.

"Of course, I'd definitely want to take you to bed," he said as a slow smirk spread across his face. "Yes, definitely. We'd need to stop time for a good long while on that one."

A flicker of hope sparked her desire for him, spreading a warmth through her body. Maybe they were veering to the "let's see where this goes" path after all.

"Is that so?" she asked, lazily running a finger over the back of his hand. "But I thought it would ruin me for other men even to see you without your clothes on?"

"Oh, it would, but you said I would be the only one to remember anything, right? If that's the case, you'd survive."

Harper laughed out loud, covering her mouth with her hand and blushing at the thought of him without his clothes.

"You're thinking about it right now, aren't you?" he asked, pretending to be shocked.

"You brought it up!"

"You're the one who came up with the game," he replied. "You had to know it would end there."

"No. Certainly not," she said. The skepticism on his face pulled the truth out of her. "Okay, I may have been testing the waters."

He studied her for a long moment without answering, his face growing serious.

"What?" Harper asked, suddenly feeling exposed by the look he was giving her.

Evan shook his head as though in awe. "I'm just trying to figure out how it is that I never noticed you when we were kids."

"You were a little busy with every other girl in Boulder hanging on your every word."

"I don't know about that, but right now it seems like it should have been absolutely impossible not to see you. You're completely stunning." He reached for her hand, lacing his fingers through hers.

"Stunning. That's one of my favourite words," she said, her voice so soft it was almost a whisper.

"You know this is probably a horrible idea, right? Wes is one of my best friends. This could turn out to be really complicated." The lust in his eyes was in direct defiance of his words. "As a rule, I avoid complicated at all costs."

"I know how to keep things simple." She blinked slowly. "In fact, I'm exceedingly good at it."

"I have a feeling you're exceedingly good at a lot of things."

Harper gave him a sultry look. "I am. But don't take my word for it. You should probably find out for yourself."

"I intend to." Rolling on top of her in one swift move, he gazed at her for a moment, his eyes full of desire. Harper's eyes grew wide in surprise and she let out a little laugh as she felt his weight pressing her to the ground. He lifted his hand to her face, skimming her lips with his thumb. And finally, he was kissing her again with an intensity that burned through her. There was nothing sweet or gentle about his kiss this time. It was rough and urgent and toe-curling, and she matched it with her response.

Harper's hands moved quickly from his powerful arms to his hair, fingers weaving through it and pulling him toward her, bringing his kiss in deeper. Time stopped. Nothing else existed outside of this moment. Tongues danced, moans and sighs escaped lips as they gave in to their need for each other.

Pulling back for a moment, he asked, "Is this—"

"Yes," she interrupted. "God, yes." She tugged on the lapel of his tuxedo jacket, bringing him back for more.

They kissed wildly, her hands now yanking at his jacket to get it off. He leaned back on his knees, ridding himself of his tie as she frantically unbuttoned his shirt, leaving his chest bare. Running her hands over his chiselled abs, she watched as he made short work of his cufflinks and shrugged off his shirt. The look he gave her as he pulled up the skirt of her dress made her feel somehow weak and fully alive at the same time. Sliding his hands up her legs, he reached her black lace panties, pulling them down, his rough hands skimming along her outer thighs.

They stared at each other, breathing heavily, as they allowed themselves their first look at each other this way in the faded light of the moon.

"Consider me ruined," Harper blurted out as her eyes locked onto his incredible body. All those years of playing sports and working construction had sculpted every muscle to perfection.

"You'll just have to forget you saw it." He let out an appreciative puff of air as he looked her up and down again. "So will I."

Their eyes met and their mouths followed quickly. In an instant, Evan lowered himself over her, his lips sucking on the nape of her neck and planting kisses up to her ear. He moved his face back in line with hers and they kissed, tongues exploring each other endlessly, losing all track of where they were. Her stomach muscles tensed as his hand finally moved down between her parted legs, finding its way to her core, now plump and wet with desire for him. He covered her with his palm and carefully pushed two fingers into her sex, rubbing and circling inside her with the most deliciously slow movements, which served only to make her wild with passion.

Harper's fingers grazed his body, starting at his shoulders, squeezing his massive biceps as they moved down to his hands, then onto his chest and finally his back. She craved every bit of him—on her, in her, all over her. She needed to take it all in, to memorize him with her body, he for whom she had longed for so many years.

And then he was moving down, pushing her skirt out of the way, his tongue gliding along her sex, tasting her slowly, carefully. Harper let out a loud moan as her legs fell away from each other of their own accord. Her eyelids lowered as she felt his lips on her sensitive core, now pulsing with electricity. Replacing his fingers with his mouth, he ran his thumbs along her sex as he sucked and licked and thrust his tongue in as deep as he could. The sensations he was giving her were exquisite. A gentle, warm breeze caressed her skin, blending with the incredible pleasure he was giving her. Gripping the fabric of her skirt with her fingers, she arched her back, bringing him in further. She was writhing under him now, her body wild, her breath ragged. She felt herself jolt as he thrust his tongue deeper. "Oh, right there, Evan, yes!" she called out as she tensed for him again and again.

When it was over, he leaned back, gazing at her as she recovered. The smile on his face was one of complete satisfaction at how she'd responded to him. Harper locked eyes with him and gave him a little nod, reaching for him. She needed to feel him inside her now.

Wasting no time, he tugged at his belt, pulling it off and yanking down his pants along with his boxer briefs, freeing himself. Harper ran her fingers over his thick length, taking in the smoothness of the skin covering his rock-hard erection. A groan escaped his chest as her hand glided over him.

Taking both of her hands, he pinned them over her head, lowering himself over her. Her full breasts rounded out of the bodice of her dress and he paused there for a long moment, kissing her satiny skin. In one slow, long thrust, he found his way inside her tight warmth, both of them moaning at the intense pleasure of it. He stopped for a brief second to look at her, making sure she was okay. The desire in her eyes was the answer he had been hoping for. She wanted him. Wanted this. Now.

Rocking his hips, he filled her completely before pulling back and almost all the way out, then thrusting forward again. Her muscles squeezed around him as he moved over her and their tongues found each other. Evan's powerful arms lifted and lowered his body over hers, the motion working them both into a frenzy that would not end until they'd satisfied their need for each other. Driving his tongue into her mouth, he worked it in sync with what he was doing inside her sex. Swirls, circles, thrusts—over and over, each time more forcefully, harder. His pace slowed, as though he were intent on savouring every second with her, before gaining momentum again, maintaining that connection where she needed him most. The hard ground below had no give, making it possible for him to go deeper than either of them had imagined. Her sex throbbed in response to what he was doing. She could feel another climax building to that perfect crescendo, every part of her tensing with an unbelievable force as she let go. Waves of pleasure rippled through her as he held her hands over her head.

She gripped him with her legs, giving herself to him completely. Slamming himself into her, he gave in to his own orgasm. After a long minute of pulsing and tensing, he pressed his forehead to hers. Their panting slowed. Cheeks flushed, body glistening, Harper wore a lazy smile of utter gratification. The frustration of two decades of waiting was now over. It was everything she had thought it would be and so much more. They stayed like that, wrapped up in each other, in this perfect moment, as time stood still. Time could wait. Life could wait.

Kissing her tenderly on the mouth, Evan murmured, "Harper, you're just so unbelievably sexy."

"So are you . . . You *have* ruined me. There is no way I'm going to be able to forget what just happened," she said, kissing him back.

"In that case, you should come home with me and stay the night."

ELEVEN

"You weren't lying," she stated, digging into her third bite of breakfast.

"Oh, I know. I've figured out the secret to the perfect waffle," Evan answered, gratified by her obvious enjoyment.

"Are you going to tell me?"

"Sorry, but I can't do that." He gave her a sideways glance to see her reaction.

"After everything we did last night and this morning, you don't think you can trust me with your waffle recipe?" Harper looked at him from under her eyebrows but her mouth curved up.

"I wish I could, but it really wouldn't serve my purpose," he replied with a phony apologetic look.

"Your purpose?"

Taking another bite, he made her wait while he chewed. "If I tell you, you'll be able to make them yourself and that would give you one less reason to stay over again."

He watched as a satisfied smile spread over her face. He hadn't been sure how either of them would feel when the light of morning came. As Harper had fallen asleep, naked in his arms the night before, Evan had had a temporary feeling of panic and guilt. His feelings for her as they lay together were far stronger than just desire, and those feelings would do nothing but complicate his life if he let them. The fact that she wasn't here permanently wasn't the biggest issue. In fact, it could serve to keep things from getting too serious, which was how he needed it. But she was still his best friend's sister, which meant that unless this was going to become permanent, he shouldn't be doing it. He had pulled her to him, forcing those thoughts aside, telling himself that they were grown adults and what they did was their own business. He wanted this, needed it. Needed her. And he was going to let himself relish every delicious moment of having her in his bed. Maybe it was actually the perfect situation. He could finally be with a woman who wasn't going to develop any unrealistic expectations of him. Maybe this could be simple.

Evan had woken her that morning, kissing her neck and gliding his fingers along the curve of her body, needing to have her again. They had let time stand still as they made love in the shower, slowly washing each other, exploring each other's bodies until the water ran cold. And now, as they sat at the table, so close together that their knees were touching, they were still keeping the world at bay. He was surprised at how pleasing he found the sight of her in his tuxedo shirt, her hair pinned up in messy waves on top of her head. She was so sexy.

"What's going on in that mind of yours?" Evan asked, pouring more syrup onto his waffles.

"Nothing coherent. You've rendered my brain useless this morning." She dabbed the side of her mouth carefully with a napkin.

"Really? I didn't know that was possible with that big brain you've got there," he replied, leaning over to kiss her lips.

"Mmm, maple syrup has never been so delicious," she said, opening her eyes as he pulled away. "What was that you were saying about my big brain? I know I have dinner plans, but right now I can't remember who with," she went on, her voice dreamy.

"Good, then maybe whoever he is will drop off the face of the planet."

"Oh, wait—I'm going to Megan's for dinner with her family."

"Well, then, I take that back. How is Megan? I heard she's got another baby and she's living with some guy from France."

"Yes, he's an old friend of mine, Luc. They're tired but wonderful. It's so great to see her happy again," Harper answered.

"I bet. She had a rough go for a long time. That's one of the things I could be grateful for when Avery and I split. No kids to get caught in the middle."

"It definitely makes things worse. No clean break if you've got kids," she agreed. She looked down at her coffee for a moment before taking a sip.

Evan could feel a tightening in his chest as he thought of his ex-wife. That was always the case when he thought of Avery. First, the initial pang that accompanied the memory of what had happened, then the humiliation, then the hurt. He had promised himself that he would never let that happen to him again. Now, as he looked over at the woman sitting next to him, he realized that she was capable of causing him that kind of pain. The kind that would last. After only one night together, he had feelings that he would never name, and they were so much stronger than lust.

His eyes were set on hers, his expression serious. "I feel like I should be honest with you, Harper. I've been down the whole marriage road before and it's not one I intend to go down again anytime soon. Maybe ever."

"Good, then we're on the same page," Harper answered. She stood to clear her plate. "I was just looking for a little fun last night."

Turning to him, she gave him a sultry smile. "Nicely done, by the way. All that rock climbing has definitely taught you some moves I've never seen before."

Winking at him, she made her way to the bedroom and closed the door, only to re-emerge a few minutes later, dressed in her gown. Striding down the hall, she smiled at him again. "I should go see my dad. I haven't been since yesterday morning, and by now he's probably wondering if I skipped town."

Evan leaned against the wall as she stopped in front of him. "Okay. I should get going anyway. I'm meeting some friends to go climbing." He ran a finger down her arm. "Too bad you have plans tonight. I wouldn't mind a replay of this morning."

"Well, we'll just have to do this again soon." Harper said, kissing him seductively before pulling away.

"Hey, where are you going?" Evan asked. "You can't just kiss a guy like that and walk away."

"Sure I can." Harper continued to the front door with a glance back over her shoulder. "That's all you get for now, Donovan."

She slid on her flip-flops while Evan watched. He tugged her in for a long, deep kiss. Just when her body started to sink into it, he pulled back with a wicked grin. "That's all you get."

"Maybe that's all I wanted," Harper replied.

"Oh, you want more. You want it so bad, you can taste it," Evan murmured, moving his mouth in closer but refusing to kiss her again.

"This was the perfect diversion. We should do it again—if you think you can handle it without getting too attached to me." Harper teased him with her mouth now, hovering it just an inch from his to see what he'd do.

"Oh, I can handle it. You call me if you decide you can." His expression was one of complete confidence, but inside he was hiding the wariness he felt.

"No. Next move's yours. Or not. See you around, sailor."

Harper could feel Evan watching her as she crossed the lawn to her dad's house. Once safely inside, she closed her eyes, feeling a pang in her chest. She was suddenly gripped by fear. She had just spent the night and the better part of the morning in bed with the man of her dreams, and she only now realized how dangerous that had been.

Being with Evan had left her torn between wanting him and knowing she would very likely get crushed if she let things go any further. If this continued, she wouldn't be able to stop herself from giving him her heart. And that was something she had long ago promised herself she would never to do. When her mother had left them, Harper came to understand that the only person she could truly rely on was herself. Not even her own mom could be trusted. She had witnessed the pain her dad had gone through as he sank into a dark fog that had never fully lifted. Harper vowed that she would never allow that to happen to her.

TWELVE

"So, that's how you left things?" Megan asked, pushing the stroller as she and Harper walked Amelie around the neighbourhood. The baby had been very fussy after dinner, so the pair had taken her up for a bath and now had her snuggled under a cozy blanket as the fresh air, along with the rhythm of the wheels on the sidewalk, lulled her to sleep. Luc and Elliott had elected to stay home to play video games, Luc seeming to sense that Harper needed some time for girl talk. "You just told him you'll see him around?"

"Correction. I said, 'See you around, sailor.'"

"That makes it so much worse, somehow." Megan winced. "But wait, I'm confused. You had this amazing fantasy night together so why, exactly, don't you want to do it again?"

"I don't know," Harper groaned, running her hands down her neck. "No, that's not true. I sort of do. I think it's because it was all just too intense, you know? It wasn't just sex, it was different. It was like there was all this passion and emotion to it. And the way he looked at me . . . I've never been looked at like that before. It was like he was peering into my soul or something."

"So it scared you a little," Megan said.

"No, it scared me a lot," Harper answered, chewing on her top lip. "It's like playing with fire. You're pretty much guaranteed to end up in intensive care."

"Maybe. Or maybe it would be the best thing that ever happened to you?" Megan inquired hopefully. "Let me ask you this: If he called you right now, would you want to rush back over there?"

"Yes. No. I don't know. Maybe. What would be the point? I'm going back to New York as soon as I can. The safest thing would be to just leave it alone. It was just sex. Mind-blowing, earth-moving sex with the man of my dreams. But that's all it was."

* * *

By the time Evan got home from work, the sun had already disappeared from the sky—like Harper, leaving only the faintest sign it had been there. He could see that there were no lights on at her house and he knew where she was. He sighed as he parked his truck, thinking about how things had been just twenty-four hours ago. They had been sitting together on a blanket, eating dinner and watching the sunset. He knew he shouldn't be going down that road but he just couldn't stop himself. She drew him to her with everything she did, every little comment, every move of her body, every look. She drew him to her with her sadness. He thought back to her sitting in the yard in her ball gown. He'd noticed her from the kitchen window first and had taken a few minutes to just watch her, fascinated. It didn't take him long to see by the slump of her shoulders that she was hurting. The need to make her feel better was instant and overwhelming. He'd come out, pretending he hadn't seen her so as not to embarrass her. If she knew that he suspected she was sad or vulnerable in any way, she would hate it

But now that he'd been with her, touched her, felt her naked body wrapped around him, he realized exactly how right he had been when he told her it was a horrible idea. He was certain that if he let things go on, he'd be making the biggest mistake of his life. He couldn't let himself be drawn in like this. Those walls around his heart were there for a reason. Harper was a love 'em and leave 'em kind of girl; she was itching to get back to her life in New York. He'd be nothing more than a pit stop for her before she disappeared again, only this time, she'd take his heart with her if he let her.

He trudged into the house and relieved his tired feet from the heavy confines of his steel-toed boots, swearing under his breath at the mess he had made of things. Everything seemed wrong at this moment, and he was hungry and tired and sore. If it weren't for the massive quantity of regret he felt, he'd be completely empty.

Showering did nothing to enliven his spirits and now, as he sat on his deck alone, eating reheated leftovers, the solitude of his life started to reveal itself to him. Hadn't he been better off the night before, sharing a meal with Harper?

* * *

A couple of hours later, he heard Roy's truck pull up. In spite of his better judgment, Evan found himself jogging down the front steps to meet Harper as she walked up the sidewalk to her dad's house. His heart pounded at the sight of her.

"Hi," he said.

Harper stopped, then gave him a breezy look. "Hi yourself."

"I wanted to talk to you about how we left things this morning." His eyes searched hers for answers.

Harper sighed heavily, rubbing her hand down her cheek. "Yes. As much as I hate to admit it, I think you may have been right about this whole thing."

Evan nodded. "You mean about it being a terrible idea."

"Mmhmm. I think we'd be fooling ourselves if we thought we could let this go on without any consequences, right?"

"Because it would be complicated?"

"Exactly. And neither of us can do complicated," she stated.

"I don't know. I bet we could find a way to keep it simple."

Harper shook her head. "I'm not so confident about that."

Evan nodded. "The last thing I would ever want to do is hurt you, Harper. I can stay away from you if that's what you need. I won't like it, but I will."

"I think that's what I need. My life is really a mess right now. I wouldn't be good for anyone, like this."

"Okay. At least I can enjoy the fact that I was right. I'll always have that." He bumped her playfully with his shoulder, hoping to lighten the mood. "If you change your mind, you know where to find me."

"I won't."

Evan swallowed hard. His heart had been in his throat as he made this one last offer, but now it had sunk down to his gut. Giving her a soft, slow kiss on the cheek, he drank in the scent of her one last time. "Take care. You call if you need anything."

"Thanks. You too." Harper's eyes mirrored the sadness he was feeling.

He stared at her for a moment before he turned and walked away.

* * *

That night, Harper collapsed onto her bed with a loud groan. Why the hell had she gone with him last night? It would have been so much easier if she had never slept with him. She'd been better off dreaming about him than knowing what it was like to be with him and needing to forget. Her time with him had been more incredible than she'd thought possible, so much more than she'd experienced with any other man.

It wasn't just his amazing body. It wasn't just how their bodies moved together, so perfectly in sync. It wasn't just the pleasure he gave her. It was the way he looked at her, the way he kissed her, the way he touched her. He made her feel like she was the only woman who had ever existed. He had taken her away, let her escape her life. And for the briefest of moments, she had felt loved and adored. She'd fallen asleep in his arms knowing the dreams she would have that night would be nothing compared to the one she was living. And then, in a blink, reality had set in, leaving her a hot mess. Tears of frustration streamed down her cheeks and into her hair. What the hell was she doing here? She should be back in New York, out with her friends or in her office, busy. Instead she was alone with her thoughts all day and night. And tonight, her thoughts were torturing her.

THIRTEEN

"Dad, this is Dr. Chan, the psychologist that Dr. Smyth recommended."

"No thank you, Dr. Chan. I already told Dr. Smyth and my daughter here that I don't want to talk about how I'm feeling."

Dr. Chan gave him a friendly smile. "That's okay. I'll just sit here anyway. Your daughter has prepaid for five sessions at one hundred and eighty dollars an hour. But if you want to spend her money in silence, that's fine too."

"That's almost a thousand dollars!" Roy turned to Harper with wide eyes. "What the hell, kid?"

"I figured this would be the only way to get you to agree to it. We talked about this, Dad. And you need this." Harper stared him down. "I'm going to sit in the hall for the next hour. Don't waste my money."

She gave Dr. Chan a little wink on her way out.

An hour later, Dr. Chan opened the door. Light spilled out into the hallway from Roy's room.

"You got him to open the curtains?"

"No, I opened them. That's the advantage of having him in that bed. He couldn't stop me."

"Did he talk?"

"Yes. Opening the curtains certainly got him talking. I'll be back in two days. I'd like to come back twice a week for now."

"Thank you. Whatever we can do to help him."

"Harper, I know you want to respect your father's wishes, but you also have to be careful not to feed into his depression out of kindness. You may need to make choices for him that he won't make for himself right now. Start with simple things, like letting some light into the room, bringing in a radio or some CDs. Play his favourite music or, if he likes, talk-radio programs. That type of thing. He needs to keep his mind busy so he doesn't spiral any further."

"Okay, I will," Harper said. "Thank you, doctor."

"You're welcome. And one last thing. Make sure you take care of yourself so his current state doesn't start to adversely affect you. Do you have a good support system here?"

"I do. I have some good friends here, and my brothers."

"Good. You let me know if you ever need to talk."

* * *

Later that day, Harper found herself wandering the aisles of the supermarket, pondering dinner, when she felt a tap on her shoulder. She turned to see Monica, an old friend from high school, who had been among the concert-goers. The pair exchanged pleasant hellos.

"Crazy how we haven't seen each other in years, then twice in a week," Monica remarked. "That was a great concert the other night. Did you all have fun at the pub? I was sorry I had to miss it."

"I didn't stay too long, actually. We'll have to do it sometime when you and Megan can both be there." Harper smiled.

"I would love that. I don't get out nearly as much as I'd like since Jayden was born," Monica answered. "Say, I wanted to ask you about something Brent told me at the concert."

Harper stiffened at the mention of Brent's name.

"He said you're going to be in town for a few months, maybe? Is that right?"

"Yes, it looks like it. I'm staying as long as my dad needs me," Harper answered, her shoulders relaxing.

Monica wrinkled up her nose as though she weren't sure if she should ask her next question. "I'm wondering if you might have a little free time. I'm starting a chapter of Fashion Forward here. It's an organization that helps women find employment. One of the things we do is provide them with business attire for interviews. I could really use an expert on staff."

"That's a great cause! We ran an article about it last year. I would love to be a part of it. Right now I actually have nothing but time on my hands. My dad won't be out of the hospital for weeks."

"Really? That's so great! Well, not about your dad, I mean. I'm sorry for what he's going through. I'm just really relieved you said yes. I've rounded up a lot of dress clothes, but I honestly don't know how to put together the right looks and accessorize them."

"Well, that's something I do know," Harper answered, just as Monica's cell rang.

"Shoot. I have to take this. I'll get your number from Meg so we can get together, okay?"

"That would be lovely."

FOURTEEN

Harper and Evan managed to avoid each other over the next two weeks in spite of both their proximity and their longing for one another. The weather had allowed Evan to spend long days working. Even though things were going smoothly at the site, he found himself short-fused and grouchy. Then he felt angry at himself for his mood, which led him to wonder how long it would take before Harper was out of his system. On the weekend, he loaded Boots into the truck and drove a few hours out of town to go solo climbing and camping. He hoped the distance and distraction would lessen his yearning for her, but it did not have the desired effect. Instead, he found himself tossing and turning in his tent, thinking of Harper when he should have been sleeping. As much as he wished he could just forget what had happened, there would be no free pass this time.

For her part, Harper split her days between readying the house for her father's return and meeting with Monica to finalize things at the Fashion Forward headquarters. Grateful that she now had a lot to accomplish, she woke each morning with a sense of purpose that helped push aside the horrible tugging at her heart when she first opened her eyes. With mere days until the opening, the office was a whirlwind of activity, with its four volunteers trying to get word out about the charity as well as making last-minute preparations. Megan joined them to take photos for the website. Excitement and a sense of community filled the air as they worked.

On opening day, everything had been set up and exhilaration flowed. The space held racks of outfits that were already coordinated and arranged by colour and size. A small play area, with donated toys and child-sized tables and chairs, had been created. The smell of fresh coffee and warm donuts welcomed clients. Four women were already booked in and three more came in without appointments. Monica introduced Harper to the clients as their personal stylist, making sure to provide Harper's credentials. Each woman received two new outfits complete with shoes, a dress coat, a purse and accessories. Harper coached each of the women on the secrets of makeup application and how to carry themselves with confidence. By the time they walked out the door, she made sure it was with their heads held high. Hair salons from around the city gave away gift cards for services to provide the final touches.

Monica and a couple of other volunteers sat at small desks assisting clients with fixing up their resumés and writing cover letters. Optimism was the order of the day, and the buzz of excitement that had started the morning hadn't worn off by the time they closed up. The friends sat around the desks, tired but filled with a sense of accomplishment as they talked about how well things had gone.

"Thank you so much, Harper. You're absolutely perfect for this work," Monica said. "We're so lucky you came on board."

"Thank you for asking me. It's funny, really. When I worked for *Style*, one of my favourite things was seeing real women wearing the looks we'd put together for our photo shoots, but it wouldn't be until months later. And I didn't get to meet them. I just had to hope they had gotten a little lift from looking good. But this is so personal and so immediate. It's just wonderful."

"Wonderful enough that you might stay?" Monica's eyes were hopeful.

Harper beamed. "How about I'll be here as much as I can until I leave?"

"We'll take what we can get."

* * *

Returning home that night, Harper went over her to-do list for the house. She vowed to get the house ready as soon as possible so her dad wouldn't have to spend a minute longer than was necessary at the hospital. She had hired a handyman to widen the bathroom door and put up bars above the bathtub. He helped her move Roy's bed into storage in the basement so a hospital bed could take its place.

Going to visit him early Friday morning, she spotted Dr. Smyth standing at the nursing station, filling in some charts. She stood beside him, setting down a box of donuts for the staff. Ignoring the donuts, the nurses and Dr. Smyth all stared at her, grinning from ear to ear.

"What? They're just donuts. Honestly, I'm not even sure how fresh they are. I had one on the way over. It was mediocre at best."

Dr. Smyth spoke up. "I think you should go see your dad. He's waiting to show you something." He nodded toward Roy's hospital room.

"Is it . . . ?" she whispered, too overcome by hope and emotion to go on.

"It's not my news to give," Dr. Smyth said, pointing to Roy's door.

Harper hurried into his room and found her dad staring down at his feet. The blanket had been pulled up, revealing his bare toes. He beamed as he pointed down. "Check out my new trick."

He wiggled the toes of both feet.

"Oh, Dad! That's maybe the best thing I've ever seen anyone do!" Harper gave him a huge hug, tears flowing down her face.

"I agree. Those wiggling toes are pure hope!" Roy's eyes were shining as he clapped his hands together.

An hour later, Harper walked down the hall to the elevator with an extra skip in her step. She was stopped by Dr. Smyth's voice.

"Harper! Hang on a second," he said, jogging toward her. "I'm glad I caught you."

She watched him as he neared. He was very handsome. Blond, with intensely green eyes and a warmth about him. His lab coat did little to hide the fact that he was some type of fitness buff. "So, that's some terrific news about my dad, Dr. Smyth! Thank you so much for everything!"

"So far I haven't been able to do much, but now I think I might be able to. I just got off the phone with the patient coordinator at the Rosewood Rehab Clinic. We might have an opening for Roy there. It would be a huge benefit to him. Twenty-four hour care, on-site occupational and physical therapy. Six weeks there would save him about four months of recovery at home. I'm there twice a week, so I can keep an eye on his progress. Now that we're seeing some of the feeling return to his legs, it would be the best place for him."

"Really? That sounds wonderful." She hesitated for a moment before asking the question that had immediately popped into her mind. "Would this be covered under workers' compensation?"

A flash of understanding crossed Dr. Smyth's face. "Right. Workers' compensation covers everything right up to the point of maximum recovery."

"Meaning?"

"Meaning I have to fill out a stack of forms as long as my arm, but with the nature of his injuries and the way the accident happened, I can't see why it wouldn't be covered."

"Thank you so much!" Harper exclaimed.

"Don't thank me yet. It's not a guarantee. The other problem is that I won't know for a few days if he can get in, so you'll need to be ready for him to come home next week just in case. There's no sense in keeping him here if we don't have to."

"The house should be ready in four days. I have a fellow coming by to help me build the ramp tomorrow. The only hold-up will be the adjustable bed, but they've promised to deliver it on Tuesday."

"Excellent. With any luck, he'll be transferred to Rosewood instead, but it'll be good to have the option open. I'll call to let you know as soon as I hear from the coordinator over there."

FIFTEEN

The next morning Harper woke to her alarm, expecting Sven, the handyman, to be there by 8 a.m. He'd agreed to come on a Saturday since the work needed to be done in short order. She dressed quickly and made a pot of coffee. Checking the time, she realized it was after eight now and there was still no sign of him. She flipped through an issue of Vogue while she ate breakfast. As she was clearing her dishes, the phone finally rang. Sven was calling to say he couldn't make it. He had been offered a much larger project and would be tied up for the next couple of weeks and no, he didn't know anyone else she could ask, but he was sorry all the same.

She glanced in the direction of Evan's house, momentarily feeling desperate enough to call him, but knowing that would only end badly. He'd be nice to her and she'd make sure they ended up in bed together. She spent the next couple of hours searching the Web for help, only to come up empty. Now what was she going to do?

As she sat stewing away, her phone rang.

"Hello?"

"Hi, Harper. It's Gordon Smyth calling."

"Oh, hi, Dr. Smyth."

"I was just filling out these workers' compensation forms and I realized there are a few blanks I'll need you to fill in for me. I wanted to let you know that I'll leave them at the front desk, so be sure to get them when you're in next."

"Thanks. I was just about to come by. My ex-handyman called this morning to tell me he's not showing up to build the ramp, so I thought I should pop in to see my dad."

"Well, I'm pretty good with tools. Why don't I come by to help?"

"Seriously?"

"Don't sound so surprised. I happen to know which end of the hammer to hold." His tone was light.

"That would be wonderful, actually." Harper answered. "Are you sure?"

"Positive. I have the afternoon off and I'd be happy to come on one condition."

"Name it."

"Call me Gordon."

* * *

Three hours later, Gordon arrived as promised. He was dressed casually in khaki shorts and a black T-shirt. In his hand was a six-pack of beer. "Building and beer seem to go together," he said as Harper let him in.

The two stepped out into the yard, finding the pile of brackets, boards and screws waiting for them. She handed him the instructions and went back inside to pour their beers into frosty mugs. When she came out, she glanced over the low fence at Evan's yard, and her heart skipped a beat to see him standing on his deck. He gave her a long, serious look and a little nod before going back into the house. Shit. He'd seen Gordon and now he would have the wrong idea. Or maybe he'd gotten the right idea? Why would Gordon be here if he wasn't at least a little bit interested in her?

As the afternoon wore on, Evan mowed his lawn and carefully pruned the shrubs in his yard. If she wasn't mistaken, it seemed as though he were keeping an eye on her and Gordon. Every time Harper glanced over, she felt a tug of guilt and had to remind herself they had both agreed that staying away from each other was for the best. Even if he was incredibly sexy. Even if she did want to climb the fence and rip his clothes off. She needed to forget him.

"Nurse, can you hold that here for a second?" Gordon teased, positioning one of the boards over the brackets he had set up.

"Yes, doctor. Sponge?" she joked back as she held the board for him.

Just as he lifted the hammer to secure the board's precut grooves into the bracket, a coughing sound came from Evan's yard. Harper was distracted by the noise and looked up, moving the board as she did. This caused Gordon to hammer his thumb instead of the wood.

"Ah, fuck!" he cursed as blood immediately pooled under his nail.

"Oh my God! I am so sorry!" she exclaimed. "Can I get you some ice?"

"No, it's fine, really." He winced, holding his thumb with his other hand, annoyance flashing across his face.

"I'm so sorry. I just got distracted for a second. Can I do anything to help?" Harper asked quickly, her cheeks turning red with embarrassment.

He shook his head. "No, it's nothing." He picked up the hammer. "Just don't move the board again," he said, trying to sound as though he were joking.

One pound of the hammer was enough. "Nope. Sorry, Harper, I don't think I can finish this today. I'm going to go into work and cauterize it to relieve the pressure. Maybe I can come by tomorrow night or sometime soon to help you get this done." He stood and swiped his keys and cellphone off the deck.

"No, no. I couldn't ask you to come back. I think I can finish it myself. I feel so terrible. Let me at least give you a ride to the hospital?"

*　*　*

A few minutes later, Harper stood on the front sidewalk as Gordon got into his car, insisting he didn't need a ride. "I'm just going to sneak in and try to fix it without anyone noticing. Then I have a dinner at my brother's house. It's my sister-in-law's birthday."

"Okay, well, call me later to let me know how you're doing, or if you need anything."

"Sounds good." He smiled at her. "Maybe we could go out sometime, somewhere without hammers."

Harper managed a laugh. "I'd like that."

She watched him drive off before wandering back into the yard. Plunking herself down into a wicker chair, she sipped the beer he had brought as she stared at the unfinished ramp. She finally decided to call Megan and filled her in on the day's events.

"That sucks. Is he going to come back to help you?" Megan asked.

"No, I think I might be able to finish it myself. We're on step twelve of sixteen. The rest can't be that hard."

"Hmm. Well, when you're done, come here for supper. I haven't seen you in a week now and that is just unacceptable."

"Has it been that long? That is unacceptable. I'll get some wine on my way over. Should be there in about three hours."

"Supper's in two hours," Megan informed her.

"I'll be there in two hours."

Harper got back to work, her enthusiasm renewed. She now had a nice evening to look forward to after she finished. She could do this.

An hour later, she dropped the instructions onto the kitchen table, having just had a quiet tantrum in her yard. When she had finally managed to get the ramp completed, she realized that it was the wrong ramp for the doorway. The screen door swung out, meaning that she should have bought the other kit. Now she couldn't get in or out of the house through the back door.

* * *

Evan had watched from his kitchen window as Harper had her tantrum in the backyard. A smile crossed his lips as she scrunched up the instructions and tossed them to the ground. Why did he find her so damn adorable as she was kicking the deck with a vengeance?

He had noticed that the ramp was going to end up a few inches too high for the door before he went inside to shower but he hadn't said anything. He understood Harper well enough to know she would have refused his help after the way they had left things. He sighed to himself, wishing things were different between them. The past two weeks had been agony for him. He couldn't get her off his mind no matter what he did. He'd stayed at work late every evening, hoping to avoid her. They couldn't be an item, no matter how badly he wanted her. It would never work. If he could take back what had happened between them, he would. It had been a mistake. Every raw, delicious second of it. He was only going to end up hurting her if she didn't hurt him first. And he cared far too much for her to let that happen. Not to mention how strong his feelings for her were after only one night together. Too strong. He had never wanted a woman the way he wanted her, and sleeping with her hadn't helped put an end to his longing. It had only made it much, much worse.

Seeing her today with that other guy had gutted him in a way he hadn't expected. From bits of the conversation he'd overheard, it sounded like the guy was a doctor, or maybe that was some role play thing they had. He shook his head as though to expel the thought from his mind. When that idiot had hammered his own thumb, Evan went into the house, unable to wipe the smirk off his face. After a few minutes of laughing to himself, he realized it was lucky that Harper hadn't gotten hurt by accident.

He knew he shouldn't have been keeping an eye on them in the first place. It was none of his business, and he knew he was partially responsible for her having moved the board. But he just couldn't tear himself away; his desire to be there in case she needed him stopped him from walking away. The longer he watched them together, the more his insides churned with regret and jealousy. He was aware of how ridiculous it was to feel upset at the thought of Harper with another man, but when it came to Harper, Evan was realizing he was far from logical.

SIXTEEN

The next morning, Harper made her way around the house to the back, glad that she had remembered to prop the back gate open the day before so she could get in. She cursed to herself as she prepared to take apart the ramp. Stopping in her tracks, she saw that the ramp had been modified. It now sat flush under the door. She walked on it, finding it much sturdier than she had left it. Opening the screen door, she discovered that she was now able to use the entrance again. Smiling to herself, she looked at Evan's house. He must have come over while she was at Megan's. She would have to find a way to thank him. Hurrying to the front yard, she saw that his truck was gone. Grabbing her purse, she set off for the store.

Several hours later, through the open window, she heard his truck pull up. She had spent the afternoon cooking up a storm. She had made crab-stuffed mushroom caps, salad and roasted root vegetables, and had barbecued a chicken. Dessert would be pastries from Ernest's. She quickly threw on some lip gloss and checked her hair before rushing out the front door and making her way over to his truck. As she walked, she hoped that her wraparound dress didn't seem like overkill. Evan glanced at her as he opened the door, holding his large lunch kit as he stepped down from his truck. Boots climbed out and bounded over to her, rubbing up against her leg.

"Thank you," Megan said, smiling up at Evan as she rubbed her hands over the dog's ears.

"For what?" He locked up his truck and tapped his leg with his hand to call Boots back to him.

"For fixing the ramp. I'm assuming it was you."

"I didn't do it for you. I did it for your dad." His voice was cool and he seemed to be avoiding eye contact with her as he walked to his front door.

Following him, she continued. "Well, even so, it's a huge load off my mind. I wasn't sure if I could fix it. I thought I'd be at it all day. Instead I had time to cook a nice dinner to show my appreciation."

He stopped, one foot on the bottom step. Turning to her, he shrugged. "No thanks. Maybe that guy you had over yesterday is hungry. You should call him. You two seemed to be hitting it off."

Harper's face burned with humiliation. "He's my dad's doctor. He called and offered to help. It's not like we're an item or something."

"A guy doesn't offer to come over and help you out unless he wants the 'or something.'"

She fixed him with a glare. "It's not like that. Well, at least not for me. He's just a really nice guy who wanted to help me out."

"That's not what it looked like to me. But it really doesn't matter what I think. You and I are just friends, remember?"

"For a friend, you seemed overly interested in what was happening on the other side of the fence yesterday." She jammed her fist against her hip, looking completely unconvinced.

"Only because I was pretty sure one of you was going to get hurt, with numbnuts there working the power tools."

"Numbnuts?" Her eyes flew open. "You are jealous."

"Of course I didn't like seeing you flirting with some other guy, not after what happened between us. Not after you told me you need to be on your own! But don't let that stop you, Harper. Go on and look for your fun wherever you can find it." His words cut through the air like a knife.

"Oh, I will. Believe me!" she returned with a look of pure venom. "And since you obviously won't be able to handle it, you better keep your blinds shut from now on." She turned on her heel and stormed back into her house, slamming the door behind her.

Harper paced around the kitchen, angrily clearing his unused dishes and wine glass before serving herself the entire plate of stuffed mushrooms. "Fuck. Him." She poured herself a very full glass of chilled white wine, gulping back half of the cool liquid then immediately topping it up. "I don't need that shit. I have enough to deal with around here."

She fanned out the cloth napkin she had bought earlier that day and placed it on her lap before slicing into a mushroom cap and taking a bite. "Your loss, Evan. This is absolutely delicious!"

By the time she had finished the mushrooms, she was halfway through the bottle of wine. A knock at the front door interrupted her angry muttering. Her footsteps were heavy, slapping against the wood floor as she made her way to the front entrance. Her best scowl in place, she swung open the door. There he was, fresh from the shower, looking and smelling thoroughly delicious. "What?" she asked, internally ordering her body not to respond to how unbelievably sexy he was. Lick. Damn it! Stop that, body!

"I'm here for supper," he said simply. "I realized you do owe me. That was a hell of a job last night, undoing the mess you two made. And I'm hungry, so I'm going to eat."

Harper scowled at him. "What? That's the most ridiculous thing I've ever heard."

"You taking back the offer? Because if you are, it really seems like you didn't actually make dinner to thank me at all. It would mean that you had some other motive." He let himself in, kicking off his flip-flops and crossing the living room to the kitchen.

Harper stood, her mouth hanging open as he stormed past her. Recovering herself, she stalked after him. "No ulterior motives here, so come on in so I can thank you!" she snapped, getting out his place setting again. After pouring his wine, she scooped a large helping of vegetables and tore a leg and thigh off the chicken for him as he seated himself at the table. Slamming the plate down in front of him, she served salad into two bowls before getting her own plate prepared.

"You missed the crab-stuffed mushrooms. They were fucking amazing, so I ate them all," she barked.

"I hate mushrooms," he replied curtly, "so I guess I just saved myself a whole lot of pretending." He ripped a piece off the French loaf she had set down and slapped some butter on it before shoving it into his mouth.

The meal was spent in a furious silence, both of them eating quickly and sucking back wine like it was going out of style.

He stabbed a vegetable with his fork and held it up. "What is this?" he asked, his voice oozing irritation.

"It's rutabaga." Harper over-pronounced the word, sounding sarcastic.

"Well, excuse me for not having spent half my life eating at fancy restaurants in New York City."

"You've got a lot bigger things to excuse yourself for," she quipped, stabbing some spinach with her fork.

He ignored her jab and continued to eat. "This chicken is delicious." It was more of an accusation than a compliment.

"I know. I'm actually an excellent cook." She narrowed her eyes at him.

Cleaning his plate, he dropped his fork, put his napkin on the table, took one last swig of wine and then stood up. "Consider us even."

"Oh, believe me, I will." She stood and cleared both of their plates, all but tossing them into the sink, as if to rid herself of the evidence of her previous gratitude. Turning, she gave him a glare. "Thank you for fixing the ramp. It's much better than before!" she yelled.

He nodded his head quickly in outright irritation. "I know! You can actually open the door now, which is kind of why they were invented in the first place!"

She thrust the bag of pastries at him. "Here's your dessert. You've been paid. You can go now."

"Oh, I know I can go. I can do whatever I want!" He glared at her, standing close enough to touch her.

"Yeah, well, you can't do whatever you want here, so you better get going," she shouted, poking him in the chest to emphasize her point.

"Don't poke me. I don't like that."

"I don't really care what you like, Evan Donovan." She poked him again a couple of times for good measure.

He grabbed her wrist to stop her, yanking her to him and kissing her hard on the lips. The gasp in her throat was cut short by his tongue thrusting into her mouth with a vengeance. Harper's hands went to his hair of their own accord, gripping the short waves and pulling him into her forcefully. Dropping the bag of pastries, Evan's hands moved straight to her ass, grabbing it roughly.

He pulled back for a minute, his eyes full of lust. "You're a fucking pain in the ass, Young." He crushed her mouth with his before she could snap back at him.

Harper's body heated up at his touch. Every fibre of her being was ablaze with an angry lust. Tugging at the sash holding her dress together, Evan pushed the fabric aside, clearly annoyed by the second tie inside, which left half of her body still covered. Yanking at it, he glanced at her cotton candy–pink bra and panties before he crossed his arms in front of his body and pulled his shirt over his head and off. Clawing at his jeans, Harper tugged the button fly open and yanked his pants down, along with his underwear. He stepped out of them, leaving himself completely nude. Glaring at her, he gripped her waist and lifted her onto the counter, moving her panties aside with his fingers as she grabbed the muscles on his back and kissed him wildly. Thrusting his fingers inside her, he found her wet. She moaned loudly, exciting them both even more. His other hand pulled down her bra, revealing her already-hard nipples waiting for his mouth. Sucking on them forcefully, he could feel her tighten around his fingers and he wanted that same sensation around his cock instead. Replacing his fingers with his thick length, he rammed himself into her, causing them both to cry out with intense pleasure. Lifting her off the counter, he held her up, rubbing her up and down on himself urgently with his strong hands. They were fucking hard now, taking out their anger on each other, and they weren't going to stop until they were drained of any hint of it.

"You can be kind of an asshole," she hissed.

"You have a talent for bringing that out in me," he answered, rocking his hips forward and pulling her onto him, pushing himself in deeper than either had thought possible.

"Oh fuck," she whispered, not wanting to allow him to pleasure her like this. She wanted only to torture him with her body, to make him miss her, but what he was doing was serving to drive her crazy instead. She was powerless to stop the orgasm that was building in her. As he slammed himself into her again, it hit, causing the wind to leave her body and her mind to go blank. There was nothing in her but pleasure from her head to her toes as she gripped him powerfully with her legs and dug her nails into his back. She could feel him empty himself into her, both throbbing together as they let go.

When it was long over, he returned her to the counter so he could wrap his arms around her back now, pressing his forehead to hers as he recovered. "I don't care. I don't fucking care what happens. We are doing this again and again until we get this out of our systems. And don't try to give me some bullshit line that you don't want this."

Harper smirked at his words, then her face grew serious. "Okay. You win. I want this. But you have to promise me something. You'll never expect more than what I can give. You'll never even think to ask for more."

Their eyes met, and in that moment, their hearts were revealed to each other. Both hurt. Both scared. Both needing. Both hiding. And agreeing to hide together.

"I promise. I'll never ask you for more than you can give."

SEVENTEEN

The next two weeks passed in a sex haze, both exhilarating and exhausting, as the pair started each morning in Evan's bed. Harper had a slightly uncomfortable conversation with Gordon to explain why she wasn't going to be going out with him anytime soon. He handled it well and made a joke about her giving him a call when things ended with the "new guy." Roy had gotten a spot at the Rosewood Rehab Clinic and had been settled in for over a week now, much to everyone's relief. He was finally on the fast track to recovering and there was every reason to be optimistic about the outcome.

Two days of solid rain found Harper and Evan together almost twenty-four hours a day, making love, cooking meals, laughing together, leaving the house only long enough for Harper to visit her dad while Evan ran to the supermarket or for takeout. No clients were scheduled for Harper at the Fashion Forward offices, so she had no other obligations. Other than that brief time out of the house, the two hid away from the world—and it was the most delectable of fantasies. Evan could see she had trouble relaxing and would pull her back to bed when she started to get up to try to get something done.

"You need this, Harper. It's good for you to learn to slow down. You can't go Mach ten your whole life."

"But we can't just lie here all day. Seriously. We're like a couple of sloths. We need to be productive. Accomplish something."

Flipping himself so he was on top of her, he planted a firm kiss on her lips. "How about we accomplish another simultaneous orgasm?"

Thirty minutes later, Evan collapsed onto the bed in a sweaty heap. "Wow. Where did you learn that?" he asked, sounding thoroughly impressed. "On second thought, don't answer that."

"I just made that up now," Harper replied. "Until a few minutes ago, I had no idea I could do any of that."

"This is a serious problem. If you keep doing stuff like that, I'm never going to get you out of my system."

Harper lifted her head and gave him a lingering kiss. "That"—kiss—"is not"—kiss—"my serious problem." With that, she let her head flop back onto her pillow, feeling her heart still beating quickly in her chest. The morning sun streamed in from its already high angle in the sky.

"I should have left for the site two hours ago. I need to get caught up."

"I thought it was Sunday."

"All that rain has me so far behind I'm going to have to put in sixteens all week to get back on track."

"So that's why you've been in bed with me for days. It was because of the rain! Here I thought you were trying to expedite the whole 'getting me out of your system' thing so you could move on," she teased.

"I'm not interested in moving on. I'm just trying to get to a point where I'll have some self-control when you're around. Totally different."

"Hmm, well, I'm not really a fan of either of those things, actually. I prefer you with no self-control."

"Funny that you're making it sound like I'm the only one with self-control issues. I'm not the one waking you up at 3 a.m. every night to have sex. That's all you."

"I'm just trying to sneak in an extra workout every day. It's swimsuit season."

"Liar," Evan said with a mock scowl. "I know you want me to stick around all day and continue to give you the best orgasms of your life, but I need to hit the shower."

Lifting himself off the bed in one powerful move, he sauntered across the room with Harper's eyes trained on his butt divots as he moved. Glancing over his shoulder, he gave her a naughty grin. "Take a good look, babe, 'cause you're going to have to wait at least ten hours to see this again."

Harper lay in bed and rolled onto her back, stretching her arms and legs in the sheets. She could feel muscles she hadn't used in a long time. Every part of her bore some evidence he'd been there, from the smell of his aftershave on her skin to her slightly kiss-swollen lips to the raw, satisfied feeling in her core. Smiling to herself, she closed her eyes while listening to the shower being turned on. She had just spent two glorious weeks with Evan-from-Heaven, fulfilling every fantasy that she had ever had about him except one. Thoughts of Harper Donovan written in big, loopy letters in her diary came to mind. He was the only one she had ever pictured herself married to, but that was before she'd outgrown such nonsense. Right now, she was simply suffering from sex brain. She could stop those thoughts before they ruined everything.

A few minutes later, Evan opened the bathroom door, steam preceding him into the bedroom. He was quite a sight to behold with his hair dripping and his hand clutching a towel around his waist. He gave her a hungry look as he crossed the room, tossing the towel aside to reveal himself ready to go. "Fuck it. I can go later. I own the company."

Kneeling on the bed, he tugged the sheet off her, leaving her fully exposed to him. "Yup. Best decision I've made all year," he said, lowering his mouth over her neck as Harper laughed and coiled her arms and legs around him.

* * *

Two hours later, Evan found himself at the next Pine Crest house he was starting, laying out the wall lines on the foundation. He preferred doing this task alone, without distractions, carefully marking out the window and door lines as he went, double- and triple-checking the angles and measurements against the blueprints until he felt certain that he wasn't even a millimetre off in any direction. This was the beginning of someone's home. The place where they would live their lives, where they'd make their memories, and he wanted it to be perfect for them. He wanted the owners to move in without unnecessary delays or unfinished details. He hoped that they would remember fondly the months spent waiting for their house to be completed, and that they would have the utmost confidence in the quality of their new home as they unpacked their dishes and collapsed into bed on their first night in it. He built a house the way he would want it done if he were paying for it. No cigarette butts tossed carelessly down the furnace vents, no garbage left scattered around at the end of each day. It was about respect and meticulous care each step of the way.

He hummed to himself, smiling as he worked, thoughts of Harper passing through his mind. Images of them cooking side by side in his small kitchen or snuggled up on the couch to watch a movie they would never see the end of. He could picture her sitting across from him at the deli as they were eating lunch two days earlier. He had talked for a long time about his work, knowing that she would really hear what he had to say, that it mattered to her. He mattered to her. She challenged his opinions and ideas and brought a fresh new perspective to his world. In a heartbeat, he had become addicted to telling her all the little things and big things that make up a life. She wanted to know, wanted to keep his secrets safe in her heart. He could tell by the look in her eyes, her questions, her expressions. She cared for him in the deepest of ways and it felt wonderful to have that.

He thought of how she loved the smell of rain so much that she couldn't help but leave the windows open, even if it meant she'd be chilly. He had teased her about leaving them open just to get him into bed to warm her up, but he knew she couldn't resist the scent of rain any more than she could resist him. Maybe this could work out after all.

But that was a thought he couldn't let take seed in his brain. That thought would grow like a weed, choking out his common sense and ruining what they had. She was leaving in a few months and this whole thing would have to end. If he could just keep his heart from getting involved, he'd be left with warm memories, like in those summer romances of youth where both people know it's just for a little while before they have to move on. No one regrets those, do they?

He could rein in his feelings. He was smarter now than when he'd thrown himself into his relationship with Avery. When they met, he was already very successful, with cash to burn. Like a fool, he had believed himself invincible. He had known nothing of heartbreak, and he had been too cocky to think that it could ever happen to him. Young and rich, he was all too happy to spend his money and time on someone so beautiful and cultured. Someone he had never thought he could get in the first place. Avery had grown up wealthy and had developed only the finest tastes. With her on his arm, he felt like he had finally made something of himself.

He thought of how the two women couldn't be more different. Avery had grown up with doting parents who gave her every advantage in life and made sure she knew she was beautiful and the best at anything she tried. Her mother had schooled her in how to catch the perfect man, to make sure she would always be cared for. Her parents hadn't been thrilled with Avery's choice of husband and Evan could tell. They were reserved, always polite, but full of questions about his business and its financial stability. The wedding had been a social event more than it had been a ceremony of commitment between two people. He had felt as out of place at the posh reception as he had at her parents' dinner table. He sensed that he would have to prove himself to these people for years to come before he was brought into the fold of privilege.

In the end, he never was accepted by her family. He lost everything first. The recession hit hard, leaving him with two nearly completed executive homes the purchasers backed out of at the same moment as every other new home was being abandoned. He had fought with Avery for weeks before putting their house up for sale. She just couldn't understand why his employees were their problem. If those people hadn't saved enough to pay off their mortgages already, it was on them. She wasn't about to suffer the humiliation of moving to some little old house in his old neighbourhood just because other people were bad with their money.

He knew it was over weeks before she moved back home to her parents. They had done nothing but fight, Evan growing more anxious as each minute ticked by and the money finally stopped trickling in. The last straw had been when she told him that she'd asked her dad for a loan. Her father had agreed to buy into the business but things would need to be run "properly" from now on, with him at the helm.

But he had his pride and he wasn't about to let anyone rescue him, especially a man who had so little respect for him. He had said some very harsh things about how spoiled and uncaring Avery was. None of it far off the mark, but hurtful all the same. And he had wanted to hurt her. She hadn't once offered sympathy about what was happening, only censure. What kind of a woman had he chosen for his wife? Someone selfish, with no idea about what really mattered in life.

She hadn't understood him at all. She didn't know that for him, building was about creating homes and communities, about providing work for honest people who were trying to live the American dream. He could help give them that dream, and for him, that was one of the best parts of his life's work. And even though he had tried to share that with her, he could see her eyes glazing over. She didn't understand the value in those sentiments. When push came to shove, none of that mattered to her.

The humiliation and pain that accompanied the end of his marriage served as a reminder of why he couldn't let himself fall again. A reminder that he needed to keep his feelings for Harper in check. Even if she was Avery's opposite, it didn't mean things would turn out any better. And the fact that Harper was leaving soon was exactly why he could be with her in the first place. He would have to stay realistic about the affair and never forget that it had an expiry date.

EIGHTEEN

"Have you heard from Wes at all?" Harper asked, opening the window to let fresh air into her dad's room at the Rosewood Clinic. Immediately, the sounds of the birds brought nature inside with them.

"Not since last week. It's hard with the time change."

"I know. I haven't spoken with him in months now. We've been emailing since you got hurt, but I have to do better at keeping in touch with him."

Roy nodded. "Yeah, you should. The thing with his job is that you never know if he'll even come home again."

"You're right. I'm going to make a better effort."

"Good girl," Roy answered.

Harper scrunched up her face for a moment. "You know, you are the only man on the planet who can get away with saying 'good girl' to me. Anyone else would get a knee to the groin."

Roy chuckled at his daughter. "You always were a tough little thing. You used to beat the snot out of Craig when you were kids."

"Well, I'm pretty sure the only reason I won was because you'd have killed him if he ever hit a girl."

"True. But you were a real fighter in your own right. Even Wes had trouble stopping you when you got going."

Snapping her fingers, Harper picked up the bag she had set on the floor when she came in. "Speaking of my competitive nature, guess what I found." She pulled out a wooden cribbage board and a deck of cards. "You up for a challenge, old man?"

A grin spread across Roy's face. "A challenge? Does that mean you're hiding someone who knows how to play crib in that bag?"

Harper laughed, loving to see her dad seem so happy. "Very funny! Laugh now, because I'm about to open up a can of whoop-ass on you."

She cleared the tray and set the board down, handing Roy the deck of cards to shuffle.

An hour later, one of the nurses came by to let Roy know it was time for his therapy session.

"We'll go best out of seven tomorrow morning. Prepare to lose," Harper said with wide eyes.

Roy gave her a little nod. "Alright, tomorrow morning it is. What are you going to do today?"

"I'm actually going to help at that charity again today."

"Nice. How's that going?"

"I love it there. It's so rewarding. I'd like to join the New York chapter when I go back."

Roy's face fell a tiny bit before he caught himself. "Good plan."

"Well, that's not for a long time, anyway," Harper said, trying to brush it off. "Oh, I was thinking about painting the living room, then maybe the kitchen? . . . Okay, and the hallway, bathrooms and bedrooms?"

"Alright, as long as you don't overdo it." Roy's tone was sarcastic. "You need to learn to take it easy, kid."

"Never," she answered, giving him a peck on the cheek.

"Well, in that case, I might as well put you to work. Oh, wait a minute. No peach or pink or other girly colours. I have a reputation as a tough guy to uphold."

"Deal. Only very manly colours," Harper answered, saluting with one hand, then picking up her purse. Taking out the books she'd brought in, she swapped them for the two that were sitting on his nightstand.

* * *

The early morning heat had Harper opening the window as she drove across town. Letting her arm catch the breeze as the truck rambled down the road, she felt a sense of freedom come over her. Her days were her own and this thought finally found a welcome place in her soul. Pulling off the road and through the open gate to the Pine Crest construction site, she parked in front of a small white trailer. She gave herself a quick once-over in the rear-view mirror, making sure her lips were still glossy, then made her way to the trailer door, giving a light knock before opening it.

Crammed into the space were four desks, several filing cabinets, a coffee station and a water cooler. Standing at one of the desks was a young woman in jeans and a T-shirt, her blond hair pulled back into a no-nonsense ponytail. She was cradling a phone on her shoulder as she spoke. Her eyes scanned the desk next to hers and she picked up the base of the phone, bringing it with her as she tried to reach for something but came up short. "Mmhmm, yes. Yes, I've got it right here," she said into the phone. "I'm looking at it now."

She glanced at Harper with an urgent expression, pointing to a grey file folder. Dashing over, Harper handed her what she needed. The woman mouthed "Thanks" and continued the call. Harper stood for a minute, looking around. At the far corner of the trailer was what she assumed was Evan's desk. It was covered in blueprints and stacked with files. She waited another minute for the woman to finish her phone call.

"Thanks for your help," she said with a southern drawl. "I'm Lacey. What can I do for you?"

"I'm Harper. Evan forgot his lunch and his briefcase this morning." She held them up to Lacey.

Lacey tilted her head as a look of understanding crossed her face. "So you're the reason he's been tapping his toes to the radio around here. I thought he must have found a woman, but you know him, he won't say a word." She picked up a walkie-talkie from her desk and pushed a button. "Boss man, there's a gal here to see you. And she's a real beauty, so you better hurry before one of the other boys gets here first."

A click sounded over the walkie-talkie before Evan answered. "Be right there, Lacey."

Harper blushed at hearing his sexy voice. "Oh no. I don't want to disturb him. I just wanted to drop this off and sneak away."

"Now, why would you want to sneak away when you have a chance to make him watch you go?" Lacey asked with a little wink.

Harper laughed. "Smart lady, I can see why Evan calls you his right hand."

"Does he call me that? How sweet. Well, he's one hell of a great boss. My husband, Chad, and I have worked for him forever. He takes real good care of his crew. In fact, we would have lost our house if it weren't for him." Lacey walked over to the counter and started making a fresh pot of coffee. "Would you like a coffee, hon?"

"No thanks. I just finished one." Harper smiled, glancing down at Lacey's emerging tummy. "Do you mind if I ask how he helped you keep your house?"

"He kept us both on the payroll even though he hadn't sold a house for over a year. We'd had our first boy about a year before the recession really started to take its toll. By then the second one was on the way. I don't know what we would have done if it wasn't for

Evan." She gave Harper a look, as though trying to gauge her reaction.

"Wow. That is really going above and beyond," Harper answered as she digested the information.

"That's Evan. He goes above and beyond in everything he does."

"Oh, believe me, I know," Harper said with a knowing look.

Lacey laughed. "You're fun. I can see why he's been in such a good mood lately."

The door swung open, revealing Evan. He was wearing work boots, jeans and a hard hat that were in sharp contrast to his crisp white button-up dress shirt. The sleeves were rolled up to his elbows, displaying his muscular forearms. His expression went from curious to delighted as soon as he saw Harper. "From Lacey's description, I thought it might be you. What are you doing here?" He hesitated for a moment before walking over and giving her a quick kiss on the cheek.

"You left these by the front door this morning. I thought I'd bring them by on my way to the hospital."

"Thanks. I haven't had a chance to go back for them." He glanced over at Lacey, who was smiling at him excitedly.

"I see you two have met," Evan said. "Don't believe anything Lacey tells you about me. I'm not really a horrible tyrant."

"Oh no, she didn't call you a horrible tyrant. I think the phrase was awful beast," Harper teased.

Lacey joined the fun. "Well, I just wanted her to know the truth before she gets her heart set on you. Us ladies need to stick together."

Evan glanced back and forth between them with a mock-concerned expression. "Somehow I think it would be in my best interest to get you out of here," Evan said to Harper. "Do you have a few minutes for a tour?"

"I'd love a tour. But do you have time for it?" Harper asked.

"I always have time for you," he said, leading her out the door.

"Lacey, your husband asked me to remind you to stay off your feet."

"Oh, tell him to mind his own business! I've had two babies already. If he thinks he can do it better, he's welcome to carry the next one," Lacey answered, clearly just pretending to be annoyed as she sat down. "Nice to meet you, Harper. I hope we'll be seeing a lot of you from now on."

"You too, Lacey." Harper gave her a little wave as she followed Evan.

When they got outside, Evan took her hand and led her around to the side of the trailer before turning her to face him and planting a lingering kiss on her lips. "Mmm, what a nice surprise to see you here."

"The drive was worth it," Harper answered, feeling a bit dazed from what his lips had just done to her. "You were gone before I woke up this morning." She pressed her hands to his chest, smoothing them along the front of his shirt. "You're all dressed up today."

"Oh yeah, a reporter from the local paper is supposed to come by this morning. I wanted to appear respectable."

Harper automatically set about adjusting the roll of his sleeves until it was just right. "You look ruggedly handsome. Every woman in town is going to be lined up outside your trailer when the article comes out," she said, giving him another kiss.

"They'll have a long wait because I'm still nowhere near finished with you." Just then Evan's cell rang, interrupting the moment. Checking it, he gave her an apologetic look. "I'm afraid this call is going to be a long one. Sorry."

"Don't be. We'll do the tour another time," Harper said, running a finger down the front of his shirt.

As she walked away, she glanced over her shoulder to make sure he was watching. From the look on his face, Lacey had been right about making sure he saw her leave.

NINETEEN

"So, what's the gossip?" Harper asked as she settled herself into a wicker chair on the deck with her phone to her ear.

"Well, a lot has happened since you left and none of it is good," Blaire answered. "Let's just say your replacement, Tina, isn't exactly up to what I would call *Style* standards. She's excellent at sucking up to Hartless, though."

"Seriously? That's awful, Blaire."

"It is awful. I miss you so much, Harper. This place is just not at all the same without you. Got any leads for me in Colorado?"

Harper laughed at the thought of Blaire in Boulder. "So far I have leads on volunteer work at Fashion Forward and as unpaid nurse-maid to my father."

"So, no, then."

Harper's voice turned serious. "God, Blaire, I don't even know what I'm going to do when my dad recovers."

"You're going to get your ass back to New York, where you belong. Shit. I have to run, but just know—each hour, I'm plotting your return."

Harper hung up the phone and sighed, suddenly feeling extremely restless. Maybe she should have resisted the urge to find out what was happening at *Style*. It made her long for her old life. She was going to have to find a way back for herself when the time was right. For now, she'd have to patiently wait until her life could start over. Not that she was anywhere near miserable lately. She loved the days she spent at Fashion Forward. It was rewarding in a way that few things were. She was also closer to her family and old friends than she'd ever been as an adult, not to mention she was having the greatest sex of her life.

Her thoughts were interrupted by the doorbell. A bouquet of two dozen red roses was being delivered. The card attached read: *Dinner tonight. Me. You. Wear something sexy. Evan*

* * *

Evan was just finishing going over some blueprints with one of the plumbers when his cell chimed, indicating a message.

As luck would have it, I'm free for dinner tonight. I'm going to wear something so sexy you'll pass out from a lack of oxygen to your brain. BTW, thanks for the flowers. They're gorgeous.

Just as he was about to replace his cell in his pocket, it rang. "Hey, Mom," he answered. "How's my favourite lady?"

"Favourite lady? That's not what I heard," Nancy replied.

"What?"

"Cut the crap, Evan. Don't play dumb with me. I know all about you and the Young girl carrying on."

"Oh, really? And where'd you hear that?"

"My spies are everywhere."

"Mrs. Morley called you, didn't she?"

"Yes. And do you know how that felt?" Her voice rose. "Finding out that my son is sleeping with that woman's daughter? She called me specifically to see if I knew. And when it became obvious that

I didn't have the first damn clue what she was talking about, she gloated like she had just won the world series of gossip."

"Sorry, Mom. I should have—"

"You're damn right you should have told me, Evan."

"I didn't really think about neighbourhood gossip, but I imagine it's a pretty hot story."

His mother's tone was reproachful. "It's the biggest news to hit Maplewood Drive since Petra Young took off with her student."

A sharp need to defend Harper hit him, causing his good mood to turn on a dime. "That big, hey? How about as big as the time your son's snobby wife left him when he went broke?"

"Oh, Evan. Everyone knows that wasn't your fault. That's not the same thing at all!"

"You know what is the same about both situations? It's none of anyone's business. Just like this thing with Harper and me now. Besides, I've got a lot bigger things on my mind than what a bunch of gossips from the neighbourhood think."

"I'm not just some gossip. I am your mother. And I think I have a right to know exactly what is going on between my son and Harper Young."

Evan lowered his voice as the plumber walked by. "You really don't, but I'll tell you anyway. She's back in town to take care of her dad. We've been spending some time together while she's here."

"Don't hold out on me, young man. Have you forgotten that I carried you for an extra month and you were ten pounds and six ounces when you finally arrived? Ten. Six."

"Now, how could I possibly forget that, Mom?" He paused, knowing she would wait him out. "What else do you want to hear?"

"You going to marry her? Because if you don't, things are going to get awful awkward between you and Wes."

"You really don't need to worry about that. Harper and I are both adults. We're more than comfortable with enjoying some time together before she goes back to New York. Nobody's going to get hurt."

"Hmph. Nobody's going to get hurt," she scoffed. "That's the dumbest thing I've ever heard. Not to mention it's a huge waste of your time. You're in the prime of your life. You should be looking for a nice woman you can settle down with—not having some fling, which, by the way, is going to keep you from finding the right girl. One who wants the same things you do."

"I think you mean the same things you do. For me to get married and give you a bunch of grandkids."

"If you knew what was good for you, you'd know that getting married and having kids is exactly what you need."

Evan sighed audibly, wishing Mrs. Morley had moved to Arizona with his parents. This was not a conversation he wanted to have. Ever. "I gotta go, Mom. I'm at work."

"You better call on Friday. It's Harry's third birthday, and he's going to want to hear from his Uncle Evan."

"I won't forget. I haven't yet."

"Alright. Love you, son. You know I just want you to be happy, right?"

"Yes, I know, Mom. It's just that your version of happy and mine might not be the same."

"They are. You just don't know it. You're father's here. Talk to your father."

"No, I'm really busy—"

"Irv, Evan's on the phone."

"Hey, son!"

"Hey, Dad. How's it going?"

"Great. I'll tell you, my golf game is getting better every week. Went three under par yesterday at Baker Creek."

"Three under? Remind me never to play you for money."

"I'll try, but you know me. Now that I'm getting older, I'm starting to forget things."

Evan relaxed a little, glad his mom had ignored his protests about being at work. "You're trying to hustle your own son, aren't you? What kind of father are you?"

"The kind that needs to pay for next year's green fees."

"You doing okay for cash?"

"Yes, yes. We're fine."

"You liking Tucson any better?"

"It's growing on me. Your mom is happy here, so that makes life nice. Lots of friends. The grandkids come over a lot too. It's just the damn heat that gets to me. I wouldn't mind spending half the year here and then coming home for the other half. I hate having to use a remote starter to cool the car off in the afternoons. Lately I've been trying to get home before lunch, when the temperatures go up."

"Good plan."

"So, what's this I hear about you knocking boots with that Young girl from next door?"

"Oh God. Can we not talk about this?"

"I'm not judging. She was always a fiery one. Your sister showed us some pictures of her on Facebook. She's quite the pretty woman."

Evan could picture his dad raising and lowering his eyebrows like Groucho Marx. "Yes. She is. Still fiery, too."

"Maybe she'll be my ticket out of here. If we had a couple of grandkids in Boulder, I know I could convince your mom to spend at least the summers there."

"Not you, too, Dad. Listen, I gotta go. Great talking to you."

"Neither of you is too old, you know. People are having kids much later in life now."

"Talk to you soon."

"Alright, Evan. I'll stop bugging you. Just promise me you'll give it some thought."

"I never make promises I don't intend to keep. Bye, Dad." With that, he hung up.

*　*　*

The evening was warm and calm, making the decision to eat on the restaurant's patio easy. Harper slid off her pashmina and draped it over the back of her chair, revealing the plunging neckline of a sexy blue dress cut from a silky fabric that flowed over her curves perfectly. Evan, who was moving in behind her to pull out her chair, leaned into her ear. "I can't wait to get you out of that dress. Sitting across from you during dinner is going to be torture."

Harper turned, her mouth an inch from his as he leaned into her. "Then it would probably be cruel of me to tell you I'm not wearing any panties."

"While cruel, I can honestly say I will always want to know that," he answered, giving her a lingering kiss.

They sat across from each other at the little table, both leaning in, fingertips touching as they read over the menu and chatted. A waiter came by to take their orders, leaving a bottle of chilled Chablis and two glasses. His eyes spent slightly longer than they should have trained on Harper's cleavage, earning him a light warning cough from Evan. Remembering himself, the young man blushed and hurried off, completely forgetting to pour the wine and wait while they tasted it.

"Hmm, now I'm not so sure about that dress. You might need to put that shawl back on or we might not get any food."

Harper laughed quietly. "Poor guy. How many years does it take before breasts no longer have that effect on men?"

"Ahh, it's not a question of years, actually. It's more a question of whether a guy is still breathing or not," he answered, filling her glass with wine. "But it really depends on the breasts as well. And yours, my dear, are extraordinary."

"Are they now?" she asked, tracing her finger over the back of his hand.

"They are. Especially in that dress. Especially when you lean forward like that. They could make a man forget where he is, what he was there for, his name . . ." His voice trailed off as he stared shamelessly at her chest.

"You're in a restaurant to eat dinner. Your name is Evan Donovan."

"Sorry, were two you saying something?" he asked her breasts, causing Harper to laugh loudly.

"I also might need you to cover up. Your warning about my brain not getting enough blood is turning out to be accurate," he said, smirking. "Especially now that I know you're not wearing any panties."

"Coco Chanel used to say, 'Before you leave the house, look in the mirror and take one thing off.' They were my one thing today."

"I had no idea Coco Chanel was a genius," Evan answered, gazing at her.

Harper smiled at him, enjoying the moment. "I hate to change the subject when we're talking fashion, but I am curious about something. You never told me what your mom said when she called. From what you did say, I gather things got a little awkward."

"Oh, that," Evan said. "Apparently, you and I are hot gossip on Maplewood Drive."

"I bet. I'm sure it's nothing compared to my scandalous mother, but I'm guessing it ranks up there anyway." Harper gestured upwards with her wine, trying to seem nonchalant.

"Why is that the first thing you thought of when I said we're hot gossip?" Evan's voice was soft.

"It's pretty obvious, isn't it? Are you trying to tell me her name didn't come up?" Harper asked.

Evan looked away, avoiding her stare.

"Thought so. It's the story that will never die. Just one of the many reasons I love it here so much." Harper rolled her eyes to emphasize her disdain.

"Why do you still care what other people think about your family?" Evan asked.

"What makes you think I care?"

"Because I'm beginning to know you well enough to see the difference between who you really are and the person you pretend to be." He reached his hand out and placed it on hers. "You can take off the armour when you're with me. I know what it's like to have to admit that my life's not perfect."

"Oh, I don't know if it's quite the same thing. Your wife left you because you were so generous that you were willing to sacrifice your own home to take care of other people. You're a hero. And I'm just the trash next door that you should stay away from."

Evan's eyes narrowed at her. "You're not trash, Harper. I don't ever want you to say that again. And I'm certainly no hero. I made my choices knowing how things would turn out. I ended up broke and alone."

"You had a downfall but you bounced back in record time. I'll always be the daughter of that woman who left her family for a teenage boy. And now I'm sleeping with you, but at the same time I'm planning to leave as soon as I can. What does that say about me?"

"It says that you know what you want and you're not letting anyone else define who you are. It would be one thing if you were lying to me about what you want, but you've been honest from the start. I knew what I was getting into and, quite frankly, the fact that you don't want more is what makes this work. We can have this simple, beautiful, sexy relationship and then move on, happy that we had it."

"But what you don't see is that it's not normal for a woman to want to live like this. I'm supposed to want the ring and the house with the white picket fence."

"Why should you want that? Just because everyone else thinks you should? Fuck them. I had that once and I can tell you it's not what it's cracked up to be. We've got it right, Harper. You and I have it all figured out. The only thing that is going to ruin what we've got here is letting other people's opinions get into our heads."

Harper stared at him for a moment, digesting his words. "You're right. I shouldn't let it get to me. I never think like this when I'm in New York. There's just something about being back here, especially this time. When I used to come back for quick visits, at least I had an impressive career to go back to. But what do I have now to feel good about?"

"Feel good about how generous you are. You've only been in town for a few weeks and already you're doing charity work. Plus, look at why you're here in the first place. How many people would give up everything to care for their father?"

"Most people," she said, trying to pull her hand away.

Evan tightened his grip. "No. Most people would hire help or pawn it off on someone else. You're different. You're better. You're an incredibly beautiful, thoroughly impressive woman. And it's got nothing to do with what you've managed to accomplish in your career," he said, his words growing thick with emotion. "You're not only one of the most thoughtful people I know, you're also the most fun woman I've ever met. Not to mention sexy as hell. And for what it's worth, I love that you're here and that I get to be with you. It makes me one of the luckiest guys on the planet."

The moment was interrupted by the waiter bringing them their food. Harper was grateful for his arrival. She needed to slow her racing pulse. For one horribly delicious moment, she had thought Evan was about to say he loved her. What had gotten her heart beating so furiously was her own reaction. In the tiny instant that hung between the words *love* and *that*, she felt a thrill she'd never experienced before. And the realization terrified her. She wanted him to love her. But he didn't. And he wasn't going to.

She heard Evan thank the waiter as her mind returned to her surroundings. She needed to shake it off. She couldn't let herself hope for a future with him, not when it wasn't what either of them was capable of. That meant this would have to end. And she was nowhere near ready to end it. She was suddenly overcome by the need to remind herself that this was just about sex. She couldn't be out on a romantic date with him. This felt too serious. She reached across to touch his arm. "Let's get out of here right now. I need to be naked with you."

Evan gave her a quizzical look. "You sure?"

"I'm sure. It's exactly what I want. Now." She gave him a look that was pure lust.

Flagging down the waiter, Evan asked him, "Can we get this wrapped up? And the bill as quickly as possible?"

* * *

"I'm sorry I ruined your plans for a romantic date," Harper said as she watched him get into the truck.

"Believe me, I'm okay with it. You can have whatever you need."

Harper slid across the seat and straddled his lap. "This is what I need."

She lowered her mouth over his, giving him rough, passionate kisses that he returned. Rubbing herself against him, she could feel how hard he was through his pants. She felt his large hands glide over the silky fabric of her dress, along her waist to her breasts. Squeezing them firmly, he leaned his head back against the seat, letting her come to him as if he needed to check one last time that she wanted this. She moved in closer, pressing her breasts against him. They stayed like that, kissing, caressing, driving each other to the brink, almost forgetting where they were.

"You're going to get us arrested," he said finally, trying in vain to hold back.

"You can stop anytime you want," she replied, licking her lips.

"Then we better hope nobody calls the cops," he murmured, letting his hand find its way under her dress, finding her naked, hot and wet. He groaned with desire as his palm covered her warm flesh.

Harper reached down, tugging his shirttail out of his pants and unbuckling his belt. Frantically unzipping his pants, she pulled them down as he lifted his hips to help her. There was nothing between them now as he pressed his smooth, hard length against her. He guided himself inside her as she lowered herself over him, taking in every inch he had to give. She squeezed her tight sex around him, drenching him as she ground back and forth on his lap.

"Oh God, Harper, you're so fucking hot," he told her, his words increasing her wild desire. She picked up her pace, moving more forcefully now. He was in so deep, nothing could be better than this. She revelled in the feeling of his powerful hands gripping her hips as he took control, slowing her to tortuously long drags now. She watched as he looked down at her full breasts, his hands raking her back and forth on his lap. But when his gaze turned to her eyes, it was full of adoration. Shutting her eyes tightly, she tried to forget that look. Forget the part of her that wished he was in love with her. *This is just sex, it means nothing*, she told herself over and over.

She gave herself over to the lie, releasing her fears and just allowing herself to feel the pleasure of what he was doing to her, in her. He pressed her down onto his lap even harder, their bodies becoming one explosive mass of flesh and bone. He covered her mouth with his as she started to come, muffling the sounds of ecstasy erupting from her throat.

When it was over, he drew her close to him as they recovered. "Wow, Harper. What was that about?"

"I don't know," she answered. "I just needed to have you."

* * *

An hour later, they lay tangled together in Evan's sheets. They'd gone straight to bed when they arrived home, stripping each other's clothes off the moment they got in the door. Now the moon had risen in the sky, and by the time they'd had their fill of each other, it provided their only light.

"I think I'll have to take you out for dinner more often," Evan said, lazily running a finger along her side.

"Agreed. That was amazing." Harper's stomach let out a loud growl, interrupting the moment.

"Now that I've satisfied your lust, I should satisfy your hunger." He got up and pulled on a pair of grey lounge pants, then tossed her one of his T-shirts. "Let's eat."

A few minutes later, they sat side by side at the kitchen table, swirling noodles with forks and sipping ice-cold water by the light over the stove.

"Even reheated, this is delicious." Harper picked up her glass and took a long gulp. "Thank you for taking me out tonight, Evan. This might have been my favourite meal of all time. I especially enjoyed the course between the bread and the main."

"Hands down. Best. Meal. Ever." He grinned over at her and rested his hand on her knee.

Harper returned his smile, plucking the last prawn off his plate with her fork and popping it into her mouth.

"My last prawn? That's just evil! I was saving it for the end!"

Harper covered her mouth as she laughed. "Sorry, it sat there so long that I thought you didn't want it."

"No, I always save my favourite thing on the plate for the last bite." He shook his head at her. "Why would I have ordered prawns if I didn't like them?"

"Good point. I'm sorry. I didn't realize you had that whole 'saving the best for last' thing going on. Won't happen again." She planted an apology kiss on his cheek. "I would offer you some of mine but I know how much you hate mushrooms."

"That's okay. I'm sure you'll make it up to me."

"Sure. You think of a way and I'll consider making it up to you." She gave him a sideways glance.

"You don't sound that sorry." Evan's voice was incredulous.

"I'm not that sorry. That prawn was delicious. Like, 'melt in your mouth' delicious." Harper laughed out loud as Evan tickled her in retribution.

"Okay! I give!" She laughed. "I'll make it up to you!"

"Good. Because my fingers have a lot more tickling in them yet."

"How about a naked massage?"

"Done. And please note that you may always eat my last bite if that is how you pay me back."

* * *

An hour later, they both flopped back down onto the bed, glistening with sweat, wearing only satisfied expressions.

"So, are we even?" Harper asked.

"And then some," Evan answered, pulling the covers over them before lying back on his pillow. He ran a finger down the centre of her chest. "Tell me one thing I don't know about you. Something you've never told anyone."

"Oh God, that's a tough one. Let me think . . ." She stared at the ceiling for a minute. "Okay, this one is really embarrassing, so I'm going to need to hear something of equal or greater value. If I don't, there will be consequences," she said, trying to sound ominous.

"No problem. I've done lots of stupid shit in my life."

Harper laughed. "True. Okay, then. When I started at *Style*, I was a lowly intern, fresh out of design school. After a few weeks, I was graced by being in the same room as Cybill Hart for a few minutes, but of course it couldn't have happened at the right time."

"Naturally."

"I knew who she was, obviously, but I had never expected to meet her in person. Anyway, I was in the closet—that's what we call this enormous room filled with row after row of racks jammed with clothes. I was supposed to be putting away a rack that had been used for a shoot that day. It was late, no one was around—or so I thought—so I decided to try something on. I had my eye on this gorgeous Valentino gown—it was a black silk duchesse with these delicate, hand-painted flowers. I stripped down and slid it on, but it was probably a size two, so there was no way I was going to be able to zip it up. I barely managed to squeeze into it and had to leave it open at the back. I was standing in front of the mirror admiring myself when who did I see standing behind me?"

"Cybill."

"Mmhmm. I was so humiliated and terrified, I think my whole body turned red. I started making all these apologies and excuses while I hurried over to this curtained-off area to take off the dress, only I was stuck. I had shimmied myself in and now I couldn't slide the straps off."

"Oh shit." Evan laughed.

"That's exactly what I was thinking as I stood in the dressing area, sweating all over this ten-thousand-dollar gown, wishing I could hide under a rock for the rest of my life. I was sure my career was over."

"So why wasn't it?"

"Turns out she shouldn't have been in their either. She'd been in one of the aisles when I came in, and let's just say it wasn't her husband who had his hands all over her ass. She thought I had seen them. The next morning she came and found me and did the whole 'I didn't see you if you didn't see me' thing."

"Seriously?"

"Yeah, in the end I think it actually might have helped my career, since I proved I could keep my mouth shut. She got divorced a year later, though."

"Wow. Crazy. But I have to know, how'd you get out of the dress?"

"I waited in the closet for an hour, then managed to find another intern and begged her to help me wriggle my way out of it. I had marks on my shoulders from those straps for two days."

Evan chuckled. "Can you describe that in more detail? Starting with what the other intern looked like?"

Harper laughed, giving him a light smack on the arm. "Alright, you're up."

"Up for what?" Evan asked, trying his best to seem authentically confused.

"You know exactly what. You owe me one embarrassing story." Harper pursed her lips at him.

"Oh, right."

"Were you hoping I'd forget?"

"Maybe."

"You should know me better than that by now, Donovan."

"Alright, I guess I owe you one. Hmm. Oh! The first time I had supper at Avery's parents' house. That's a classic. But you have to promise not to tell anyone."

"That bad? Ooh, yay!" she exclaimed.

"So you can imagine how nervous I was to be going there. Went out and bought new clothes, picked up a ridiculously large bouquet of flowers for her mom, and then I must have spent over half an hour staring at labels on wine bottles, trying to pick the right one on my way over. When I got back in my car—I had just leased a little black Porsche at the time—"

"Nice." Harper interjected.

"It was. Anyway, when I got back in the car I realized I was going to be late. A total no-no when you meet the parents. I jump in and zoom over, weaving in and out of traffic, running yellow lights, basically driving like a total asshole. So I go in, give her mom the flowers and the wine and notice that her dad's not at the door to greet me. A couple of minutes later he comes in the door, looking thoroughly pissed off. He points at me and says, 'You!'

"I didn't know what to do so I extended my hand and said, 'Good evening, sir,' trying to think of why he could possibly be so angry with me. He says, 'Don't *sir* me, and don't think you are ever going to be driving my daughter around in that little death trap of yours!'"

"Oh shit."

"Exactly what I was thinking. Turns out he had been one of the people I had zigged and zagged around. He saw me run a yellow. He claims it was red; he may have been right. I had scared the shit out of him when I cut in front of him, and he spilled his coffee all over his pants."

"So you might have been better off being a few minutes late, then."

Evan laughed. "Possibly. As it turned out, it didn't matter in the end. We were never going to like each other anyway."

"God, that must have been insanely awkward."

"Yes. Yes, it was."

"What did Avery say?"

"Turns out it did a little something for her. She liked the whole bad-boy thing at the time."

"I shouldn't have asked."

"In the end that doesn't matter either, does it?" Evan replied with a shrug.

"Do you miss it? The Porsche, I mean," Harper asked, happy to change the subject from that of his ex-wife.

"A little, once in a while. It was pretty sweet. But to be totally honest, it was never that comfortable. Sports cars aren't great for tall guys."

"I never thought of that."

"Sad but true. It's one of the great tragedies of life."

"There must be a support group somewhere for that."

They lay together for a moment, Evan running his fingertips along the length of her arm. "You know what? I think this is my favourite moment of us together so far."

"Of course. We've had sex three times this evening and we're both naked."

"No, I mean, this moment right now. Just really talking." He planted a kiss on her forehead.

* * *

A little while later as Harper drifted off to sleep, Evan lay awake watching her, a sinking feeling in his stomach. He thought of how she'd used the term trash to describe her family, and it made him ache for her. On the outside, she was a tough, savvy, sexy woman, but tonight he'd had another glimpse behind the mask. The pain of her past was so carefully hidden away that no one would ever see it. He'd gotten too close tonight and she had done the only thing she knew how, which was to take them back to being just physical. But he was way beyond that now. He thought of the anger he'd felt when his mom had brought up Harper's past. The instinct to protect her was automatic then, just as it was now, as she lay in his arms. He was going to protect her for as long as she would let him. Even if that meant protecting her from his own unwelcome feelings.

His mind wandered back to the promise he had made her, that he would never ask for more than she could give. But tonight he'd come close. He had wanted to ask her to stay. Forever.

TWENTY

"So, that head shrinker you've got me seeing says we need to talk about your mom. She's pretty sure that what happened is stopping all of us from moving on with our lives." Roy paused to spoon some oatmeal into his mouth. "And I think she might have something there."

Harper lifted her chin defiantly. "Well, I can only speak for myself but I'm pretty sure I've managed to move on just fine."

"Have you? According to her, there's a difference between running and moving on. It seems to me like you've just been running, like the rest of us."

Harper set her gaze at the window. She hadn't yet asked Roy if he still missed Petra and this seemed like the perfect opening. "You probably don't remember, but when you first woke from your surgery, you called me Petra. You said you missed her."

Roy nodded slowly as though trying to take in this bit of news. "If you had brought that up a few weeks ago, I would have lied to you, but I can see now that it's time to face the truth about everything. Part of me has always missed her—well, what we had more than her, really. It felt like we had a family when she was still here. But it kind of dissolved when she left, didn't it?"

Harper nodded but stayed silent.

"I don't want her back, Harper. I never will. I *do* want to have my family back, though, and in order to do that, we need to talk about what happened."

"I'm fine. We're fine," Harper answered firmly.

Roy waited a moment before speaking again. "We're not fine. And as much as I have to sort all this out for myself, you need to do the same. The thing is Harper, it's my fault—"

"It's certainly—" Harper started but Roy's finger in the air silenced her.

"And I want to fix this if I can. I should have gotten you and the boys some help when the whole thing happened. But I was so wrapped up in my own . . . head . . . and I didn't know what to do. I wanted the whole thing to just go away. I figured bringing it up would be a lot worse for you than trying to forget about it."

"It's been twenty years, Dad. We can just forget it now."

"I don't think we can. When I think about you kids, I can see that it's not over, no matter how much I wish it was. I know how hard it is for you to be back here. I know you're ashamed when you've got nothing to be ashamed of. You should hold your head high wherever you go, because you're a good person—a strong, successful woman. But I worry about you and your brothers. Not one of you has gotten married or had kids. Hell, I don't even think any of you have shacked up with someone. It's not a coincidence, is it?"

Harper glared at her father. "Just because I haven't gotten married doesn't mean I don't have the life I want. I have—had—a pretty kick-ass career and a terrific life, and I'm going to get it back when the time is right. I don't really care what your therapist says." Harper tapped her chest with her finger. "I get to choose the life I want."

Roy tilted his head thoughtfully. "You do, kid. You get to decide for yourself, but just make sure you aren't ruling out some wonderful possibilities because they scare you, okay? Make the life you really want. Really, deep down."

"I have. I'm fine, so let's just drop it, okay?" Harper's bottom lip trembled. She bit down on it to force it back in line. "I should go. I have an appointment with one of the Fashion Forward ladies at eleven." She stood to leave.

"Okay. I'm sorry, honey. I didn't mean to upset you. I just really want you to live the life you want. I know what it's like to look back and see that you didn't. I've spent months now with nothing but time to think about all the things I regret." Roy reached for Harper's hand and took it in his. His eyes filled with tears. "It's too late for me in a lot of ways. I can't go back and change my life, but nothing would make me happier than seeing you and your brothers live your dreams."

Harper screwed up her chin, trying to stop her tears. "It's not too late for you. Don't say that, okay?"

Roy nodded. "Well, it's too late for a lot of things. I can't start over with you kids, I can't go back and do a better job of things after your mother left, but if I can help you somehow, it'll mean I didn't fuck all this up completely."

"You didn't fuck anything up, Dad. Mom did that on her own. You did the best you could to clean up her mess."

"There's still a lot left to do. And I aim to do it. I need you to let me finish cleaning up." Roy squeezed her hand.

Harper nodded. "Okay. I won't fight you, but really, know that I'm okay, Dad."

"Good girl. I love you, kid. So much." Roy smiled through his tears. "You're strong and smart and you're good to the core. And I know I haven't told you this enough, but I'm so proud of you."

* * *

The next morning, instead of going straight to the clinic, Harper drove downtown for breakfast and a little shopping. She parked

{155}

and strolled across the quiet street to the little diner where she and Megan had agreed to meet and saw her waving enthusiastically as she approached. Giving each other a quick but warm hug, they went inside and settled themselves into a booth to get caught up. Because neither woman needed to scan the menu, knowing she would order the same thing she always did, they were able to dive right into girl talk.

"Dish. I need details," Megan said.

Harper laughed. "It's like . . . volcano-hot sex."

Megan's eyes grew wide. "Wow. That good?"

"I'm having so many orgasms I'm starting to worry I'll run out."

"Not possible."

The waitress came by with two waters and a pot of coffee. They ordered before picking up the conversation where they had left off.

Megan gave her a questioning look. "But what else? Do you think it's going to go anywhere?"

"Definitely not. Which is exactly why it's working so well. We both knew the score going in. I'm only here for a while, then it'll be done. I'm thinking that actually adds to the heat, knowing it's temporary."

"Really?" Megan wrinkled up her nose. "You're sure neither of you is going to start thinking about a future together?"

"No. Not a chance. We're both being adult about it." Harper glanced down at her friend's hand, seeing a shiny rock where there had been nothing before. She gasped, grabbing Megan's hand with hers. "Oh my God. Is that what I think it is?"

Megan nodded, eyes suddenly shining with excitement. "It is. But we were talking about you."

"Forget me! I need details! Now!"

"Okay, good. Because I was about to burst if I couldn't tell you soon!" Megan laughed. "It was a total surprise. We had agreed a long time ago that the whole wedding thing really didn't matter to either of us, but Luc just decided he wanted to make it official. Last Saturday he took Elliott out for a few hours. I thought they were going to the playground, but really Luc took him for lunch to ask him if he would be happy if we got married. I guess Elliott jumped up from his seat and ran to Luc for a hug. I wish I had seen it. Just the thought of it brings tears to my eyes." Megan fanned at her eyes for a moment. "Okay, anyway, after lunch, he brought Elliott with him to help pick out a ring."

"Oh, that Luc. In all the years I've known him, I didn't think he had it in him."

"And yet he does," Megan said. "So, he had this whole plan to get my mom to babysit so he could take me out for a fancy dinner, but he realized that he wanted the kids there to share in the moment. So instead, he stopped at the bakery on the way home and had them write 'Will you marry me?' on a carrot cake."

"Your favourite dessert. Aww. Very sweet!"

"I know. When they got home, I was a total wreck, still in my pyjamas, passed out on a lounge chair in the yard with the baby. I probably had drool hanging from my mouth. He and Elliott came outside with this box from the bakery, and Elliott says, 'Mom, can we have dessert before supper tonight?' and I said, 'No, I might be tired but I'm still the same mom you've always had.' But then I see this grin on his face, and I look at Luc and he is so excited he can hardly stand still. So I asked them what was going on."

"Oh, I wish this was all on video because I would kill to see it!"

"I'm glad it isn't. I was super gross that day," Megan said quickly. "So, then Luc says, 'Just take a look at the dessert. I think you'll like it.' He gives Elliott this little nod and Elliott opens the box and says, 'Not me. Luc.'

"So I start crying and nodding, and before I know it, Luc's on one knee with the ring box, and he says, '*Mon ange*, say you'll be mine forever, because I will always be yours.'

{157}

"I sat up and we kissed and woke Amelie, and she started fussing while Luc slipped the ring onto my finger, and then we were all hugging and laughing and crying together." Megan's eyes shone with tears as she finished her story, just in time for her plate of eggs Benedict to be placed before her.

Harper got up and gave her a huge hug. "I am so friggin' happy for you. All four of you. I think I might be the happiest for Elliott. He's needed a real father for so long. It gives me hope that life really can turn out beautifully."

"It can!" Megan said. She paused, smiling at Harper as she watched her return to her seat. "And it will turn out beautifully for you too. I just know it."

"God, I hope so," Harper replied. "But back to you. Have you started making wedding plans?"

"We have. It's going to be a lot sooner than you'd expect. Luc's aunt and uncle are coming in three weeks to meet all of us and we thought we'd do it then. They're really the only family he's got. It's going to be very simple. At home, just family and a few friends. My brother and his wife can come up with the kids then as well. We're going to have it in the late afternoon out by the pool and then have a caterer serve dinner right after the ceremony. Nothing big. No gifts."

"Sounds perfect."

"I think so too. I've already done the big wedding and I really don't want to do it again. Luc has hardly any family, and his friends wouldn't all be able to come this far anyway."

"It'll be wonderful," Harper replied, pouring some ketchup next to her hash browns. "Good for you, Megs. Can I do anything to help?"

"Well, I do want to ask you something important. We're not having a best man or a maid of honour, but I do need a photographer. And there is no one I'd rather have than you."

"What? Seriously? That's a little intimidating for me. Are you sure you don't want to hire someone in the industry?"

"Positive. I love all the photos you've taken of us over the years. You're the one who will be able to capture who we really are. I don't want a bunch of staged, phony smiles. I want the real moments. And you have an incredible eye. If you need help setting up a few family shots, I can get you started and you'll just have to press the button. But you won't need help. You know what you're doing."

"Well, Megan, if my best friends want me to take photos on their wedding day, I will take photos. And it will be an honour."

"Yippee! I'm so glad you said yes!" Megan looked elated as she tucked a lock of angel-blond hair behind her ear.

"Now, have you thought dresses?"

"I have not. I was hoping you, as my style guru, would guide me in the right direction."

"Gladly. I already have about fifty ideas in mind."

"I really only need one."

"Is that what we're shopping for this morning?"

"It is! And I'm going to need your help, since my figure will not be ready yet for anything too fitted by then."

"Well, we're going to have to play up your huge boobs, then."

Megan laughed. "I'm thinking Luc will like that, but nothing too showy. We have to remember my son and our other relatives will be there. We don't want to gross them out."

Harper put up a finger. "Got it. Tastefully done boobage."

*　*　*

Late that afternoon, after shopping and a visit with her dad, Harper stopped at the deli and bought the fixings for a picnic. She had decided to surprise Evan at work, knowing he was in for a long day. She hurried home and put together some sub-style sandwiches, iced teas and donuts she had picked up. After a glance at what she'd prepared, she decided to bring along a kale salad for herself, which she knew Evan wouldn't eat. She freshened up her makeup and replaced the dress she had worn shopping with a pair of jeans and a cute T-shirt that fit just right. Smiling to herself, she made her way over to the building site. As she pulled up, she could see Evan was alone, and she knew he must have let the crew leave.

He stopped what he was doing when he saw her pull up, a broad grin crossing his face under his hard hat.

"Hey, beautiful!" he called as she got out of her dad's truck. "What brings you here?" He jumped down onto the dirt surrounding the now-framed house and strode over to her, taking off his hat and wiping the sweat from his brow.

"I thought you might be hungry," she replied, holding up the bag of food. "I also assumed you'd be missing me terribly by now."

He gave her a long kiss. "How do you know me so well after only a few weeks?"

"You're a man. Men are not that complicated. You're either hungry or horny."

"And here I thought I was a man of mystery."

"No such thing, really. Even James Bond is either looking for food or sex. The espionage just gets in his way most of the time."

Evan laughed, taking the bag and leading her over to the house. Setting the bag down, he lifted her onto the raised floor so she wouldn't have to use the stepladder. Pulling himself up in one quick move, he planted himself next to her. Harper gave him a lingering kiss.

When she pulled back, he said, "I'm a mess. I'm sure I smell like a locker room."

"Not really. You somehow manage to still appeal to me. That's the real mystery," she teased, pulling the food and drinks out of the bag.

As they ate, Harper told him about Megan's big news, excitedly describing the proposal and the dress they had picked out. When she had finished, she stared at him for a moment. "Hey, your eyes didn't glaze over even once when I was telling you all of that. And now that

I think of it, you probably don't care in the slightest about chiffon versus charmeuse."

"I was riveted, even though I don't have the first clue what either of those words means. For reasons that I can't explain, if you are telling me about it, I want to know every detail."

"God, you're perfect," she said with a happy sigh. "All thoughtful and caring, wrapped up in that sexy package."

"Glad you like my package," he said, leaning in for a deep kiss.

"Mmm," Harper moaned as their lips met. When it was over, Harper took a moment to open her eyes again, returning to reality. "I should go. I promised myself I was just going to feed you and then get out of your way so you can get home earlier."

"But now I don't want to get back to work. I want to go home and get you into the shower with me."

"That sounds good. Too bad I can't help you so you could get home sooner."

"Maybe you can."

"Really?"

He stood, pulling her up with him and plunking his hard hat onto her head. Grinning as the hat wobbled there, he led her over to his tool box and selected a long level from the top drawer. "Your tool, Madame. You ever used a level before?" he asked.

"Nope, but it's long and hard so I'm sure I'll be good at it," she answered in a sultry voice.

Evan's eyes grew wide and a short bark of laughter escaped him. "You should come to work more often. This is going to be fun. Alright, I was just going to check one last time that all the walls are framed straight and square."

Giving a quick nod to show she was back to being serious, she replied. "I don't know what any of that means, but if you're teaching me I'm happy to learn."

They worked until the sun had almost disappeared. Harper

quickly picked up what he needed her to do, and they laughed together when she got confused. He was a patient teacher and showed appreciation for her help, repeatedly insisting that she was saving him a lot of time even though she was sure that in fact she wasn't. In the end he would only go so far as to admit that even if things weren't getting done faster, he had never had such a good time at work before.

* * *

That night as he fell asleep, Evan realized he had never been happier in his life. Harper was everything he had always wanted in a woman without even knowing it. She was his perfect match and here she was, asleep in his arms, trusting him completely and letting him in. He felt lucky to have her, even if it was just for a little while.

TWENTY-ONE

"I haven't been here since I was a teenager. I forgot how pretty this lake is." Harper inhaled the fresh scent of summer mountain air and pine before filling her arms with bags of plastic plates, cups and cutlery. She stared for a moment at the sandy beach that led into the clear blue water while she waited for Evan to unload a large cooler from the flatbed.

"I love it out here. It's the perfect spot to host the barbecue," Evan said as he started toward the picnic shelter. "Say, thanks again for helping me get everything ready for today. I really appreciate it."

"No problem. It's been pretty fun, actually. I just can't believe that you normally get all this ready for fifty people by yourself every year."

"It's no big deal, really. It's my little way of saying thank you for all the long hours they've been putting in all summer."

The two worked quickly for the next twenty minutes, covering picnic tables with red-and-white checkered tablecloths, stringing some balloons to the shelter and getting the food and drinks set up. Evan had brought a large bin of lawn games for the children who would be joining them and he started setting them up on the grass.

"You've thought of everything," Harper said as she watched him pin croquet wickets into the ground.

"Well, it's a lot more fun for everyone if the kids have something to do."

"Lacey's right. You are a horrible tyrant."

"I thought it was awful beast?"

"Right. That."

A little while later, the first of the guests started arriving. Evan greeted them all warmly and introduced Harper to everyone. The pair started the party by handing out Popsicles to the children and cold drinks to the adults. The heat of the day was now peaking, making the refreshments all the more welcome. The kids quickly made their way to the games, giving their parents the opportunity to relax and visit.

Next, much to the group's delight, the start of the annual Labour Day Donovan Builders football game was announced. Never one to back down from a challenge, Harper joined in, finding herself on the opposing team to Evan. The first huddle of the game broke up and the teams faced off. Harper's team started with the ball, which was quickly intercepted by Evan. He weaved in and out of the players, passing the ball to one of his smallest teammates, a boy of about ten. When they neared the end zone, Evan picked him up and carried him in for a touchdown. Cheers and jeers filled the air, and the boy he was holding laughed hysterically and held his hands up in victory.

"Cheap, Donovan!" Harper called to him. "You're better than that."

"You guys just wish you had thought of it first," he gloated.

During the next huddle, Harper told her team to leave Evan to her. As soon as the ball was snapped back to him, Harper charged ahead, hoping to cut him off. Leaning forward, she tried to tackle him, which only made it easier for him to pick her up with his free hand, sling her over his shoulder and run the ball in for a touchdown.

He put her down with a celebratory smirk. "Not a chance, Young," he said, kissing her hard on the mouth. "Nice try, though. I have to admire your spirit."

The game continued like this, the two of them flirting their way through each play until Evan's team claimed victory. When the high-fives and trash talk had ended, most of the players made a beeline to the lake to cool off, while Harper and Evan returned to the picnic shelter to wash up and start dinner. As they walked, he wrapped his arm around her shoulders lazily and pulled her in for a kiss. "That was fun. Let's get these people fed and out of here. I want you all to myself again."

"Mmm, sounds wonderful," Harper replied as they reluctantly parted ways to start preparing dinner.

A few minutes later, some of the other women joined Harper, helping to slice open hamburger buns and put out salads.

"So, Harper, this must be pretty serious if he asked you to help host the Labour Day picnic," Lacey said.

"Oh, no, he just asked me to come along because I didn't have plans today." Harper gazed over at Evan, who was flipping burgers on the grill. He glanced at her at the same moment, his expression saying how much he wanted her.

One of the other women at the table caught their exchange. "I don't know. He seems pretty smitten, if you ask me. You lucky bitch. There's not a woman in town who'd kick that man out of bed for eating crackers."

Lacey gave the woman a light swat on the arm. "Heidi's just teasing, of course. She's madly in love with her husband."

Heidi nodded. "I am, but that doesn't mean I would turn down a roll in the hay with his boss."

Harper laughed, putting her hand over her mouth. "He is easy on the eyes, isn't he?"

Heidi flashed her a knowing smile. "If by that you mean unbelievably hot, no one is going to disagree with you. But even better than that, he's a really good man."

"Agreed. So, Heidi, which one of these lucky guys is your husband?" Harper asked, changing the subject. A distinctly uncomfortable feeling had started to set in on her. Part of her felt as though she wouldn't be deemed worthy of Evan by these women. But why should she really care what they thought of her? She pushed the thoughts and their accompanying feelings aside, telling herself it was all in her head.

* * *

When the meal had been served and all the guests were seated at the long row of tables, Evan made his way over to the head of the last one and addressed the group. "As you know, I'm not big on speeches, but I thought today I better make an exception. We've had an amazing year so far and I owe it to all of you. First, to the families—for understanding and supporting these tired guys. I know they can't always make it to every Little League game, and that they've missed a lot of dinners, especially lately. And I know that's not easy for any of you. It puts all that extra work on you wives, particularly, and I want you to know that your sacrifice means a lot to me. So, thank you.

"Second, to the crew—you guys get up at the crack of dawn every day and put in the long hours, which is the reason we aren't running two months behind all the time. You work hard, you never cut corners and you take pride in what you do, which means that every house we build is one we can be proud of. My reputation as a contractor really comes down to what each of you does every day. It's the reason we were awarded the Pine Crest development and it's the reason why when we're finished, it's going to be the best place to live in Colorado.

And I am grateful to you all. One more thing, and then I promise I'll go sit down. Everyone gets a paid day off tomorrow."

He paused for a moment to let the cheers die down. "So eat up! If you're not driving, drink up. And have a wonderful extra-long long weekend. You've earned it and then some!" He held up his beer to toast them, receiving a round of applause. Picking up his plate, he started toward the empty spot next to Harper.

Just as Evan sat down, Lacey's husband, Chad, stood up and cleared his throat. "Well, since it's open mic, I thought we better say something nice to our illustrious leader." Chad paused, giving Evan an appreciative smile, before his face shifted into a more serious expression. "I think I speak for everyone when I say I'm proud to work for someone with integrity, someone who cares—not just about the bottom line—but about doing things right, about the people who work for him and the people they love. So here's to Evan." He raised his cup and the others joined him.

One of the men at the far end of the table leaned over to look at Harper. "He paid Chad to say that, Harper. He told us we had to make him look good in front of you."

"I assumed it was something like that," Harper said, joining in the fun.

After dinner, a few of the guests helped clean up and load the leftover food into coolers, while others spread blankets on the grass to get ready for the fireworks. Lacey worked alongside Harper, chatting as they wiped down the tables. "So, you can see, we're all pretty attached to Evan."

"Yes, it's very obvious you all love your boss. It's sweet, really."

"Speaking of sweet, you two are about as sweet as a Krispy Kreme donut dipped in chocolate."

Harper grinned. "We do have a lot of fun together."

"It's none of my business, but I sure hope you two'll make it stick.

I've known Evan for a lot of years, and I'm not kidding when I say I've never seen him this happy. He just lights up when you're around."

Harper was saved from having to respond by Evan's approach. He gave Lacey an easy smile. "Lacey, why don't you go relax? Chad's got the boys all set up for the fireworks. You should get off your feet too."

"Oh, alright, but only if you promise you're bringing her back to the picnic next year," she said, handing him her cleaning rag. "This one's a keeper, boss."

Evan took the rag. "She'll be sick of me by then," he teased.

Lacey pursed her lips at him. "Keeper. As in, you better keep her," she advised before turning to go.

When she was out of earshot, Evan said, "You two seem to have hit it off."

"I really like her." Harper picked up the bucket and plunked the rags into it. "I'm going to go empty this in the bathroom sink. I'll catch up with you in a minute."

Harper hurried to the bathroom, her shoulders slumped. An uncomfortable feeling had come over her, brought on by Lacey's mention of the future. By this time next year she wouldn't be around to be part of another such wonderful day. She stood in front of the bathroom mirror, staring at the woman looking back at her. "What are you doing?" she asked her reflection.

A few minutes later, she found Evan lying on a blanket that was set back a little from the rest of the party. "There you are! Come take a load off, the show's about to start."

Harper flopped onto the blanket next to him, lacing her fingers through his. "What a great day. You really showed everyone an amazing time."

"This was definitely our best picnic yet. Thanks, in no small part, to you." He paused, picking up her hand and bringing it to his lips. "I'll have to find a way to make it up to you later."

"I like that sound of that," she replied, but there was something about her voice that sounded small.

"You seem a little upset. What's wrong?"

"Nothing. I'm happy."

They were interrupted by the first crack that filled the air as the fireworks began. She smiled reassuringly at Evan. They lay back with their heads together, holding hands as they watched the sky light up then grow dark. The heat hung in the air, allowing everyone to hold on to the last moments of summer before it gave way to autumn. Although they were surrounded by people, Evan and Harper were suddenly alone again in their own perfect world. The sound of *oohs* and *aahs* faded in her ears as she snuggled closer to him, feeling safe and cared for. How could anything that felt so right be so wrong?

* * *

Later, as they bid goodbye to the sleepy children and grateful parents, Lacey stopped to give Harper a hug. "I sure hope you two are going to have a happy ending, but if you don't, just promise you won't break his heart, okay?"

"I'll do my best."

When the last of the stragglers had gone, Evan pulled Harper in for a long hug. "Thank God they're gone. I thought I'd never get you alone." He kissed her from the nape of her neck to her earlobe. "We've been so good all day. I say we do something really bad to make up for it."

"Mmm. What did you have in mind?"

"I thought I'd get you out of those clothes and we'd go for a swim together," he murmured in her ear, letting his hands wander up into her tank top.

Harper gave him a naughty look. "I like how you think."

"Then let's get to it," he said, picking her up over his shoulder and carrying her down to the water.

"Ack!" She squealed with laughter. "Put me down!"

"Nope. You walk too slow and I've been waiting all day for this!"

TWENTY-TWO

The day Roy came home was a mixture of relief and worry for all concerned. Black clouds swirled overhead, threatening to open up and pour down on them as Craig pushed an empty wheelchair up the ramp to the back door of the house. Roy, who had now progressed to using two canes with arm braces, walked ahead of his son, annoyed at the need for the support but grateful to be going home again, where the food was good, where he could sleep in his own room, where his private space was waiting.

"Dad. Welcome home." Harper smiled at him from the kitchen, where she had been waiting for him.

"Yup. It's about time, isn't it?" he asked.

"That it is," Harper replied, hovering a bit as he slid his shoes off.

"Back off, kid. I've got it covered," he said with no hint of anger, only pride in his accomplishment.

"Where do you want this?" Craig asked Roy, referring to the wheelchair.

"The dump, for all I care. I'm not using that damn thing." Roy's voice was determined.

Craig looked at his sister, his eyes wide with exasperation.

"Would you like a drink, Dad?" Harper asked.

"Yes, but I'll get it myself. I've been waiting to have a beer for months now, and it just won't taste the same if someone serves it to me." He grunted a little as he carefully made his way over to the fridge. Trying to act like everything was normal, he said, "The place looks terrific, Harper. Thank you so much. I saw all those plants out front but I really want you to go with me and show me everything you did."

Harper lit up, glad he had noticed. "I'd love to. Do you need to have a rest first?" She moved to the stove, stirring the chili she had made.

"Yeah, I probably should. They work you hard at therapy. It's like a boot camp for cripples."

His attempt to joke about his predicament fell flat, bringing tears to Harper's eyes.

"Don't go getting all soft on me now, kid. This is going to be hard enough. We should at least keep our sense of humour about the whole thing."

"Of course, Dad." Craig stepped in, giving Harper a moment to recover. He grabbed himself a beer and sat at the table, cracking open the can. "So, Harper and I were thinking I could stay with you part of the time, when I'm home from work. I'm going to stay here for the next few nights. I don't have to leave until Monday morning."

"I don't see the point in either of you staying, really," Roy said. "I'm fine."

"Well, we'd like to hang around all the same, at least while you get used to everything." Craig took a sip of his beer. "Besides, Harper here is homeless and jobless. You wouldn't kick her out now, would you?"

"It's true. I'm like one of those boomerang kids you hear about who keep moving back home," Harper added.

"You sure as hell better not be," Roy said, trying to hide his delight. "I didn't raise any lazy-ass kids. Speaking of which, don't you need to get to work today?"

"I told the ladies at Fashion Forward I was spending the day with you. We have a couple of clients tomorrow, but nothing pressing today." Harper checked on the chili again, lowering the heat.

"Well, thanks, kid. I appreciate that."

* * *

On Monday morning, Harper unlocked the front door to Roy's house, opening it as quietly as possible. Craig waved to her from the kitchen and held up a pot of coffee, silently offering to pour her a mug. Nodding, she put her bag down on the living room floor and crossed to the kitchen. It was so early that a few stars still hung in the sky. Craig seemed tired as he handed her the warm mug.

"What day are you back?" she asked. He had come over to Evan's to watch baseball and unwind while Roy was sleeping, so he had filled her in on how things were going. She knew that the next month wasn't necessarily going to be pretty and she had readied herself for it.

"On the tenth. It's hard to see him like this, isn't it." Craig poured himself a travel mug of coffee and secured the lid.

Harper nodded without saying anything.

"I better go. Call me if you need to talk, okay? I'm off shift by eight every evening."

"Will do, but I'll be fine. I'm not made of glass, you know."

"You're not made of iron like you pretend you are, either." He gave her a little wink before he opened the back door, making the "call me" sign before he left.

Harper sat at the kitchen table, coffee in hand as she contemplated the day. A few minutes later, her dad's door opened and she could hear him negotiating the narrow hall with his canes. He looked old to her as his eyebrows knit together in concentration. Seeing her, he stopped briefly before continuing on.

"Morning, Harper." He relaxed the muscles in his face in an attempt to make walking look easy.

"Morning, Dad. How'd you sleep?"

"Not bad. That bed you got me is pretty comfortable, actually. I might want to keep it."

"Yeah? I'm glad to hear it. I was worried about that."

Her first impulse was to get up to pour him some coffee and offer to make breakfast. Fighting that urge, she sat still, knowing he'd want to do it himself. She watched as he struggled to get a mug out of the cupboard and then pour the hot liquid, spilling a little as he did. He turned to the fridge, opening it and getting the milk out, but not before knocking one of his canes with the door and having to correct himself in order to avoid falling.

Harper dug her nails into her palms to prevent tears from forming in her eyes, finding it heart-wrenching to see her tough-as-an-ox father weakened like this. She'd gotten used to seeing him lying in a hospital bed but somehow this was so much worse. Staring up at the ceiling for a moment, she reminded herself that this was only temporary and that he'd make a full recovery. The last thing he needed was for her to burden him with her sadness.

He returned the milk to the fridge and gingerly picked up his mug, taking a sip where he stood. He finished half of it before bringing it along for the bumpy journey to the table. Once he was settled, Harper stood and crossed the room, opening the breadbox and dropping two slices of bread into the toaster. "I'm having some toast. You want any while I'm up?"

"Couldn't help yourself, could you? Watching me get the coffee was all you could stand to see."

Harper refused to look back at him, not wanting him to see the truth in her eyes. "You managed that just fine as far as I can tell. I would make the same offer to anyone I was sharing breakfast with."

Her father nodded a little as if accepting the logic behind her explanation. "Okay, then. I'd like a couple of slices with some peanut butter. But not that New-Age crap you like. I want Skippy."

A small grin crossed Harper's lips. "Sure thing, Dad. Skippy it is." *Skippy. Four out of five tough guys prefer it,* she thought to herself.

* * *

Late that evening, Harper lowered herself onto Evan's front step and placed a Thermos of homemade beef-barley soup next to her, her grin touching both ears. She had seen his truck pull up and had come over to meet him as he gathered his blueprints and briefcase from the passenger seat. A slight chill in the air had her wrap her cardigan around herself a little tighter.

"You're a sight for sore eyes," he said, his dimples making their regularly scheduled appearance as he shut the truck door and made his way over to her. "And from your face, I'd say you've got something to celebrate."

"I do. It's not a major accomplishment or anything, but I got through day one of looking after my dad without any tears."

"Good for you. It must be so hard to see your dad like that." Evan sat beside her on the step, and they gave each other the sweet, lingering hello kiss that they'd both grown accustomed to.

"It is. But I just have to keep reminding myself that we're lucky he's even alive and that it won't be too long until he's much better," Harper said.

"That's true. Just think of how far he's come. In the spring, it didn't look like he'd ever walk again."

"It's actually amazing, isn't it?"

"It is. I'm so glad for him. For all of you." He paused to look at her for a moment, putting his arm around her. "I want you to promise me something. If you have a rough day or you need to talk, you'll call me. Or, at the very least, come by when I get home so I can hold you until you feel better."

Harper felt a lump in her throat at his words. He wanted to take care of her, which was a completely new experience for her. She was both touched and terrified at the same time. "That sounds nice, but I'll be fine."

Evan gave her a look. "Why can't you just let yourself lean on me a little? I promise it'll feel good."

"That's the problem. If I start doing things like that, this'll end up feeling a lot less casual than it is," she answered, glancing up at him. She could tell by his expression that he didn't like what she'd just said. But there was no way Harper would let that conversation go any further. "You're home late tonight. You must be beat."

As if he understood that she needed him to drop it, he allowed her to steer them to a new topic. "I am both. One of the electricians had an apprentice who was a no-show, so I spent the last five hours pulling cable. That is a young man's job if ever there was one." He stretched his arms out straight in front of him to relieve the sore muscles in his back.

"You were pulling cable for the last five hours? No wonder you're sore." She tucked her lips into her teeth, doing a poor job of hiding her delight.

Evan shook his head. "I don't know whether to be turned on by your dirty mind or concerned that I'm with a woman who has the sense of humour of a fifteen-year-old boy."

"Would both somehow be an option?"

"Oddly, yes," he answered. Spying the container on the step, he asked, "That wouldn't be some soup for me, would it?"

"It would be. Beef barley."

"Thank you. I was just wondering what I was going to make for dinner," he replied, pressing his lips to her cheek. "I've always wanted a sexy neighbour who would show up with food when I was starving."

"Oh, I know. Sex and food. You men are so simple it's almost unfair."

"You're a little bit patronizing, you know that?"

"And even still, you can't resist." She let her lips hover over his.

"How is that possible?" he asked, pulling back to glance at her lips. "If every muscle in my body wasn't aching right now, I would carry you into the house and have my way with you."

"How about a massage instead?" Harper replied in a low tone, trailing a finger down his thigh.

"One with a happy ending?" His eyes lit up with hope.

"Sure, if your jaw isn't as sore as the rest of you," she answered before bursting out laughing.

TWENTY-THREE

"So, you look pretty relaxed for someone about to take the plunge," Harper remarked. She and Megan sat side by side at the salon, soaking their feet in the swirling warm water.

"I'm too tired to be nervous. Amelie was up half the night. I think she's cutting another tooth."

"Well, you're absolutely radiant in spite of the lack of sleep," Harper replied.

"That's because I'm marrying the right guy this time."

"He is sickeningly perfect, I have to say."

"I know. I can hardly stand us myself, sometimes." Megan gestured with her champagne flute. "Speaking of sickeningly perfect, how are things with Evan?"

"He's just . . . I had no idea it could be like this. Not even the tiniest clue. We just have so much fun together, and he really listens to me when I talk, and he's so thoughtful. The other morning, he came home with the September issue of *Style*. He told me he couldn't decide if he was being disloyal by supporting it now that I'm not there anymore, but in the end, he just really wanted to look at it with me so I could show him what I do. Did. What I did."

"Wow. That is really sweet," Megan said.

"There's more. We went for a breakfast picnic and he brought it along so we could go through it from cover to cover. He must have asked me a hundred questions, trying to understand how we put an issue together and what, exactly, I did there. I've never been with a guy who showed such interest in my work. Except that prick who was only dating me so he could meet models."

"Oh, yeah. I forgot about that guy. Hot bartender bastard, right?"

"That's the one. Evan's been a nice change of pace."

Megan looked up from the nail colour samples she was studying. "I know you don't want to hear this, but it's my wedding day, so I get to say what I want and you're not allowed to get mad at me. I'm keeping my fingers crossed that you two will stay together. He's a good man. He's funny and smart and really thoughtful. For the first time, you're with a man who I think actually deserves you."

"Ooh. That's low, Megan. Really low. I'll be calling you first thing tomorrow morning with my response."

"Knew you would, but I'm hoping that if you have the next twenty-four hours to let it sink in, you'll realize I'm right."

Harper rolled her eyes to end the discussion, then pointed at a nail polish sample called Petal Pink. "That's the one for you today."

* * *

The very earth itself seemed to approve of Megan and Luc's nuptials, offering perfect blue skies without even the tiniest wisp of white. Summer seemed to have returned for them, adding a welcome warmth to the air. The birds sang their love songs as the bride, the groom and their two children made their way to the arbour where the officiant, Mr. Grady, a short, bald man in his sixties, was waiting with a smile.

Luc, dressed in a simple, light grey suit, a crisp white dress shirt and steel-blue tie, held little Amelie, who was adorable in bare feet and a beautiful white dress with tiny blue flowers. She chewed on her fist happily as the ceremony got underway. Elliott, looking sharp in grey plaid dress shorts and a short-sleeved button-up shirt, had a grin plastered from ear to ear as though it was permanently in place. He walked between Luc and Megan, his hands tucked neatly into theirs. Megan was a vision in a simple V-neck goddess dress in ivory silk. A belt beaded with pearls sat just above her waist, letting the skirt flow out to hide her tummy while tastefully accenting the large breasts she would have for a few more months. Her blond hair was up in pincurls, with a few pieces left down to frame her beautiful face.

Harper had placed herself a few steps behind and to the side of the justice of the peace so that she could capture the moment. She had spent hours with Megan in the days prior to the wedding learning the intricacies of Megan's camera equipment. Megan had assured her that she would be fine, but Harper had been obsessive about making sure she wouldn't miss a single shot. Now, as the event began, Harper felt herself breaking out in a cold sweat and wished she had gone with the black dress with the tiny floral pattern instead of the metallic lace–embellished sheath dress she had on. How had she let herself get talked into taking photos of a photographer's wedding? Horrible idea. Her hands shook a little as she zoomed in on Elliott's face, a seven-year-old in pure bliss, just as he reached up and gave his little sister's foot a kiss. *Got it!* she thought, shifting her position to catch Luc's expression as he glanced at Megan, his eyes full of that adoration he always felt for her.

When Megan and Harper had arrived earlier, Luc had been rushing around, trying to ready the yard. Excitedly overseeing every detail, he had surprised Megan by purchasing a wrought-iron arbour and hiring a florist to decorate it with roses and hydrangeas in lavenders, purples and blues. Large urns overflowing with arrangements matching those on the arbour trailed from the end of the driveway to the entrance of the house. In the backyard, they continued from the house to the shaded grassy area that had now become the focal point of the intimate gathering.

Evan stood off to the side at the front, holding up a video camera that Harper had thrust at him before the ceremony began. Planting both feet firmly, he steadied the camera as he slowly zoomed in and out to focus on the faces of the happy family.

Mr. Grady welcomed the group to the beautiful ceremony, making a few kind remarks and teasing the couple on their order of events before asking Luc to recite his vows. Luc handed Amelie to Helen, his soon-to-be mother-in-law, before turning to Megan and taking both of her hands in his.

"Megan, it's no secret that I didn't believe in love until you came along. You changed my mind about everything with your smile, your laugh and your beautiful heart, and I will forever be grateful to you for that. You have shown me what true love can do, and you've given me a family with two beautiful children and a home filled with laughter. You've shown me what life is all about and how rich it truly can be, even if I were to lose every dollar. And I have you to thank for all of it. So thank you, *mon ange*, for giving my life meaning." He paused to wipe a tear from her cheek before continuing.

"I, Luc, take you, Megan, to be my wife. I promise to love you, respect you, remain faithful to you and honour you for the rest of my life. I will be here to take care of you in the face of whatever comes. I will support your dreams and be the voice of encouragement when you need a little push. For now and always, in sickness and in health, for richer and for poorer for the rest of our lives. You are stuck with me."

Megan dabbed at her eyes with a tissue, glancing up at the sky for a moment in hopes of regaining her composure. "Well, how do I follow that?" she asked, getting a light laugh from their guests.

Smiling at him, she gave his hand a squeeze. "Luc, before you came along, I was content with my life, just Elliott and me. I had stopped believing in fairy tales years ago, but you swooped in and showed me what romance really was, and then you showed me love. I was scared to try again, to let you in, but you just kept proving to me that you were real, that this was real and that it could be easy and it could be forever. And now, my life is full. Elliott and I have you, and we all have Amelie, and there is so much more love and fun in our home. And I will always be grateful that you came along and that you stayed and that you're mine." It was Megan's turn to wipe a tear, this time from Luc's cheek.

"I, Megan, take you, Luc, to be my husband. I promise to love, honour and respect you, and to be faithful to you for the rest of my life. I will be here to take care of you in the face of whatever comes. I will support your dreams and be the voice of encouragement when you need a little push. For now and always, in sickness and in health, for richer and for poorer for the rest of our lives. Whether you like or not, you are stuck with me."

As Mr. Grady led them through the exchange of rings, there was not a dry eye to be found in the yard. "And now, Luc would like to make a pledge to Elliott."

Luc crouched down so he would be at eye level with his stepson. "Elliott, from the moment I first met you in the hospital waiting room, and you quickly pointed out my funny accent and the fact that I was overdressed, I knew I was going to like you a lot. You are wise beyond your years, you are so full of love and acceptance of others, you are full of life and wonder, and I have been honoured to watch you grow this past year. Thank you for accepting me into your life with open arms. Elliott, I may not have seen your first steps, but I promise to watch over you for all the rest of the steps of your life, big and small. Life is full of opportunity, and nothing has been more important than the opportunity to help raise you and your little sister. I love you, Elliott, and nothing will ever change that."

Elliott wrapped his arms around Luc's neck, hugging him with everything he had in his little sixty-pound frame. Tears filled Luc's eyes as he kissed the little boy on the head. Megan was weeping uncontrollably now, seeing her son and her new husband share such a tender moment. Harper snapped away, her vision blurry from her own tears as she watched the beautiful scene unfold through the camera lens. Taking a second to glance over at Evan, her face fell a little when she noticed he was frowning. She made a mental note to ask him about that later. Or not. Maybe it was better not to know.

The party dined under the stars as evening fell, chatting and laughing together at four round tables set up poolside. Candles floated in the blue water, fairy lights sparkled around the pergola above, glasses were raised in happy, heartfelt toasts and cake was cut and savoured. A quartet of musicians strummed guitars, providing a romantic musical backdrop with a hint of Spanish flair to the warm night. As Harper let the scene unfold around her, she found herself wondering if maybe this was something she wanted after all. She watched as Luc led Megan over to a clearing near the band and pulled her in for their first dance. The love they shared had beaten the odds and had created a beautiful family in the most impossible of circumstances.

Her eyes fell on Evan, who was standing at the bar talking with Megan's brother. He laughed at something Mark said, which made him look all the more handsome. He had a warmth that drew others to him. Sighing to herself, she felt her heart swell. How could anyone be so perfect?

As she watched him, an uneasy feeling came over her. The closer she got to him, the deeper she fell. And the deeper she fell, the more terrifying this all became. Suddenly she realized that somehow her heart had started counting on a future with him. She was in love with him in a way she'd never been with anyone before. For the first time in her life, she wanted forever with someone. With him. But there wasn't going to be a happy ending for them and she knew it. The only person she could rely on was herself. Anyone else might leave at any time. Including him. She would have to fight for ownership of her heart again and get it the hell back from him. Downing another glass of champagne, she told herself she was feeling this way only because of the wedding. Maybe just for tonight, she could let herself be in love. Tomorrow she'd come to her senses.

TWENTY-FOUR

Driving home under the bright moon, Harper leaned sleepily against the seat as she absent-mindedly rubbed the back of Evan's neck with her fingers. "You're looking pretty fine in that suit, Mr. Donovan. It's the kind of look that makes a woman want to do very naughty things."

"That's why I wore it."

"It's a smart man who knows the power of a well-cut suit," she remarked. "What a wonderful day. It feels like all is right with the world." Harper sighed happily. "I get all choked up even thinking about it. They're just so perfect together, and it's so amazing to see how much Luc and Elliott love each other too. Everything has just fallen into place so beautifully for them."

"Yes. It was very nice to see. I hope I managed to get it all on video. That was a lot of pressure for a contractor, you know."

"I know. I'm sorry about that. I realized at the last minute that we hadn't thought of getting a videographer and I figured that catching the moment, even if it wasn't on a pro video, would be better than missing it. I'm sure what you did will turn out just fine."

Harper paused for a moment, thinking back to that expression on his face, and decided to plunge into the deep waters of his mind. She'd been treading in the safety of the shallow end long enough to work up the courage. "So, Evan, was that why you had such an uncomfortable look on your face during the ceremony?"

"What?" he asked, in a way that seemed like he was trying to stall.

"It was hard to miss that scowl." Harper's heart quickened a little as she removed her hand from his neck, placing it on her lap awkwardly.

Evan stared straight ahead without answering for a moment. "To be honest, I was worried for them. I was thinking, they better damn well mean all of those nice words because if they don't, two little people who are relying on them for everything are going to be destroyed."

Harper nodded. "I wondered if it was something along those lines. I don't think you need to worry, though. I've known them both for years, and I can honestly say I don't know two people more suited to each other. It's going to last."

"Don't be fooled. It's all sunshine and roses at the beginning, especially when you've got so much cash you don't know how to spend it. But I'd hate to see what would happen if they suddenly found themselves with nothing. The smiles would fade pretty quickly. I know from experience."

Waiting a beat without getting a response, he continued. "I'm sorry, but that's just how I feel. I know they're both great people and I'm not trying to upset you or anything. Just being honest."

"Hmm, right. So it's got nothing to do with Meg and Luc. It's just marriage in general that you disapprove of," she stated evenly.

"I'm sure that won't come as a huge shock to you, Harper."

"Not really. You told me you didn't intend to ever get married again after our first night together." She shrugged. "I can see why you might feel that way after how your marriage ended."

"Exactly. Once was enough," he replied. "I hope you're not going to let that bother you."

Harper kept her eyes on the passing houses, trying to ignore the sinking feeling in her chest. "Why would it? It's not like I've been picking out china patterns or something."

"I know. But I think it's probably important to lay our expectations out on the table just in case."

"Okay. Thanks for clearing that up for me. Message received loud and clear. No commitment for you." Harper's voice exuded a sarcasm that hid the hurt gripping her. Why was this bothering her so much, anyway? She'd never wanted to fall in love or make a life with someone.

"Not no commitment. No wedding. I'm not about to make promises no one on earth can really keep."

Harper glared at him, wishing she had stayed in the shallow end. "Marriage has worked out for billions of people throughout history. Literally billions. I know it didn't work out for you, but that doesn't mean you can say it would never work for anyone ever in the future of all mankind. That's a little ridiculous, don't you think?"

"That's not what I'm saying. I'm not saying that marriages can't work out. I'm saying that the promises made at a wedding are bullshit. There is no way to know with one-hundred-per-cent accuracy if a marriage is going to succeed or fail. How the hell can someone who is twenty-five—or forty-five, for that matter—know what they are going to want when they are eighty-five? They can't. That's the answer. There is no possible way to know. And you should never make a promise you can't keep."

"That's where the whole trust thing comes in. When two people get married, they're trusting each other with their very hearts, they're committing to keep working on it no matter what. They're promising that they are going to be there for each other for all of it. The good, the bad and the morning breath. Is that really such a bad thing?"

"Yes. It always ends badly. Your best-case scenario is that you get really old together and then one of you dies and the other one lives out the rest of their days broken-hearted. That's the best you can hope for. More often than not, though, someone gets bored, someone cheats, someone doesn't treat the other one with enough respect, someone leaves and both people are left broken-hearted. Either way you get crushed. It's a dumb thing to do."

"So, we're not really talking about wedding vows then, are we? We're back to talking about commitment in general. And apparently, you're not a fan of that either."

"Commitment is fine. But there's no need to be all public or permanent about it. It should be a quiet agreement between two people who understand that they can't really know what's coming in life, but they can agree to be together exclusively."

"How is that any better, you meathead?" she asked, raising her voice. "If you commit to someone and things go along smoothly until you someday grow old together, one of you will be heartbroken when the other one dies. It's the same friggin' thing, whether you've made a pinky swear like a couple of nine-year-olds or you've stood in front of a thousand people making vows."

"Meathead? That's a little harsh. Sounds like you're getting defensive, which makes me wonder if somewhere deep down inside, you do want the ring and the dress and the cake."

"I'm not . . . No! We're not talking about me. We're talking about you and your messed-up version of relationships. It's got nothing to do with me."

"Messed-up? The way I see it, I'm the only one with a clear view of the whole topic! The problem is everybody else out there who is naive enough to believe that any of that shit is real. They're the ones with the blinders on."

"Oh, I had no idea I was in the presence of the all-knowing Evan Donovan, Smartest Man Alive. You should have said something sooner." Harper was spewing venom now. "Imagine my embarrassment, not knowing I was supposed to be bowing when I entered and left your presence this whole time."

"Alright. Relax," he spat out "You asked the question. Don't blame me if you don't like the answer."

"It's a little more than that!" she exclaimed.

Evan pulled up in front of his house, parking the truck in the driveway. "Yeah, I know it is. You're pissed because deep down you want the 'I do's,' and now you're realizing that I really don't."

"Really? Is that why I'm mad?! Thank you for telling me! But of course you would know, since you do know everything!" Harper climbed out, slamming the door behind her before realizing she had left her clutch on the seat. She opened the door and snatched it up, getting a second chance to take out her frustration on his truck.

Evan got out, giving her an exasperated look. "Take it easy on the truck. It's not the one you're mad at."

Harper snapped open her purse to get the keys to her dad's house. "Believe me, I know exactly who I'm mad at. That would be the Dalai Lame-ass standing in front of me." Finding the keys, she held them up triumphantly before heading down his driveway.

"What are you doing? You're leaving because we're having a disagreement?" He watched as she stormed away and then rounded back on him.

"Yes, I am going home. I don't want to be around someone so high on himself that he thinks every woman he sleeps with must want to marry him!" she scoffed. "What would ever make you think I would even want to get married to you? We're just having a little fun here, Donovan. That's it. This means nothing!"

Evan's head snapped back. "It means nothing?" he asked quietly. "That's a little cold. I know we aren't in anything long term, Harper, but it still means something to me."

He stared at her for a moment before turning toward his house.

* * *

An hour later, Evan sat at his desk, failing miserably in his attempt to concentrate on some paperwork. He heard a small knock at the front door, followed by Boots announcing the guest with a happy bark. Getting up, he made his way over to answer the door. There stood Harper on the steps, now dressed in jeans and a white tank top, her hair dripping wet. She shifted uncomfortably, hooking her thumb into the belt loop of her jeans and biting her lip. Something about seeing her like this tugged at his heart. She wasn't the picture of sophistication she had been at the wedding. She seemed vulnerable now in a way that made it impossible for him to stay angry.

"Come here," he said, taking her hands in his and pulling her inside with him. "I'm sorry that I upset you. You were having such a wonderful day, being happy for your friends, and I killed the moment."

"Slaughtered it. Which was kind of a shitty thing to do. But I'm sorry too. I shouldn't have gotten all personal and insulting. And I definitely shouldn't have said this means nothing. It was horrible of me and it's not true. I just got so angry because it felt like you were accusing me of wanting to push you into marriage when really there's nothing further from my mind."

"You're right. I was definitely implying that. But you have to admit, you got very defensive about the whole thing pretty fast, which means I must have touched a nerve."

Harper pressed her lips together for a second. "I know I did. But that doesn't mean I want to get married. Couldn't it just mean that I really disagree with you?"

"I guess it could. But was that really all it was?"

Pulling her hands away, she leaned against the wall to distance herself from him. "I think maybe we should break up. Or whatever you call it when you're not officially in a relationship with someone but you should definitely stop sleeping together."

Evan folded his arms across his chest, his jaw set tightly. "Over one argument?"

Harper stared down at her feet. "It's not that. I think I may have been fooling ourselves about being able to do this without getting too involved. I've been thinking about how everyone around us has trouble accepting what we're doing here. It's because they might be right. We are heading down a dangerous road, and I think we should stop before it's too late."

"No."

Harper's head snapped up. "What do you mean, 'no'?"

His voice was crisp as he answered. "I mean no. We tried that when you first came to town. We tried to stay away from each other and it was useless. So, no. We're not going to stop." He took a couple of steps to reclaim the space between them, lifting his hands to her face and kissing her mouth. "I know you're only here for a little while and then you need to go back to your real life, and I won't try to stop you. But as long as you're here, I can't just pretend I don't want you. And I'm not going to pretend that this doesn't matter. This matters. Whatever this is. You matter. And I'm going to be with you. I'm going to get you naked and kiss every part of that gorgeous body of yours and feel your legs wrapped around me as often as humanly possible until it's time for you to go. I'll take whatever I can get."

Harper swallowed hard, looking like he'd just shredded the long list of reasons she'd come up with for them to break up. "When you put it that way . . ." she answered, her voice thick with desire.

Evan lowered his mouth over hers again, giving her a long, deep, passionate kiss. Harper's lips parted, and he accepted the invitation, sliding his tongue in to search for hers. He ran his hands over her neck and shoulders, then down her sides. When he reached her waist, he tugged her shirt up and over her head, tossing it onto the floor. His fingertips skimmed the outline of her lacy ivory bra as he gazed down at her with adoration. Harper frantically unbuttoned his shirt, then ran her hands over his smooth skin as he yanked his shirt off. Evan's hands were immediately on her back, undoing her bra so she could slide the straps off her arms and let it fall to the floor. His mouth hovered over her left breast, his tongue reaching it first, swirling over her nipple. Pleased at the results he was getting, he moved to the right. She moaned, arching her back against the wall, wishing she had done away with her jeans by now.

As if reading her mind, Evan picked her up by her bottom and carried her over to the pool table, his mouth never leaving hers. He set her down, giving himself access to easily undo her jeans and pull them off, along with her panties. Harper leaned her arms on the table and lifted her hips in cooperation.

"On the pool table?" she asked, surprised. "Won't this wreck the felt?"

"Totally worth it," he said, tugging his pants down and off. Lining himself up with the table, he pulled her to him, bringing their bodies together where they most wanted to connect. Kissing her hard, letting his tongue find hers, he pressed himself into her sex for a deliciously long moment. Giving her a look of greedy anticipation as he pulled away, Evan dropped to his knees in front of her. Parting her legs with his hands, he gently held her thighs as he let his tongue dip into her already wet core. Moaning at the taste, he licked her slowly, over and over, with long drags before plunging his tongue into her. "I love how you taste. I could never get enough of it."

Harper's back arched involuntarily, begging him to go deeper. Harder. Faster. Her fingers gripped the edge of the table as she lowered her bottom and lifted her legs over his shoulders. Gliding her hands along her tummy and up to her breasts, she caressed herself as they surrendered to this moment. They were back in their own world again, where no one else existed and time had no meaning. There was no past, no fear of tomorrow. There was only tonight.

Evan slid his hands from her thighs to her centre now, parting her with his thumbs, making room for his tongue to delve in as far as possible. Rubbing, licking, rolling his tongue over and over until he could feel her tense around him and heard her cry out with the pleasure he was giving her. That sound—those moans—had somehow become that which he craved endlessly. When her body finally relaxed and she released him, he stood, skimming his large hands over the silk of her skin. Up from her thighs to her neck, then back down again. He gazed at Harper, her breasts rising and falling as her breathing slowed, her cheeks flushed, her waves of beautiful hair resting on the felt of the table. He revelled in the pleasure of what he saw and what he felt as his fingertips moved over her. She was his and he would let nothing stand in the way of this. She was worth the risk.

Harper reached for him, interlacing her hands in his, pulling him down to her, kissing his lips. He pressed his thick length against her sex as he felt himself throb with pleasure and desire. He needed this. They needed this. He watched her as he lifted his hips toward her, his body tensing with excitement as he moved over her. His eyes met hers and he heard her breath hitch as he gazed back at her with the full intensity of his need. He entered her slowly, ever so slowly, each inch bringing new intensity. He filled her completely, touching every nerve in her body as he pulled her up so that she was sitting, their chests meeting as their mouths joined. Pivoting back and forth, harder and harder each time, he thrust himself into her as if his very life depended on it. He kept his eyes on hers as they became one tangled mess of emotion, longing and passion. And now, clutching each other as they came undone, they were one.

TWENTY-FIVE

"You outdid yourself, Harper. Seriously." Megan had forced herself to wait four days to look at the wedding pictures, so that she could do it when both Harper and Luc were there. The three crowded around her computer, scrolling through the shots for the second time. Megan's hands moved at lightning speed as she selected the best ones, depositing them into a folder of shots to be edited.

"Thank you, Harper. You did a wonderful job," Luc remarked, leaning toward the screen to examine each photo closely. "I guess it makes sense that you would have an eye for it, but you really seem to know how to work the camera as well. Have you had any formal training?"

"Never any classes or anything. I was a photographer's assistant for two years while I worked my way up. A couple of the photographers were excellent teachers."

"Well, you're quite talented." Luc said. "That one of Elliott kissing Amelie's foot is perfection. I want to frame that one."

Megan glanced up at him. "Definitely. It just captures the spirit of the day. Pure joy."

"Oh, it was. Elliott was just one big grin all afternoon," Harper said.

Megan turned to her friend. "Say, you wouldn't want to do this professionally, would you?"

"You mean like start my own business and try to compete with you?" Harper teased.

"No," Megan laughed. "I mean like come work with me. You know how I've been struggling to keep up since Amelie was born. With your eye for setting up shots and your knack for getting people's best angles, I think we could do well together. Really well. I mean, look at this one—you captured exactly how Luc and I feel about each other, right there. You chose the perfect moment to take the shot. The lighting, the way you zoomed in and blurred out the background. It's as good as any photo I've ever taken, and I've been at this for years."

Megan was interrupted by Amelie waking from her nap. Luc kissed his new wife on the shoulder. "I'll go. You two talk business," he said as he started toward the stairs. "But first, let me say I think it's a terrific idea. You two would complement each other so well, and with Harper on board, there would be an entirely new way to market your services."

Megan wore a thoughtful expression as she watched Luc walk away. "He's right. You could do consults for brides who are having trouble picking out their wedding dresses. You could blog on my website about it. It could be huge, actually."

Harper sat back in her chair, staring at the screen. "That sounds like a lot of fun. That I could do, but I don't know about the photography part of it. You've been doing so well on your own. What if you send me to cover an event and I botch it? I'd ruin your reputation, and this really is a word-of-mouth business."

"I just can't see that happening. Listen, we could take it slow. I'm not accepting that many jobs right now. Neither of us can throw ourselves into this full-on right now anyway. Why not come with me to a few jobs here and there if you can? I can give you my old Nikon to play with for a while you think about it."

"What if I break it? No, no, I couldn't."

"You won't break it. And if something does happen, we either fix it or replace it. It's not the end of the world." Megan crossed the room and plunked a bag down in front of her. "Harper, you and I both have the same work ethic. Besides, it'll give you something to do when Craig is with your dad. And Luc's right—having a former art director from *Style* as a partner would be a huge boost. Do you know how many brides and new moms will want you?"

Harper shook her head.

"All of them."

TWENTY-SIX

Over the course of the next week, Harper settled back into her routine as Roy's caregiver. She would make him breakfast and take him to his lengthy physical therapy appointment every morning. She would read in the waiting room or run a few errands. When they returned home, she'd make lunch, then practise with Megan's camera or work on the Fashion Forward website while Roy napped in his recliner to recover from his morning's work. After he woke, they would play a few games of cards in the kitchen while supper was cooking. Each day, she noticed her dad growing stronger and happier. He was doing well enough that she started to spend her nights at Evan's. If Roy got into any trouble, he could call and she'd be there in minutes. The easy pace of the days started to become more comfortable for Harper. Her contempt for Boulder itself lessened as she drove through the gridlock-free streets or found herself with time to sip some tea and enjoy the autumn splendour surrounding her.

"How'd it go with that reporter this morning?" Roy asked as he and his daughter seated themselves at a booth. They'd picked CJ's Deli for lunch after Roy's psychologist appointment.

"It was good. It should give the organization the extra publicity we need. Two of the clients had agreed to come back and share success stories, which was wonderful. The reporter focused mainly on them, which I think is the important part."

"I can't wait to read the article. It's such an impressive thing you're doing."

"I think I get more out of it than the clients, actually." Harper set aside her menu. "Hey, how was your appointment?"

"Good," he answered with a nod. "We talked about your mom again. Actually, Dr. Chan told me I shouldn't refer to her as your mom, but as Petra. She said that when I link her to you and your brothers as your mother, it somehow makes you feel responsible for her actions."

"Fascinating." Harper's voice was devoid of enthusiasm as she flagged down the server for a coffee. Maybe if she only half listened she would only half feel the emotions associated with the dreaded topic.

"We talked about you. She figures that it must have been tough for you, especially since you look so much like your mom, er, Petra."

"Hmm." Harper held out her mug to the waitress. "Thank you."

"Anyway, all these appointments got me thinking. I haven't ever explained what happened between Petra and me. You and your brothers deserve an explanation. You're all scared that the same thing is going to happen to you, but it really won't."

Harper stirred some cream into her coffee, mesmerized by the swirl of white in the dark liquid. "Are we? It's actually highly unlikely that I'm going to fall in love with a high school student and leave the husband and children I don't have. I'm surprisingly unconcerned about that."

"No need to get snippy, kid. I'm trying to tell you something you need to know." Roy levelled her with his dad glare. "Now, as I was saying, your mom's and my situation was totally different from anything you'll ever find yourself in. First of all, we were teenagers when we got married. Petra's parents were incredibly strict. She knew better than to get out of line in that house. My shrink says because she grew up in such a stifling environment, she hadn't rebelled yet or figured out who she was. Unfortunately, when she finally did, there was a lot of collateral damage. Does that make sense?"

"Yes, but—"

"Good," he cut her off. "Backing up a bit, when she got pregnant with Wes, we took off together to Montana to get married. She needed to put some distance between herself and her parents. Turns out I didn't understand her much better than they did. We never did relate well. I just figured we'd stick it out and make it work because that's what you do when you have a family." Staring down into his own mug, he shook his head. "I don't know, maybe it wasn't as bad for me as it was for her. I liked my work; I went out once in a while with the guys to blow off some steam. There were lots of other stay-at-home moms on our street that she spent time with. I made decent money, we were getting by, and I wasn't mean to her or anything, but I didn't really listen to her either. There wasn't a lot in common. And she was always sort of restless, even after she went back to school to become a drama teacher."

Harper sat, fully attuned to her dad's words now, realizing she didn't know the first thing about her parents as young people.

"Every year, she seemed to grow more dissatisfied. You probably remember we fought a lot. What you may not know is that she and my boss started a relationship just before we moved here."

"I knew that. Everyone knew that."

"Oh. Here I thought we'd managed to cover that up the whole time." Roy shook his head. "Shows how much I know. So then you probably figured out that was why we moved here. I couldn't keep working for a man I wanted to murder with my bare hands, and your Uncle Jim was able to get me on at Park Construction here. Petra apologized, said it wouldn't happen again. Said she'd be happy here. We tried to make it work for a while but, well, you know how that turned out."

"Why didn't you leave her after the first time?" Harper wrinkled up her nose.

"Because of you kids. You have to remember, twenty years ago men didn't have the same custody rights they do now. And I didn't want to be one of those dads who saw you only every other weekend. I didn't want to leave you with your mother either. To me, she just never seemed all that involved with you kids."

"No, she really wasn't, was she?" Harper shook her head.

"She's the one who missed out. My point in telling you all this is to show you that you're not in any way in the same situation we were. You're not a teenager. You didn't grow up under the same circumstances as your mom. You're a successful, stable, generally well-adjusted adult, and you're capable of having a successful, stable, well-adjusted relationship. You just have to find a man who understands you better than I did your mom. A man who's going to really listen when you have something to say and who'll support you when you want to live your dreams."

"I'm sorry, but it's not that simple. First of all, you say it as though that man even exists—"

"What about Evan? He doesn't fit that description?"

Harper shook her head in exasperation. "Evan has no intention of ever getting into a permanent relationship, so it wouldn't really matter if he did fit your magic formula for husband material."

"Then what are you doing with him?"

Harper felt her heart constrict at his words. Their relationship was becoming more difficult for her to justify, even to herself, but she had her lines memorized. "To be honest, I'm not interested in anything permanent either, so it's kind of a perfect scenario for me. We're just enjoying some time together before I go back to New York. Which brings me to my 'second of all.' I may be capable of a relationship, but that doesn't mean I should be dumb enough to trust that someone else will be. When Mom left, I learned that the only person I could rely on was me. That little nugget of wisdom got hammered home pretty hard."

Roy looked closely at his daughter. "What about the lessons I was there to teach you?" He tapped the table with his index finger as he spoke. "I was there for you every day. I stayed. I chose you and your brothers. And I'm still here for the three of you. Shouldn't you have learned something about love from that too?"

* * *

That night, Harper sat on the edge of the bed, watching Evan as he shaved in front of the bathroom sink, wearing only his boxer briefs. She watched as he cleared the steam from the mirror, his muscles flexing as he moved. Her dad's words floated though her head in spite of her attempts to push them away. What if she'd been wrong all this time? What if she could rely on someone else? Other people did it. And it worked out for them.

Evan glanced over at her. "You seem a little quiet tonight. You okay?"

"I'm good." She gave him a tight smile.

He stopped and leaned his shoulder against the door jamb. "You sure? If something's bugging you, I'd like to fix it if I can."

"Unless you have a time machine, there's no fixing this."

Wiping bits of leftover shaving cream off his face, he tossed the washcloth into the hamper and crossed the room to Harper. Crouching in front of her, he put his hands on her bare knees. "What happened?"

Harper bit her lip and shook her head a little. "Just a conversation my dad and I had today about my . . . You know what? It's nothing." She lowered her eyelids seductively. "Come here. My lips miss your lips," she purred, pressing a finger to his mouth.

Evan's brows lowered as he pulled back onto his heels. "Why do you do that?"

"Do what?"

"Why do you try to distract me with sex anytime I attempt to have a real conversation with you?"

"We have real conversations all the time. But not this. This would make things . . . awkward."

"I can handle awkward."

"Well, it would also make things less casual," she spat out, feeling a sense of desperation overtaking her. "You promised you'd keep things casual."

"That's not what I promised. I promised not to ask for more than you could give," Evan answered evenly.

"Having that conversation would be more than I can give. So let's just forget about it, okay?" Harper ran her finger down his chest. "I could use a good distraction, though." She lowered her mouth over his, but he pulled back.

"As tempting as that is, Harper, I don't love the notion that I'm just here to distract you from the things you don't want to think about. I'm more than that." He got up, turning away from her to pick up his jeans and slide them on.

"What are you talking about? I don't do that to you." Harper's tone was defensive.

He glanced down at her as he zipped up his jeans. "Of course you do. You did it at the restaurant that time, but I decided to let it go."

"And if you'll recall, that turned out to be a very wise decision."

"Yes, and I enjoyed it, Harper, but at some point, you're going to have to deal with this stuff. It's not healthy to just hold it all in like this."

"Actually, I really don't have to deal with any of it. It's ancient history, and none of it bothers me in the least when someone's not bringing it up," Harper answered. "Besides, you're not exactly a Zen master yourself, Donovan. If I'm not mistaken, you're also lugging around a fair bit of baggage."

"You're doing it again. Trying to distract yourself from whatever's bothering you. But since sex didn't work, now you're trying to pick a fight. I don't want to fight. And I don't want to fuck. Not when neither of those things has anything to do with me in the first place. What I'm interested in is something real." Evan grabbed his T-shirt off the chair and walked out of the room, leaving Harper alone with her thoughts.

"Shit," she said, flopping back onto the bed.

She found him a few minutes later in the backyard, sitting on the steps of the deck, sipping a beer and throwing a ball for Boots to retrieve. In spite of the fact that it was almost dark, the dog never seemed to lose sight of the ball.

"Can I join you?" she asked, her voice small. She pulled her sweater tight around her in an attempt to keep out the cool air.

"Sure." His voice was devoid of emotion.

"There may be some grain of truth to what you were saying." Her tone was reluctant.

Evan stared at her from under his brows.

"Okay, you're mostly right," she admitted. "But I think it's okay if I don't want to talk about my mom. Or my past. And I don't think anyone, especially you, should try to push me into doing that."

"I'm not trying to push you. But I want whatever we've got to be a hell of a lot more than just sex. I want you to let me in. To lean on me when you need a shoulder. Why can't I be that for you, even for a while?" he asked, his voice gentle.

"I can't rely on you, Evan. When people rely on each other, it never works out. You, of all people, should know that."

Evan took a pull on his beer and threw the ball again. "I feel sad for you, Harper. Not just because of what happened when we were teenagers, but because of how you still let it control you. You deserve better than what you let yourself have. You deserve to have everything. You're just too damn stubborn to admit that you're scared."

"You say it as though you're not scared, Evan, but you are too. You try to pass it off as logic, with your whole 'marriage is for morons' speech, but that's just fear and you know it!" Harper scoffed.

"I may not want to get married again, but I'm not the one who's spent an entire adult life running. At least I stay and face down my demons." Evan set his eyes on hers, seeming unmovable in his resolve.

"You want to see me run? I'll show you running." Harper got up and walked back into the house, letting the screen door slam shut behind her.

TWENTY-SEVEN

The next morning, Harper woke in her bed at her dad's house. Alone and tired. She'd barely slept, thinking about her conversation with her dad and her fight with Evan. Maybe they were both right. Maybe she was going to have to face her demons. It's not like she could get away from them anytime soon. She dragged herself out of bed and into the shower.

Her dad was in the kitchen playing solitaire with a deck of cards when she made her way in for some coffee.

"Morning," he said. She was grateful that he didn't ask why she'd spent the night there. She didn't want to talk about it.

"Morning, Dad," she answered. "What's on the agenda today?"

"Thought I'd go to physical therapy. You know, for a change of pace."

Harper grinned. "It's nice to try something new, isn't it?" She grabbed a yogurt out of the fridge and stood against the counter as she stirred it with a spoon. "Well, maybe I'll give you a ride. You know, for a change of pace."

* * *

That evening, Harper knocked quietly on Evan's front door. When he opened it, he gave her a terse nod.

"I think you're right. So are my dad and Megan. I probably do need to sort through what happened. Apparently, it's turning me into a total bitch when it comes to the men I date."

"You're not in any way a bitch. More like exceptionally adept at denial, which makes it kind of hard to be with you."

"I'm sorry. I'm sorry about what I said last night. And I'm sorry for making you feel like I'm using you. I love what we have together and I want to be able to be in a healthy relationship. I honestly don't know how to do this, though. This whole relationship thing." She sighed, looking up at him.

"Let's figure it out together." Evan stepped forward and took her hands.

* * *

Three weeks later, Harper went straight to Evan's house from her first major client meeting with Megan. Craig had come back and was staying with Roy, and Harper had been spending most of her time at Megan's house, learning the business. She and Megan had decided that they would work together until Harper went back to New York. It was the perfect scenario for both friends, allowing Harper to exercise her creative genius and giving Megan the help she needed to keep her business thriving. Harper quickly set to work, blogging on Meg's website about how to choose the right wedding dress for your body type, the best dresses for mothers-of-the-bride, how to style groomsmen, and updos versus hair down, among other topics. Things were going very well, but it left her with less time to spend with Evan.

Anticipation came over her as she turned the key to Evan's front door. Hanging up her wool coat, she made her way down the hall to his bedroom and crouched down to pet Boots. "I had a very good day today, buddy. Yes, I did! Those rich people are very interested in hiring Meg and me."

The door to the bathroom swung open and Evan peered around the corner. "You're here? This is a nice surprise! I feel like we hardly see each other lately." He grinned, rubbing his wet hair with a towel.

"I know. I feel like I practically live with Megan and Luc these days. How was work?" Harper smiled appreciatively at the sight of Evan in nothing but a towel. She took off her earrings and deposited them in the travel jewellery case she had left at Evan's weeks ago.

"Everything's on schedule, which is like a miracle." Evan walked up behind her, running his lips along the nape of her neck. "Too bad you weren't here a few minutes ago. You could have joined me in the shower." He wrapped his arms around her waist and pressed into her back.

Harper leaned into him. "Mmm, this feels so good. I've been missing you lately. We're both working so much."

"I know. I was thinking about those rainy days we spent in bed in July. I could use another week like that with you."

"Well, we'll have to make the most of Thanksgiving next week. But for now, we could pretend that it's raining, couldn't we?" Reaching behind her, Harper let her hands wander to the front of his towel. Hooking her thumbs under the fabric, she gave it a little tug, letting it fall to the floor.

Evan glided his hands down her legs, bunching the silk of her dress up to give himself access to what was underneath. Reaching for her panties, he slid one hand into them and rubbed her already wet sex. In their time together, he had paid careful attention, discovering what she liked, what she needed and what made her weak in the knees. It had been the most pleasurable form of education he'd ever had. He felt like an explorer charting new territory, staking his claim all over her body, each time discovering some new cove, a new secret that he could enjoy. The gratification of seeing and hearing her pleasure in what he was doing to her was like nothing he'd ever known. Harper was full of passion for him, always ready, always willing, as if she couldn't help herself.

Turning her head, she searched for his mouth with hers. Their kisses were urgent, hungry. It had been days since they'd been together and it felt like far too long for both of them. His fingers moved inside her, indulgently, carefully, possessively. His other hand reached over her dress and up to her full breasts, squeezing them firmly. Harper tugged at her panties, letting them drop out of the way as Evan pulled her dress up above her waist and pinned her against the wall. Gripping his cock with one hand, he guided himself inside her, just an inch at first, circling her sex, feeling the wet heat that was his for the taking. Rocking his hips forward, he thrust himself in all the way as she arched back, bringing him in deeper, causing them both to moan. He could feel the silk of her dress on his chest and her soft skin around him as he fucked her. Slow, hard thrusts, feeling each inch, each squeeze of her core, the hard wall giving them both the intensity of each tiny movement.

"Yes! Evan! Yes. Like that!" she cried out, ready to come. Waves of ecstasy washed over her, leaving her boneless as he held her up, pressing her body against the wall as he emptied himself into her.

They stayed like this, bodies intertwined for a long time afterward, feeling the bliss of connecting again after so many busy days. This was the sweet relief they had both needed.

"Wow. What a nice way to say hello." Her voice had a dreamy quality.

"Agreed." Evan released her from his hold, turning her toward him so that he could kiss her again. "I've been missing you."

"Me too."

"You hungry?"

"Starving. We didn't have time for lunch, so Megan and I split a package of almonds."

"Grilled cheese?"

"Perfect. You cook, I shower?" Harper asked.

"Be fast. I want to hear about how the consult went today."

A few minutes later, as Harper stood under the spray of water, she thought of the wedding consult she and Megan had finished that afternoon. They had spent two full days preparing. Megan had put together a new sample album to show the bride, groom and their parents. Harper had reorganized and redesigned Megan's online portfolio to make it more attractive and easier to navigate.

Both families were prominent in Colorado. The father of the groom was a congressman; the parents of the bride, both surgeons. It was going to be a spectacular April wedding. The happy couple also wanted engagement shots taken within the next two weeks, followed by photos documenting a lavish engagement party to be hosted by the congressman and his wife. They were very interested in having Harper assist with the choosing of dresses and tuxedos for the entire bridal party, and were willing to pay a considerable fee for the privilege. Securing the contract would generate Megan and Harper a lot of business through word of mouth, as well as referrals if things went well. The bride and both mothers seemed particularly impressed with Harper's background at *Style*, though the men seemed a little confused how that would translate into usefulness for wedding photos. Harper and Megan both had a good feeling when they left the meeting. They'd managed to balance the need to make personal connections with discussions of logistics and contracts.

Now, as Harper rinsed shampoo from her hair, her excitement at the possibilities ahead grew. The families were meeting with two other photographers, but there was just something about the look on the bride's face that said she had made up her mind already.

Shutting off the water, she quickly patted herself dry and rubbed some lotion onto her legs. She could hear the radio playing in the kitchen and Evan's voice singing along. Something about the whole situation felt very real to her. Too real.

She realized that it had been days since she had thought of New York or her life there. Between Evan, Megan, her dad and her new work, she had somehow fallen into a life she had never wanted in the last place she would have ever agreed to live. Glancing at the counter, she stared for a moment at her and Evan's toothbrushes leaning against each other in a glass. Everything suddenly became clear. Without meaning to, she had created a life for herself. Complete with a man to spend it beside. She was letting herself fall in love. Fear gripped her as she pulled her shirt over her head. Her heart pounded as she stared at the radiant woman in the mirror, the one glowing from having just been so thoroughly satisfied. Resolving again to push through the fear, she flicked the light off and followed the smell coming from the kitchen. Evan smiled over at her before flipping a grilled-cheese sandwich in a pan. The table was set and at her place, a glass of wine was waiting.

He turned to her. "Hungry?"

"I am," she said, walking up behind him and wrapping her arms around his waist.

"Then let's eat. I think I may have perfected grilled cheese."

They sat together, taking their first bites of food. "This is perfect. What type of bread did you use?"

"Whatever you put in the breadbox yesterday. I don't know what kind it is, actually." He stopped mid-bite. "Wait, are you mocking me?"

"Teasing, maybe. Mocking, no."

"And what exactly is so funny about this gourmet meal I've made for you?"

"Nothing. I just love how you want to perfect cooking, one dish at a time. It's really cute."

"Cute," he said, giving her an annoyed look. "I don't know if you know this about men, but we don't like being called cute. Same for adorable, sweet, little, or any other adjective used to describe babies or baby animals."

Harper wore a wicked grin, knowing she had his number now. "Aww, but it is cute. How you get so excited about your little sandwiches. It's adorable, really." She gave him a patronizing smile.

"That's it. When I'm done eating, I'm going to take you into that bedroom and show you how adorable I'm not."

"Ooh, so it worked then."

Shaking his head at her, he took another bite. "I'm serious. You won't be calling me cute when I'm done with you. You'll be calling me Mr. Donovan from now on, out of respect." His words were muffled by the gooey sandwich in his mouth.

TWENTY-EIGHT

Christmas felt as though it was arriving only moments after Thanksgiving. For the first time in Harper's adult life, she wasn't dreading the holiday. What had always been something to avoid was now something she was actually looking forward to. Wes was coming home for two weeks from his deployment on December twenty-second, and Craig was already back for his month off, which meant that for the first time in years, they would all be together to celebrate. Roy, who normally spent winters in Cabo San Lucas, was in a surprisingly happy mood as he awaited the return of his eldest son. Having worked extremely hard to rebuild his strength, he had progressed to using only one cane now. Neither Craig nor Harper were staying at Roy's house at night anymore, which was a relief to all three of them.

Standing in the airport arrivals area with Roy and Craig, Harper spotted her big brother first and ran to greet him. Throwing her arms around his neck, she exclaimed, "You're here!" as he dropped his duffel bag and returned her hug.

"I am! And am I ever fucking glad!" he said as she let go of him. Craig and Roy moved in to give Wes hearty back pats and deep-voiced greetings. Harper laughed in excitement at seeing them all together, all four of them relieved that Wes had once again made it home safely.

Tears brimmed in her eyes for a moment, but she fought them back with everything in her. She would not cry in front of these men.

Roy handed Wes a winter coat he'd brought for him and Craig picked up his brother's bag as they started for the doors. "Hungry?" Harper asked.

"Starving."

"Good," she said. "I've been cooking up a storm. Roast beef and mashed potatoes are waiting for you."

"Excellent. Glad you're here for once, Harper. We won't have to stop at the supermarket for Hungry-Man dinners for Christmas this year."

"Aww, you make it sound so sad, Wes. But you know, just because none of you have ovaries doesn't mean you're not capable of putting a turkey in the oven," Harper teased, earning herself a light punch on the arm from her brother.

"Still a sassy brat, I see. Some things never change." Wes shook his head with a little grin. "Now, what's this shit I hear about you and Donovan carrying on?"

"Mrs. Morley has a long reach. I didn't know she was providing direct intel to the military now. Or is she one of your Facebook friends?" Harper retorted in an indirect admission of his charges.

Wes looked down at her with an exasperated expression. He was an intimidating figure in his fatigues, with his perfectly straight posture and crewcut. "Dad told me, dummy. He treatin' you right, or do I have to kill him?"

"Well, he never calls me dummy, so I guess you could say he does treat me right."

"Touché. I'm sure you'll understand that I'll still be putting him on notice."

"I figured you would."

* * *

Evan arrived just in time for supper, bringing both beer and wine as his contribution to the meal. Wes answered the door and led him into the kitchen as they exchanged hellos, and Evan remarked upon how good it was to see him home in one piece. It didn't take long for Wes to harden his eyes at his old friend. "What's this I hear about you tapping my little sister? You do realize I know at least twenty ways to kill a man with my bare hands."

Evan matched the look on Wes's face. "Careful, now. I don't appreciate you talking about anyone tapping her, even if it is me. You do realize I know at least thirty ways to kill a man with my drill."

Wes let his face relax into a grin. "Just making sure we understand each other."

Harper glanced over at them. She couldn't quite make out their conversation over the one Craig and Roy were having at the table, but she felt a bit of hope at the casual appearance of things on the other side of the kitchen.

"She seems really happy, so I'm okay with the whole thing—as long as you understand that if you hurt her, I will tear your limbs off and feed them to you," Wes said, looking over at his sister, who was heaping potatoes onto plates.

"I'd expect nothing less."

Wes gave him a hard slap on the back. "Good. Glad we got that straight. Now, what are the chances we can eat in the living room so we can watch the game?"

"It's up to Dad," Harper interjected. "But first, he has some big news to celebrate."

All eyes were on Roy, who pretended to be annoyed. "It's nothing. I got cleared to start driving again."

"That's not nothing, Dad," Wes said. "That's great news. Good for you!"

Roy waved off the congratulations from the rest of the group.

"Well, I'm guessing it's nicest for Harper. She won't have to chauffeur my sorry ass around anymore."

Harper's face dropped a little. "I've actually been enjoying it. I'm going to miss the terror in your eyes when I run a yellow light."

"Well, I'm sure as hell not going to miss it. She treats every road like it's the Indy 500," he teased. "I'm starving. And, since it's apparently my choice, I say we watch the game while we eat."

* * *

"So, Wes seemed to take it pretty well. I mean, for Wes." Harper's voice was loud so that Evan could hear her over the sound of the shower. She stood in front of the sink, flossing her teeth.

"Yeah, other than the part where he promised to tear me limb from limb if I hurt you, he took it pretty well."

Harper laughed. "What a goof. Sorry about that."

"I'm not offended. It's his job, really."

Rolling her eyes, Harper slipped off her dress, followed by her bra and panties. Moving the curtain aside, she stepped into the tub with him. "You men are so silly. As if threatening violence ever helped anything."

Evan gave her an appreciative once-over before picking up the soap and going straight for her breasts. "Hey, you'll kindly remember that I'm not the one threatening violence."

Stealing his spot under the shower head, Harper lifted her hands to her hair, letting the spray of the water relax her. "Never even with one of Karen's boyfriends?"

"Karen is four years older than me. It's different with big sisters. You grow up knowing they can kick the shit out of you, so you tend not to worry about them." Pause. "God, I like watching you wash your hair."

Glancing down at his obvious show of appreciation, she pressed her lips together to hide a grin. "I can see that."

* * *

The next evening was a long-overdue poker night for the guys. Craig was hosting, and Evan, Wes and a few of their other friends were going to attend as a sort of welcome-home party. Roy was invited but had turned them down, saying he'd rather pick out his own eyes with a toothpick than spend an evening listening to that bunch of hens natter on. He had passed the better part of the afternoon watching hockey with his sons anyway, so for him it had already been a perfect day.

Around eight in the evening, Evan arrived at Craig's, his arms loaded with cases of beer and grocery bags filled with chips and several varieties of beef jerky. Wes answered the door, taking the beer from him as he held the door open with his foot.

"Put the beer outside on the step," Craig ordered. "I'm out of room in the fridge and it's colder out there anyway."

Evan and Wes did as they were told.

"Why's the fridge full?" Evan asked. "You normally have one bottle of ketchup and some expired orange juice in there.

"Craig's been seeing someone," Wes answered. "Apparently, he wants to trick her into thinking he's an actual grown-up."

"You're seeing someone, Craig? Good for you. What's she like?" Evan asked.

"Yeah, Craig, tell us. What's she's like?" Wes asked, motioning with his hands in front of his chest as if attempting to determine her breast size.

Craig levelled him with a dirty look. "And he says I'm still a child. She's nice. Her name's Rita. She owns a clothing store on Pearl

Street. Harper dragged me in for some new shirts a few weeks ago and we hit it off."

He opened the fridge and took out a premade tray of cheese, crackers and pepperoni.

"Wow. We're getting the royal treatment tonight," Evan observed. "Must be in your honour, Wes."

"Really makes every day on the front line totally worth it," he answered.

The evening passed quickly. Six guys managed to make it. They played poker, smoked cigars, drank beer and ribbed one another in that way men do. One guy, Todd, was cleaning everyone out, and clearly loving every minute of it.

Todd stretched and got up for that one beer too many. "So, Evan, I hear you and Harper are an item these days. I wish I had known she was back in town before you found out. There's one skirt I wouldn't mind getting into."

"Heyyy!" Wes and Craig hollered in unison as Evan scowled and said, "Don't be a shithead, Todd."

Todd's eyes widened at the reaction. He put his hands up, signalling surrender. "Okay. Touchy subject. Won't happen again. Unless she's single again and she wants to. Oh yeah, then it'll happen," he said out of the side of his mouth.

"Don't make me kick your ass, Todd. You really won't enjoy it as much as you think you will," Evan said. "Besides, aren't you forgetting about your fiancée?

"Aww. I'm just kidding around. A guy can dream, can't he?"

Wes, Craig and Evan all shook their heads at him. Craig leaned toward him ominously. "No. You can't."

Wes took his cigar out of his mouth and blew a ring of smoke into the air. "It's bad enough we've got this fucker hanging around her. We should have shipped her off to a convent when she was fourteen.

Married her off to Jesus. That would have been a lot better for my blood pressure."

"You do realize you are abnormally overprotective, right?" Evan ventured. "I mean, she's almost thirty-six, for God's sake. And she can take care of herself, believe me."

Wes looked at his friend. "You know all that stuff last night about me tearing your limbs off was just for Harper's sake, right?"

"It was?" Evan asked, seeming unconvinced.

"Yeah." Wes puffed on his cigar and fixed Evan with a steely glare. "If I ripped your limbs off, you'd bleed out too fast. I'm going to make you suffer for a real long time if you hurt her."

Their friend Geoff, who had always been the voice of reason, cut in as he watched the men stare each other down. "Are we here to play poker or are you ladies going to sit around and talk about relationships all night?"

His words managed to restore harmony.

* * *

That night, as Evan stumbled into bed beside Harper, she woke and turned to him. "How was poker night?"

"It was fun," he slurred, his words so thick with beer she imagined she could see them floating in the air. "Your brothers are fucking psychos when it comes to you, though. I can see why you moved to New York to get away from them."

"Shit. Were they giving you a hard time?"

"Yeah, but not the whole night. Only when your name came up." His eyes closed and his breathing became heavy. "Stay away from Todd, by the way," he mumbled as he drifted off to sleep and left her wondering.

TWENTY-NINE

The next day was Christmas Eve. By the time Evan got up, it was close to noon and Harper had been up for hours, wrapping presents and singing along to festive songs on the radio. He looked a little rough as he lumbered down the hall in his boxer briefs, scratching his bare chest. His eyes looked like they wouldn't be opening fully for a while, and he headed straight for the coffee pot. Harper turned down the volume on the radio and gave him a sympathetic look, trying not to laugh.

"Hey," he said, his voice hoarse as he grabbed a mug out of the cupboard and filled it.

"Hi, honey. I would ask how you're feeling but I think I can see for myself."

"I'm fine. I just need a coffee and a shower." He sipped the hot drink with one eye still shut. "Fucking bright in here, though," he muttered.

Harper could no longer contain herself and broke out into a giggle.

"What? You laughing at me?" he asked. "That's okay, wait till it's your turn. See how funny it is after you and Megan go for a ladies' night out."

"Oh, I don't get hungover like that. I discovered my limit a long time ago."

"Really? I'm going to remember you said that."

Harper laughed. "I doubt you will remember. You probably killed thousands of brain cells last night." She knew that would get under his skin and just couldn't help teasing him. Feeling a twinge of guilt, she walked over to give him a little kiss on the forehead. "Can I get you some toast?"

"That would be spectacular."

She popped some bread into the toaster, saying, "Merry Christmas Eve, by the way."

"You too."

"I need to run these gifts for the kids over to Megan and Luc's a little later. I'm sure they'd love to see you if you're up for it. Then we're going to my dad's for our new Christmas Eve tradition of ordering Chinese food."

"Oh, nice to see that the Young family spends Christmas Eve the same way Mary and Joseph did, eating pineapple chicken balls and fried rice."

"Oh, that coffee must be kicking in. Your sense of humour is coming back."

"I took two Advil in the bathroom before I ventured into the light."

* * *

A couple of hours later, Evan held his arm for Harper to steady herself on the icy walk from the Chevaliers' door to his truck. They'd just delivered presents for Elliott and Amelie, staying for a quick visit to watch Elliott tear open the gifts. They'd left as Amelie was about to go upstairs for her nap and Elliott and Luc were getting started on building the Star Wars Lego set Harper had given him. It had been a cold, sunny day but as evening fell, clouds moved in and started blanketing the city with fresh snow. They drove for a few minutes in contented silence, enjoying the Christmas lights that gave the city a festive glow. Evan glanced over at her. These were the little moments that created a life together. He put his hand on her leg.

"What are you thinking?" she asked, seeing the expression on his face.

"Nothing. I'm just really happy."

"I'm glad."

"No, I mean it. I've never been this happy before. This is just one of those days you don't forget, you know?"

"You mean spending the day really hungover?

He laughed. "No." Reconsidering, he said, "Well, yes, I guess. This all feels very real to me. It's just been such a fun afternoon, and now we're going to spend the evening with your family. Just being together, you know?"

"Yes, it has been a great day." Harper fiddled with her bracelet, suddenly feeling uneasy.

"I wish you were coming with me tomorrow. I don't want to go to Tucson without you," he said, reaching for her hand and giving it a squeeze.

"I know," she answered, resting her head against the seat back. "But it's the right decision. If I went to visit your family, especially at Christmas, it would send the wrong message."

"I don't know. Would it?"

Not knowing how to answer, Harper let the question hang in the air.

* * *

When they got home, Evan unlocked the door and ushered Harper inside and out of the chilly air. "Let's open each other's gifts now."

"Deal!"

The pair scattered to get the presents they'd bought each other and met back in the living room. They flopped onto the floor in front of the small tree they had put up earlier in the week.

"You go first," Harper said, beaming at him.

He tore the wrapping paper off a box to reveal a tote for his hand tools. "Is this the Klein Tough Tote with durable feet to protect the bag from the elements?" he asked, quoting the product description from memory.

"Yes," Harper confirmed excitedly. "I remember you stopping to look at it when we were at Lowe's. Open the box. There's more inside."

"More? This is already more than enough," Evan said, pulling the tote out of the box to find each pocket filled with a wrapped gift. "What's all this?"

He unwrapped the presents quickly, his face lighting up each time he opened a new gift. He stopped after every one to tell her how much he liked the item or how much he needed it.

When he finished, he leaned over and gave her a long kiss. "Thank you, Harper. I love it all. You clearly put a lot of thought into it."

"I did, actually," she agreed, clapping her hands together. "Okay, my turn. Let's see who out-thoughtfulled who."

"I had no idea this was a competition. You really bring new meaning to Christmas spirit," he teased, watching as she ripped open the paper on her gift. Her face fell.

"It's the Nikon D800," she said quietly. "Holy shit, Evan. This is way too expensive. No. I can't take it. You have to return it."

"Why?" His face dropped, along with his heart.

Harper put her hands out, palms forward as if trying to stop what was happening. "Lots of reasons. First of all because this is way too much for you to spend on me. Second, I could buy it for myself if I needed it, which I don't. This is a professional photographer's camera. I'm not a professional photographer."

"Have you been earning money taking pictures for the past few months?"

"Yes, but—"

"Then you're a professional photographer. You need the equipment to go with that."

"Evan, that would be necessary if I were going to make photography my permanent job, but I'm not. It's just something I've been doing to help Meg and fill my time while I'm here. I'm sorry, but I can't accept it. Please don't ask me again." Harper got up and walked down the hall into the washroom, shutting the door behind her.

* * *

Evan waited a few minutes before making his way down the hall and gently knocking on the bathroom door. "Harper? You okay?"

The door opened in response to his question. She gave a quick nod and moved past him. "Fine. Just freshening up so we can get going. My dad'll be expecting us."

"Hang on," he said, following her to the front door. He placed his hand gently on her arm when she stopped to open the closet. "I think we should talk about this before we go."

"What's to say?" Harper turned to face him. "It was very thoughtful of you. I appreciate the gesture, but I can't accept."

"Harper, I can see you're really upset. I'd like to know why."

"I'm not upset. I just overreacted. It's a big gift and it made me panic a little, thinking maybe there was some expectation behind it." She smoothed her hand over his chest and patted it.

He gave her a hard stare for a moment, saying nothing. Finally, he shrugged. "It was just an impulse buy. I couldn't think of anything, so I picked it up last night when I got off work. I thought you'd like it. In light of the fact that it doesn't mean anything, I hope you'll decide to keep it."

"I won't, but I hope you can see why," she said, pulling away from him and putting on her coat. "We should go."

* * *

"To being together!" Roy held his glass in the air.

The sentiment was shared around the table and everyone had a sip of their drink.

"Since we're all together, I want to say a couple of things." Roy swallowed hard. "I want to thank Harper and Craig for everything. Especially Harper, who gave up her career for her old dad. I've been through a lot this year and as it comes to an end, I feel lucky. I'm alive. I have a wonderful family and we're doing a lot better than we ever have. In fact, going through this was worth it, because I got my family back. We're mending, just like my spine is. Might have a few tender spots, but we're getting stronger."

Wes turned to Harper. "What the hell did you do to Dad while I was gone?"

THIRTY

Evan returned from Tucson in the afternoon of New Year's Eve. After days apart from Harper, he wanted to have her all to himself, but the evening was to be spent at the Chevaliers'. The foursome had planned to go out, but Megan and Luc couldn't find a babysitter.

"Well, it wasn't so much that we couldn't find a sitter," Megan confided when she and Harper were alone in Amelie's room together. "Luc won't trust anyone other than my mom to watch the kids."

Harper giggled as she held Amelie's little hand while the baby was getting her diaper changed. "Is your daddy a little bit over-protective? I think he is! Yes, he's a little bit crazy, isn't he?" she said in a high-pitched voice. Amelie beamed at her, displaying her four teeth.

"There! All changed," Megan said, fastening the last snap on Amelie's cozy sleeper. "Now, will this child please go to sleep easily tonight?"

"She can't go to bed yet. It's her first New Year's Eve! She needs to stay up and party with her auntie." Harper lifted the baby off the change pad and carried her out of the room.

When they reached the kitchen, Luc cleared his throat. "I'll have you know that I'm not crazy. When you have your own baby, we'll see if you find it easy to just leave her with some random teenager who might start doing drugs as soon as you leave the house."

Harper looked confused for a moment before Evan pointed at the monitor on the kitchen island. "Ah. Baby monitor. I see. That was just a little girl talk, Luc. Nothing for you to worry about."

Evan walked over and made a huge smiley face at Amelie before starting a rousing game of peekaboo over Harper's shoulder. Amelie squealed in delight, reaching for his nose.

"So, what's it like to not have Elliott home?" Harper asked her friends.

"Very odd," Luc answered.

"Quiet," Megan added. "Too quiet. But he's having fun. He's called every day since we dropped him off at the ranch."

"What ranch is he at?" Evan asked, gently taking the baby out of Harper's arms.

"Some friends of Ian's, Ben and Alicia, own it. Well, they're more like Ian's only family. Ben played ball with Ian when they were just starting out and his family basically adopted Ian. They have a guest ranch near Colorado Springs. Ian asked if he could bring Elliott there for the week."

"That sounds really nice."

"I think it has been. He's gone horseback riding and has been staying up late playing board games. Georgie, Ian's girlfriend, is there, so Elliott's getting a chance to get to know her a little. Ian's doing much better these days, so they can start having a real relationship." Megan seemed happy as she spoke, but Luc wore a concerned expression.

"Yes, well, we can only hope he doesn't relapse," he said.

Megan looked over at her husband. "Luc's worried about it. I am, too. It would be horrible if Ian started using again and dropped out of Elliott's life. But we have to meet him where he's at and hope for the best, right? For now, he's doing really well and Elliott's in a safe place. The Mitchells would never let anything happen to him. And

Georgie seems terrific. From the sounds of things, she's pretty good for Ian."

Harper gave her friends a thoughtful look. "I can only imagine how tough it would be to have all those worries on your mind. From the outside, parenting seems like a gut-wrenching experience."

Evan, who was holding Amelie above his head, making her laugh, interjected. "I don't know. It looks pretty amazing, too."

The three adults in the room all turned to him, surprised expressions on their faces.

"What? I like kids. Is that so hard to believe?" Evan's voice was a little defensive.

"Not at all," Luc answered for everyone. "You're terrific with our kids."

"Thanks, Luc." Evan nodded in his direction before looking from Megan to Harper, both of whom were trying to avoid eye contact with him.

"What? Harper, you know I like kids. You've seen me with kids before."

Harper glanced up from the hors d'oeuvres that suddenly held her full attention. "I know you do."

Megan hadn't looked up at all from her position in front of the oven, peeking in on the rack of lamb.

Looking at the baby in his arms, Evan spoke to her, his eyes wide. "Can you believe this, Amelie? For some reason, these ladies think I don't like kids."

"Nobody said that, Evan," Megan retorted. "It's just that you've made it pretty clear you're not interested in getting married and having a family."

"I'm not going to do the marriage part, but the children thing I could do. Could be fun," he answered.

Luc, who had been waiting for Amelie's bottle to reach the perfect temperature, took it out of the bottle warmer and dried it with a dishtowel before securing its top and testing the temperature of the milk. "I'll give you one word of advice about having children. Don't wait until you're as old as I am. Having no sleep is harder to bounce back from when you're past forty. So if you're going to go for it, get started right away." Giving Evan a knowing look, he handed the bottle to Megan.

"I'm going to get this little pumpkin to bed," Megan said, as Amelie reached for the bottle and popped it into her mouth. The others bid the little girl good night with lots of kisses to her chubby cheeks before her mom took her upstairs. Luc continued the dinner preparations with the skill and flair of a chef. Harper excused herself to go to the washroom, leaving the men alone.

"More wine?" Luc offered, holding the bottle out to Evan.

"Thanks, I think I will," Evan answered. "So, Harper said you're selling your nightclubs."

"Yes. I don't want to be away from home so much. I'm trying to sell all of them but the one in Aspen. It's much easier for me to go there than to Europe. I'll keep my real estate holdings. They don't need as much of my attention. I've been looking for the right buyer for months now, but I can't find anyone I would trust. I'm not going to turn the clubs over to just anyone. I want someone reputable who will treat the staff well."

"That's good of you. Most people would just take the best offer and run."

Luc trimmed some mint leaves with herb scissors as he considered Evan's comment. "I think turning your life's work over to someone who will honour your accomplishment and take care of those who helped build it is much more satisfying than a few extra dollars. From what Megan has told me, you are also someone who cares about those who work with you."

Evan nodded. "Yeah, well, I wouldn't get very far without them. Having a loyal, skilled crew is worth every effort to keep them."

"I agree. I'm also of the opinion that it takes a certain kind of boss to inspire dedication and hard work on a continuous basis."

"I suppose that's true," Evan answered.

"From what Megan tells me, you've gone above and beyond to earn their loyalty. No matter how things turn out, at the end of the day you'll know you've lived a generous life and made sacrifices that matter." Luc paused for a moment to take the lamb out of the oven. "You know, that's what it takes to be a good husband and father. Generosity. Selflessness. Commitment. You would be an excellent candidate for both roles."

"I was a husband once. And once was enough for me," Evan answered.

"But it was with the wrong woman. Maybe with Harper . . ."

"Harper's going back to New York. Besides, marriage isn't for me, Luc. I'm not really the type to commit. I'm more of a 'keep it simple' kind of guy."

Luc smiled. "You remind me of me. All my life, I thought I would never be capable of committing to anyone. But you know, I realized that I was already committed to those close to me—my friends, the few relatives I have, my employees. I had been doing it without really realizing it. And if I'm not mistaken, you seem to have many people in your life who depend on you."

"That's different."

"Yes. Those other commitments don't require the same risk, do they?"

Evan tilted his head a bit, considering Luc's words. "I think I know where you're going with this but, honestly, our situations aren't really all that similar. You and Megan already had a child and were living together, so it wasn't exactly a big jump to get married."

"It was, actually. For me, it meant the end of my pessimistic view on love. Finally letting go of how I grew up—very bitter and hurt. I had always been so convinced that falling in love and getting married were the stupidest things you could do with your life, a meaningless ploy to sell diamonds. Getting married to Megan was like telling the world that I was wrong. And I was. Because when you find that one person who will always love you and care for you no matter what, you know it and you want the world to know that she is yours and that you would do anything for her. For the rest of your life. And more importantly, you want her to know." Luc paused as he started to dish roasted potatoes onto the dinner plates. "But that's me. Feel free to disagree about the matter. That's your right."

Evan nodded a little, trying to digest Luc's words. The collar on his shirt suddenly felt tight. He had been so hell-bent on protecting himself, but what was he really protecting himself from? Maybe all he'd been doing was letting Avery stop him from moving forward with his life. And there was no way he should allow her that much power over him. She had decided not to share his life, so he sure as shit shouldn't be letting her decide how he spent the rest of his days.

He watched as Harper walked back into the room. She was so lovely in a black cocktail dress that perfectly highlighted her curves. She had her hair down in soft curls and he could see she'd just reapplied her lipstick. The sight of her tonight was enough to take his breath away. How could she still have that effect on him? They'd been together for months now. He should have grown used to seeing her face and yet every time he saw her, it was as though it were for the first time. His eyes followed her as she crossed the room. Suddenly it hit him with a violent force. He was in love with her. How had he not realized this before?

She sauntered over to the fridge and reached for a jug of water to put on the table. Evan took it from her and gave her a kiss on her cheek. "You're amazing," he murmured in her ear before filling the waiting glasses. It was a statement he'd started making without realizing it—they were the words he spoke when "I love you" was on the tip of his tongue.

* * *

The next morning, Evan woke Harper with a lingering kiss on her neck. Nothing had changed since the night before. The fear hadn't returned. He felt only relief at admitting to himself that he was in love with her. He wanted her to be his forever. Incredibly, instead of being scared off by the thought, he was brimming with a warm happiness. She was lying on her side, facing the other way, and the sight of her under the white sheet was irresistible to him. His hand roamed down the front of her naked body as he pressed himself into her back.

"Mmm, morning." Her voice had the sleepy, raspy sound he loved. His cock twitched with excitement as she wriggled in closer to him.

"Morning," he murmured. "Hope you don't mind me waking you up so early. You're just so delectable, I couldn't resist."

"I'll put up with it this time," she answered, taking his hand and guiding it over her sex. She pressed his hand slowly and firmly along her warm skin as he nibbled on her earlobe. Together, their fingers indulged her masterfully. Their bodies intertwined as they moved together. He wanted to feel himself inside her. The need was as intense as it had been the first night.

They stayed like this for a long, perfect moment as he brought Harper to the edge of ecstasy and then gently pushed her over, feeling her body writhe with pleasure. "Yes, Evan!" she called as the waves built up and passed through her over and again. As she started to come down from her high, Evan pushed himself into her wet, throbbing sex, gripping the wrought-iron bed-post with one hand to propel himself up and into her. He felt the effects of her orgasm as he began to move. He angled himself so he could get in deeper still, and he could tell another climax was building in her by the way she tightened her muscles around his thick length and her breathing became more frantic.

He thrust himself into her more forcefully now, deeper, slowing down and then building his rhythm again as he glided up and down behind her. Their bodies glistened as the morning sun brought a warm glow to the room, bringing an openness to the moment, to the intimacy of seeing each other like this, in their truest and most honest form. Nothing to cover up, nothing to hide from each other and no need to. Even without giving words to it, they loved each other deeply and purely. It was a love so strong and unconditional that it could heal every pain of the past, every feeling of doubt about forever. The intensity of it had him calling out her name as he finally gave in to his own powerful release. She went with him to that place where time stopped, the world stood still and only they existed. It was perfection.

* * *

Harper slid into the hot water of the bath, replaying how Evan had woken her. She could feel a lump forming in her throat. Something had shifted in him the night before. She had seen it when she walked back into the kitchen. There was something new in his eyes, a sureness that hadn't been there before. The way he held her had felt different. But he'd yet to say it. Maybe she was imagining what she secretly hoped was there.

Sinking down until her head was under the water, she tried to shut out these thoughts. Attempting to tell herself that she could handle this whole thing wasn't working today. Overnight, things had become intense in a way that terrified her. Suddenly, it was all too much. She felt her chest constrict as fear crept in. Deep down, a voice was telling her to start looking for a way out before he could crush her heart.

Later, as she combed out her wet hair, she reminded herself that neither of them had crossed the line. No one had ventured an "I love you," and she would make sure that no one would. She could control the direction this was heading. Bring it back to where it all felt safe. And if she couldn't, she could run.

THIRTY-ONE

"Okay, guys, I need to go take care of a few things. Phone if you need me," Evan called as he walked out of the office trailer and headed to his truck, opening the door for Boots to jump in. For once in his life, he was taking the afternoon off. He needed to go somewhere to clear his head.

It had been over a week since the New Year's Eve dinner, and Luc's words about love and marriage had been flooding Evan's brain ever since. He had never considered the possibility of getting married again and having kids, but now that the idea had crept into his mind, it was starting to take shape. If he was ever going to have a family, he wanted it to be with Harper. Even though he had yet to say it out loud, he was completely in love with her. She was the one. And if, by some miracle, she decided to stay with him, maybe she'd want all that too.

Parking in front of his property in the country, he got out of his truck. Boots sprang out of the cab and bounded into the snow as Evan climbed over the gate. He made his way through the trees to the clearing on the other side. The crisp air filled his lungs and there was nothing to hear other than the sound of snow crunching as he walked. He laughed a little as the dog ran in a huge circle, clearly thrilled to have the space to do so. It was the perfect spot to build his dream home—their dream home. Five acres, with rolling hills and lots of mature trees surrounding the property. He would situate the house so that the bedrooms, kitchen and back deck faced west to take advantage of the sunset. The house would be solid, built to last. He wanted a lodge feel to the place, something warm and welcoming, somewhere a person could really relax and put their feet up. High, wood-beamed ceilings in the living room and master bedroom, a long wraparound covered porch, a hot tub just off the deck to soak in with Harper after a long day's work. But hell, if she wanted some postmodern glass house, he'd build that for her, as long as she would stay.

Evan could imagine them there together, snuggled up in the hot tub, watching the sun go down. Making love. There would be no neighbours nearby to intrude. No Mrs. Morley to pry. Just him and Harper. Here, he could shield her from the bad memories. Save her from all of that. Then, maybe not too far down the line, a couple of kids. He'd like that. They could all walk down to the creek and drop a fishing line in, and he and Harper could lie on a blanket together and watch the kids play.

Everything became so clear to him. He was starting over fresh, only this time he would do everything right, beginning with the right woman. The woman who saw him for who he really was and loved him exactly the way he was. At thirty-eight, he felt like his life was finally beginning. He filled his lungs again with fresh mountain air, then released it in one long, satisfying push, letting go of every fear, every reservation he'd had about making a life with Harper. Standing there in that moment, he knew. His gut told him it was going to be okay. He just needed to approach the whole subject carefully so he wouldn't scare her off.

* * *

"So, you are never going to guess what just happened!" Blaire spoke quickly, her voice brimming over with excitement.

"I'm all ears," Harper answered as she took the turn toward home from the consult she had just finished. She turned up the volume on her hands-free as she slowed for a yellow light.

"There's been a huge shakeup. Cybill's been fired, along with Tina and the head of ad sales and some junior staffers. It happened just this morning."

"What? Are you serious?"

"Dead serious. Three more clients pulled ads this past week, and circulation has dropped fifteen per cent in the last six months."

"That's insane," Harper answered. "She's been there for over thirty years! Who the hell is going to torment the fashion industry now?"

"You're talking to her," Blaire answered proudly.

"WHAT? Are you friggin' kidding me? Blaire, I'm so happy for you!" Harper practically danced in her seat in spite of the seat belt.

"The board called me at six this morning to see how quickly I could take over after they fired her bony ass. I told them I just needed enough time to take a shower and I could be right in and ready to work."

"Good for you! That is the best news ever!"

"Thank you! There's a lot of pressure right now, but if I play my cards right, I can turn this ship around and put myself at the top of the industry. And guess what my first card is going to be?"

"What?"

"To hire back the best art director in the business, but as creative director now."

"Oh, Blaire, really?" Harper asked, feeling momentarily elated, then immediately sick to her stomach.

"Yes, really! What do you say?"

Harper hesitated. She was finally being offered her way back to the life she'd spent over a decade building. This was supposed to be her dream come true. So why didn't it feel like it should? Why did she feel queasy? "Wow. Thank you, Blaire, this is incredible . . ." her tone was flat, expressing her true feelings.

"Harper? Why do you sound so unenthused? I'm offering you the one thing you've been wishing for since last summer. Only much better, because it's not only a promotion, but Hartless is gone!"

"I know. I know. I am very excited about it. It's, um, just that I have commitments here I need to consider. Can I take a day to sort things out?" Harper answered, pulling up in front of her dad's house.

"This isn't about Evan, is it? Dear Lord, tell me you aren't giving up this opportunity over some man?"

"Of course not!" Harper scoffed. "What do you take me for?"

"Oh, thank God! If I thought you'd suddenly become so pathetic I'd have lost all respect for you. Just think of how wonderful it's going to be. It's everything we always talked about. We'll be unstoppable. No Hartless to put up with. We can do all those things we said we would. We can revolutionize the fashion industry, starting with using models who eat and have finished middle school! I promise you, Harper, it's the smartest decision you'll ever make."

Harper shut her eyes, trying to push away that annoying heavy feeling in her stomach. "Sounds amazing. How long can you give me before I'd start?"

"In a perfect world, you'd be here tomorrow, but what if you work from Colorado for, let's say, three weeks until you can wrap things up there? I've got four issues that need your expert touch immediately. They're god-awful and I just can't pull them together without you. I can overnight a laptop to you."

"Okay, I'll call you first thing tomorrow morning."

"I'll be holding my breath until I hear from you."

* * *

An hour later, Harper put a large homemade pizza into the oven at Evan's house. Her mind raced as she cleaned up the mess from making the dough. She had gone over to her dad's after her call with Blaire to tell him about the offer. He tried to seem happy for her, even though his eyes had betrayed his true emotions. Their talk had given Harper a taste of what was to come if she decided to take the position.

Even though she'd made no secret of her plans to leave, now that it might actually be happening she didn't like how she felt. Instead of being completely elated, she was nowhere near sure that this was the right decision. Her stomach lurched when she heard Evan open the door.

"Hey, babe!" he called. She heard his heavy boots drop to the floor as he took them off. Walking to the entrance of the living room, she leaned against the wall, watching him as he hung his winter coat in the closet. He picked up a large bouquet of flowers and crossed the room to her. "For you," he said, kissing her on the cheek. "Smells delicious in here. I was actually going to surprise you with dinner out, but I see you've beat me to the punch."

Harper took the flowers. "Thank you. These are gorgeous. What's the occasion?"

Evan's eyes shone down at her. "I have some things to talk to you about, but first I need a quick shower."

"Do you? That's odd. I need to talk to you, too." Harper stared at him. He seemed so happy and she felt sick that she was about to change all that.

He put his hand on her waist. "Really? Well, I can't wait to hear what you have to say. Maybe we'll have to open that wine we've been saving so we can celebrate. I have a feeling it's going to be a very good night." Giving her a lingering kiss, he pulled back a little. "Be back in a few minutes smelling good."

* * *

Evan scrubbed shampoo into his hair vigorously, wanting to shower and shave as quickly as possible. Today, he'd decided without a doubt that he wanted to start his life with Harper, and he didn't want to wait another minute. He would take her for a drive up to the property and tell her everything right in the spot where it had all started so many months earlier. He'd left a bottle of champagne in the back of his truck to stay cold and had hidden the ring in his coat pocket when he got home, so that the surprise would be complete. He just needed to figure out a way to smuggle two glasses out of the house without her noticing, but that shouldn't be too hard. Everything would turn out beautifully.

Their time together had shown him that they were perfect for each other. He was in love with her and he knew in his heart that nothing was going to change that.

* * *

Evan walked into the kitchen with damp hair and that fresh-from-the-shower look he wore so well. When Harper handed him a glass of wine, he rewarded her with a kiss on the neck.

"I must be the luckiest guy on the planet to get to come home to you and this wonderful meal." He pulled her to him for a long, deep hug.

"Mmm, you smell pretty delicious yourself right now," Harper murmured, experiencing that sinking feeling in her stomach again. "Let's eat before this gets cold."

Evan was the picture of happiness as he scooped salad into bowls for each of them. Harper added two slices of pizza to their plates and returned to the table. Sitting across from him, she fanned her napkin onto her lap and then watched as he took his first bite of pizza.

"Wow, that's good. How is it you've never made this for me before?"

"I kind of forgot about it."

"This might have to replace Friday night steaks."

Her heart squeezed at the thought of him talking about their future together. Suddenly she had no appetite. She took a sip of wine, wanting to postpone the inevitable.

"So, what's your big news?" he asked, looking up at her expectantly.

"I was just about to get to that," she replied, putting her glass down. "Blaire, my friend from *Style*, called today. Cybill got canned this morning and Blaire's been hired by the board to replace her on a temporary basis."

Spearing some salad with his fork, Evan said, "Wow. That is a crazy turn of events. I bet everyone there's pretty thrilled." He looked a little puzzled.

"They are. And you're wondering what this has to do with me."

Putting his fork down, Evan gave her a serious look. "I think I can guess."

"Blaire asked me to come back as the creative director. It would be a big step up." Seeing the shock on his face, she quickly continued. "I haven't given her an answer yet but if I take it, I'd have to leave in a few weeks."

Evan took a long gulp of wine before answering. "So what are you going to do?"

Harper hesitated, trying to read him, but his expression gave nothing away. "It's really everything I've ever wanted. I'd be at the top of the entire fashion industry. Well, one step from the top. I'd be a fool not to take it," she said, her eyes boring into his. Until this moment, she hadn't realized that she wanted him to ask her to stay. Very badly.

Evan's gaze shifted from her for a moment to the camera he'd bought her. It was still sitting on the counter, waiting for him to return it. He looked back at her. "It's your dream, right? It's been the plan all along, so I guess you should take it."

Harper swallowed hard. So that was that. He didn't want her to stay. And the reality of it filled her with pain. Doing her best to pretend it didn't matter either way, she nodded. "It would be the smart thing to do."

Evan opened his mouth to speak, then closed it, a smile crossing his lips but not touching his eyes. "If it's what you want, you should do it. Good for you, Harper. Congratulations."

He stared down at his dinner, cutting a small piece of pizza using his knife and fork.

Harper blinked back tears, glad he wasn't looking at her. Taking a swig of wine, she fortified herself. "I guess I'll call Blaire back in the morning and accept."

"Well, that's settled then," he answered in a cavalier tone. "How soon will you be leaving?"

"Why? You in a rush to get rid of me?" She asked it as though she were merely teasing but the edge in her voice told a different story.

"Not at all." He narrowed his eyes at her a little. "Just thought it would be good to know so I don't make any plans you won't be around for."

"Oh, of course. I have to find out for sure, but I think I can take maybe three weeks to wrap things up before I move back. I'll work from here in the meantime."

"Alright. Good to know."

They sat in silence for a few minutes, Harper pushing the food around on her plate, unable to bring herself to eat. She hoped changing the topic would help ease the tension. "I almost forgot that you had something you wanted to talk with me about."

"Oh, that. There was a ridiculous mix-up with some paperwork for the city, so I need to head back to the job site for a while tonight. I didn't want to make Lacey stay and do it."

Harper stared at him. "You got me flowers because you have some paperwork to do?"

He cleared his throat. "Those were just because. I actually don't know why I even said I had news for you. It's more of an update. Lacey'll be going off on maternity leave soon, so I'll be working a lot more than usual."

"Oh, right. I guess that makes sense." Harper did her best to sound casual.

Glancing at the clock, he announced, "I better get back to work. Anyway, good for you. I'm really happy for you. Really." He wiped his mouth and stood up, giving her a quick peck on the cheek.

* * *

Evan drove straight to his office, then sat at his desk for the next few hours trying in vain to concentrate on his work. It was useless and he knew it. He just stared off into space, thinking about what had happened. The image of the camera sitting on the counter kept coming back to him, reminding him of why he couldn't go home and tell her the truth. Just when she'd asked whether he thought she should go, his eyes had landed on that damn camera, reminding him of her reaction to it on Christmas Eve. The mere hint of him wanting to make things permanent had sent her running to the bathroom to get away from him. She'd thrown up her guard again.

But then had come New Year's Eve, when he realized he had what it took to go the distance, and he'd decided he wanted to do that with her. He thought things had felt different between them, but maybe it had all been in his head. He stared down at the engagement ring in its box, feeling like an idiot. What had he been thinking, buying her this? Over the past few days he'd managed to fool himself into thinking she might want to marry him, and now he knew full well that her thoughts couldn't have been further from marriage. She was leaving him, just like she had told him she would. He had no one to blame but himself for letting it get this far. But that didn't make it hurt any less.

Evan got home long after Harper had fallen asleep. As he crept into the bedroom and stripped down, he could feel the loneliness settling over him already, in spite of the fact that she was there in his bed. What he felt and had let himself believe wasn't her doing. She had been honest with him the whole time, but he'd let himself fall in love with her anyway. And now he was going to have to face the pain of letting her go.

He slid under the covers behind her, pressing his body to hers and inhaling the scent of her shampoo. She made a happy little sigh in her sleep as he held her close to him. Sadness overtook him. "You awake?" he whispered.

He listened for a moment. Her breathing was steady, so he knew he could risk it. He felt his heart quicken in his chest. His voice was almost inaudible. "I'm in love with you. I want you to stay. I want to marry you." He hoped the words that came straight from his heart would find their way to hers.

THIRTY-TWO

Grande Lisboa, Portugal

"That's it, everyone. It's a wrap! Thank you all for your hard work," Harper called out, motioning to the production crew to begin break-down. For a moment, she stared out at the incredible view from the top of the Sintra Mountains, wishing Evan was with her. He would love it here. They had captured some gorgeous shots at the medieval Castle of the Moors, making the trip a complete success, but Harper now felt completely drained.

It had been two weeks since she had accepted the job and instead of working from Colorado as Blaire had promised she could, Harper had somehow let herself be talked into a whirlwind trip to Portugal. As she began gathering up her things, she realized that after only a few months away from the magazine, she now found it hard to imagine that she used to do these forty-eight-hour location shoots so often and would be doing so again from now on.

"That might be some of our best work together, Harper. I've missed you," Assaf said, coming to stand beside her and admire the view.

"It was great, wasn't it?" Harper agreed.

Their conversation was interrupted by her cellphone ringing. A picture of Evan lit up the screen. "Excuse me," Harper said, stepping away. "Hey, you. How are things?"

"Good. I just wanted to apologize for not calling you yesterday. I got caught up at work and when I finally had a moment, I was sure you'd be asleep already."

"No problem. I completely understand," Harper answered, trying to sound breezy. But she didn't feel breezy. She felt a little hurt. In the weeks since she'd started back at *Style*, things with Evan had felt strained and awkward. The end was hurtling toward them at a furious pace and neither of them knew exactly how to handle it. They'd taken to pretending things were back to being very casual but it now felt hollow.

"How's Portugal?"

"Things couldn't have gone better, actually. We're just wrapping up now, so I'll be back tomorrow night." Harper gave a wave to one of the models as she left. "Listen, if you're busy, I can just catch a cab. You don't need to pick me up."

"No, I should be able to make it. I'll see you at eight?"

"Only if you're sure. If anything changes, just text me."

Boulder, Colorado

Warm water rained onto Harper's face and chest as she stood in the shower at Evan's. She was torn between relief at being back where he was and a sense of doom knowing that things were drawing to an end. Closing her eyes, she tried to shut out what was to come. The feeling of Evan's hands on her naked skin had her disappearing into his world again. Harper's melancholy started to subside as his hard body pressed against hers. Longing overtook her as Evan's lips skimmed along the nape of her neck. He sucked carefully in that little spot he knew drove her wild. Working his way up to her earlobe, he nipped gently with his teeth. "You're"—kiss—"completely"—kiss—"amazing."

Turning, Harper met his lips with hers, kissing him hard, letting her body relax and lean against the shower wall. She arched her back so that her chest met his. Evan's hands glided over her ass and back up again. He ran his fingers up her tummy to her chest and, cupping her breasts, he rubbed her nipples with his thumbs before lowering his mouth over them, one at a time. Sucking, kissing, rolling his tongue over the pink buds until they were firm. Letting one hand drop down to her core, he rubbed the sensitive skin. "I've missed you, missed this."

"Me too," Harper whispered. Her heart tugged at the thought of missing him, but the pain was soon overridden by what he was doing to her body at the moment. He was going to make her forget.

Running her hands over his wet skin, she wanted to feel every inch of his powerful body. She stopped when her hands found his rock-hard length. She gripped it, rubbing him while gently twisting her fingers at the same time. A moan escaped Evan's throat as he lifted his face to hers again, crushing his mouth over hers. Thrusting his tongue between her parted lips, he showed her what he wanted to do with his cock. Letting one hand slide down to her outer thigh, he lifted her leg up along his body, giving himself full access to her. Harper wrapped that leg around him, arching her back even more so they could finally join together. She took his cock and brought it to her, rubbing him against her wet heat in deliciously slow, long drags. "Yes," she said, her eyelids lowering.

Evan bent his knees, then slowly slid himself inside her throbbing core, feeling each inch as she drew him in further. Sighs.

Kisses. Moans. Thrusts. The intensity and pace grew as he pulled away and thrust himself back inside her. Gripping her ass with both hands, he lifted her onto his cock so that her full weight was now resting on him. She could feel him filling her completely as she neared her own climax. She tensed her core, squeezing him, feeling him hit her in that perfect spot. This was everything she'd been wanting for so many nights. She didn't know how she would ever give this up. Opening her eyes, she gazed at him, watching him as he lifted and lowered her over himself. His expression was one of possessiveness, of need. It made her feel wildly feminine and beautiful. "Yes, Evan, just like that," she whispered as she felt that first wave overtake her. It was a million sensations at once. The incredible release of her orgasm, his lips on hers again, his tongue dancing with her tongue, the warm water rushing over them, her back pressed against the cold tile, her front pressed against his warm, hard body. And that moment, that perfect moment when she could feel him pulse inside her, each wave bringing her more and more pleasure.

He held her there, up against the wall, as they recovered. Harper clutched him with her arms, her legs, not wanting him to ever put her down, ever pull out of her. "How are we ever going to give this up?" she asked finally.

"I don't know," he sighed. "For now we'll have to just savour the last tastes," he answered in a low tone. Carefully, he lifted her up and off him, lowering her to standing again. Pressing his forehead to hers, he closed his eyes. Harper was grateful for the spray of the water that prevented him from seeing her tears. He kissed her on the mouth again, this time letting his lips linger on hers as though he never wanted to stop.

*   *   *

The next morning, Harper's alarm went off at six thirty, far too early. For the last two weeks, she'd worked fourteen-hour days, and after her gruelling flight back from Portugal and a late night of sex, she was beyond exhausted as she dragged herself out of bed and into the bathroom to shower and dress for the day. Twenty minutes later, she made her way to the kitchen to have a quick bite before Megan arrived to pick her up. They needed to leave for the mother of the bride's house by seven forty sharp. Grabbing two apples and tossing some trail mix into a sandwich bag, Harper then pulled on her coat and shoes and waited by the front door. She didn't want to make Megan wait for even a second after having left her in the lurch over the past week. Megan had handled the rehearsal and dinner the night before as well as the bridal shower the previous Sunday, both of which Harper had been scheduled for. When she saw her friend pull up out front, she hurried out, quietly shutting the door and locking it behind her. Megan popped the trunk from the driver's seat and waited for Harper to load up her bags and get in.

"Hi," Harper said as she buckled her seat belt.

"Hi." Megan stared at Harper for a moment. "No offense, but you look like hell."

"Thanks. I'm so unbelievably tired."

"You sure this is all going to be worth it?"

Harper rested her head against the seat back and closed her eyes. "At the moment, I have my doubts."

Megan put the car in gear and pulled away from the sidewalk. "So, maybe don't go."

Still keeping her eyes closed, Harper answered, "I have to. It's what I've worked my whole life for and now it's being handed to me, Megan. I can't just give that up."

"Why not?"

"What do you mean, why not?" Harper asked with a distinct edge in her voice. She sat up and turned to glare at Megan.

"Well, in case you haven't noticed, you've built quite a nice life for yourself right here. You've got family and friends who love you, a great job with your BFF, you've been doing some really rewarding volunteer work, not to mention you have a hot man you're totally in love with. The way I see it, you actually have a lot more to give up here than there."

"I already told Blaire I'd take the job."

"So what!" Megan scoffed. "What do you even owe Blaire anyway? I mean, when you lost your job, was she there for you? No. Not until she was up shit's creek and needed to use you as a paddle. So why the hell are you giving up everything and dropping all the people who actually love you?"

Harper slumped down in her seat but said nothing.

Getting no response, Megan went on. "I know you think what I do isn't that important, but in its own quiet way it has value. We document the most important and beautiful moments in peoples' lives. The moments that they will look back on fifty years from now and their great-grandkids will look back on a hundred years from now. And it means something."

Harper's voice was shaky as she spoke. She was both overtired and overly emotional. "Well, maybe I don't want to spend the rest of my days documenting something I'll never have. Did you ever think of that?"

Megan glanced over at her friend. "Oh, Harper, there's no reason on earth that you can't have those things if you want them."

"With whom? The guy I'm sleeping with who doesn't want a future with anyone ever?" Harper's voice was incredulous.

"You don't know that. From the sounds of things, you've both done nothing but dance around the truth, which is just totally unlike you! I've never seen you so scared to speak your mind. And until you do, you'll never know for sure!"

"The thing is I do know, Megan. He's been very clear about the whole thing and no amount of wishing is going to change that. So, if you don't mind, I'm going to take the sure thing. I'm going back to fucking Manhattan so I can live out my fucking dreams! And I really don't want to hear another fucking word about it from anyone! Least of all my friend who grew up in the perfect family and now has one of her own!"

Megan's head jerked back in surprise. Her voice was quiet. "Wow. I had no idea that's how you felt."

They drove on in a pained silence for a few blocks.

"I'm sorry. I shouldn't have said that," Harper admitted finally.

"No, I'm sorry. I should stay out of it. It's your life. You don't need me to give you a hard time about how you choose to live it."

"It's okay, really. I know you're just trying to make sure I'll be happy."

Megan pulled up in front of their destination and put her hand over her friend's. "I really am. I love you so much, Harper. And I'm worried about you. And I'm going to miss you so much when you go." Her voice broke.

Harper blinked furiously, trying to stop her tears. "I know. I'm going to miss you too. But it's what I have to do, okay?"

"I know." Megan's eyes glistened as she gave her friend a sad smile.

* * *

The rest of the day went relatively smoothly. As the event wore on, they fell into their natural rhythm, getting the shots they needed without being obtrusive during the ceremony or the dinner. It was close to midnight by the time Megan drove Harper home. The air had all but cleared between them, but Harper still felt some residual guilt about what she'd said that morning.

"Do you want to come in for tea or a glass of wine?" Harper offered. Staring at the dark house, she realized that Evan must have gone to bed already.

"No. I better not. I'm wiped and I have to be up early with the kids. Luc will have had a long day with them."

Harper turned to her friend. "Megan, about our conversation this morning. I still feel really bad about hurting your feelings. I didn't mean what I said about your family."

"I know. It's okay. I'm sorry too," Megan said. "Part of me is going to keep hoping you'll stay, though. In my heart of hearts, I believe you'd be happy here."

"The life I'm going back to isn't one you should pity me for. It's going to be fabulous. It's the smart choice."

* * *

Late Sunday morning, as Evan and Harper lay in bed in a blissful post-sex moment, Harper's cellphone buzzed, indicating an email.

Evan held her wrist as she reached for it. "Leave it. The magazine had you for the last week. Megan got you yesterday. Today is my day. Let's just have twenty-four hours without thinking about anyone or anything but us." He gave her a lingering kiss on the neck to help make his case.

Harper moaned. "Mmm, you're certainly very convincing, especially with that thing you're doing with your lips right now."

"Glad you can be persuaded," he said, pulling back and lifting himself off the bed in one move. "Give me a couple of minutes. I'll be right back for round two," he said as he got up and pulled on some low-slung pyjama bottoms.

"Hey, you can't just give a lady a kiss like that and then walk away," Harper called to him as he left the room.

"I need to refuel, and believe me, so do you." He flashed a killer grin back at her before turning down the hall.

Harper flopped back onto her pillow. Smiling to herself, she heard the sound of water running at the kitchen sink, followed by the sound of the coffee grinder. She had a full day in bed with Evan to look forward to, and she was going to drink in every delicious drop of it. Sex was the only thing that took her mind off what was happening, the only thing that pushed out that nagging feeling of dread that had been following her everywhere since she agreed to take the job. As long as he was touching her, she could forget.

Stretching, she suddenly felt chilly and got up to grab her bathrobe. Glancing down at her phone as she tied the sash on her robe, she sat down on the bed, deciding that it couldn't hurt just to check who the message was from. If she didn't look, she would be distracted from focusing on Evan. It was probably something that could wait. But just in case, she better check it while she had a minute.

Opening her inbox, she saw the words *Red Alert!* in the subject line under Blaire's name.

"Son of a . . ." she muttered, her heart sinking as she opened the email. A moment later, Harper was rushing down the hall to get her computer. Evan looked up from his position in front of the counter in time to see the panic on her face.

"What's wrong?"

"Somehow a section of the June issue has gone missing. Twenty plates have just disappeared from the printer's. The run was going to start tonight at eight, and the crazy part is that those same pages are not anywhere in the saved versions of the file on the server. Blaire needs me to check to see if I've got them backed up somewhere on my hard drive. If not, we're screwed." Harper spoke quickly as she turned on her laptop and sat down.

"What? How could that happen?" Evan asked.

"They don't know. This has never happened before, but it looks like someone is trying to mess with Blaire. There were twelve pages of ads by some really key clients that have just gone up in smoke. It doesn't make any sense. I'm so sorry, Evan. She needs me to call her right away. Can you give me a few minutes and then we'll pretend it never happened?"

"Sure. You want some cereal?" Evan nodded, then handed her a mug of coffee.

"No thanks, babe. I'll eat in a few minutes."

Taking a bowl of cereal and some coffee, he walked into his office and turned on the computer. An hour later, Harper was still on the phone, and now three more members of the team had been patched into the call. No one had been able to find what they needed, and they would have to recreate the files within the next few hours. At least twice every five minutes, the conversation oscillated from speculation about how this had happened to how the problem could be solved.

Evan showered and dressed, then wandered back into the kitchen. Lowering his head and waving to get her attention, he realized it was no use, so he wrote her a little note. *Going to the job site. Looks like you'll be at this a while. Call me when you're free and clear. I have a long list of naughty things to do with you . . .*

Starting up his cold truck, Evan let it run for a minute, staring back at the house. Inside was the woman he loved as he'd never seen her before. She was a ball of excited energy, contained but clearly so alive at that moment. Everything about her work, including this latest crisis, seemed to somehow light her up in a way he'd never seen before. He thought of the expression on her face as she had read his note, gave him a grateful look and mouthed "Sorry" to him. She lived for this. It was obvious to him. And now that she was back in that world, she was quickly leaving his. Soon she'd be gone for good. Starting down the street, he sighed to himself, knowing that the end was hurtling toward him at the speed of light.

He returned six hours later, having heard nothing from Harper. She was talking to someone on speakerphone while working away on her computer. The man on the other end was laughing at something as Evan walked into the room. Harper was laughing along with him, but her hands never stopped moving as she resized and cropped a photo. She stopped long enough to wave at Evan and give him another apologetic look. She was still in her bathrobe, the coffee mug he had given her earlier still on the table, now empty. A banana peel sat next to it, making him wonder if that was all she had eaten that day. Walking down the hall, he undressed to have another shower. He had gotten a lot of work done, but he hadn't been behind to begin with. The last two weeks, he'd been at the job site late every evening because he had no reason to go home. Now he was ahead of schedule, having wrapped up almost every detail.

Making his way back to the kitchen a few minutes later, Evan found Harper in exactly the same position as when he'd left. She didn't know he was standing behind her as she spoke. "Christ, this would be so much easier if I were there . . . Damn it, I never should have come back this weekend."

Wincing, he wrote her another note. *Going out to grab supper. Too hungry to wait for you.*

He placed it next to her on the table and walked out without saying anything. When he got home, he could hear the shower running. She had finally pried herself away from the computer. He put a bag of Thai food on the table and went in search of a corkscrew to open the wine he'd bought.

Harper's cellphone rang. Seeing that it was Blaire, he decided to answer it.

"Hello?"

"Um . . . hi. Is this Evan?"

"It is. Harper's just in the shower right now. Can I get her to call you in a bit?"

"Yes. Can you tell her I need her to call me right away?" Blaire's tone was brisk. "There's one last thing I need her to finish up tonight."

"I'll let her know."

"Thank you," Blaire answered before hanging up.

When Harper emerged from the bathroom, she was dressed in jeans and a long-sleeved black T-shirt. As he watched her walk into the kitchen, his heart started to break. She was completely lovely to him as she used a towel to squeeze the excess water from her hair.

"There you are!" She made a beeline to him and kissed him hard on the mouth. "Thai food? That smells divine. I've only had a banana all day."

"Thought you could go for a little coconut rice and some red curry chicken." He attempted a smile but his eyes were full of sadness. He pulled away and turned to get some plates down from the cupboard.

"I'm so sorry about today, Evan." Harper rubbed his back with her hands, then wrapped her arms around him, leaning against him for a moment. "We were supposed to have a day to hide away from the world, but it was completely ruined."

"These things happen, right?" He turned, careful to avoid her as he took the plates to the table. "I guess that's one of the sacrifices if you're handed the opportunity of a lifetime, right?"

"I suppose." Harper's voice was tentative.

"Blaire called. She needs you to call her right away."

"Well, forget her. I'm going to sit and eat with you first."

"Either way, it doesn't really matter. I've been thinking maybe you should stay at your dad's until you move back to New York," he replied. "We both need to face the fact that this is over. Let's not drag it out any longer."

Harper's shoulders dropped. She reached for his hand, covering it with her palm. "Why does it have to be over? We could still see each other after I move. People do it all the time."

"The thing is, Harper, I'm not going to be that guy you sleep with when you're back in town for a few days here and there. A lot of guys would love that type of arrangement, but I'm not one of them. I've realized I want more than that. But you don't. And that's okay, but it means we're done here."

Harper rubbed her temples with her fingertips. "Why right now?" she groaned. "Why do you have to pick this moment to do this? With everything else I'm trying to deal with?" she asked, tears threatening to escape her eyes.

"Oh, I'm sorry. Should I have called your assistant in New York to have her schedule a breakup when it was more convenient for you?" Evan's tone was pure sarcasm.

"Wow. You know what? Fuck you," she said, her body and words devoid of emotion, before she walked out of the room.

Harper spent the next twenty minutes packing up her things, hoping he would stop her. She didn't want it to end this way. If she were really honest, she didn't want to end it at all. She wanted him to ask her to stay. Evan had gone into his office and was sitting at his desk working on some spreadsheets. She walked past the office several times as she collected her things. He didn't look up once. Instead he kept working. Finally, standing at the front door, she pulled on her coat and boots.

Evan appeared around the corner, his jaw set. "So, this is it, then."

"I guess so. It's a shame you want to end it like this."

"Does it really matter how it ends? We were just having fun, remember?"

"It doesn't feel so fun right now." Harper stared at him, her face expressionless. She wouldn't let him see how much this hurt.

"It's reality, babe. So, I'm sure you'll go running from it." His eyes were ice cold. "You need help getting your things out of here?"

"Not from you," she replied firmly. Opening the door, she picked up her laptop bag and slung it over her shoulder, followed by her overnight bag and her purse on the other shoulder. Gathering all of her things, she overloaded her arms, straining every finger to grip every bag so that she could spare herself the indignity of coming back. Unable to see over everything, she went out the door, carefully testing her footing on each step down as she made her way to the sidewalk. The last thing she needed was to trip over her own feet and fall, especially if he was watching her. It was dark out now and the night air was cold, causing her to shiver. Dropping several bags in the snow along the way, she swore to herself. Her arms ached as much as her heart by the time she reached the front door of her dad's house. Humiliated, she let everything fall at the bottom of the steps and went back to pick up what she had lost en route.

Glancing across the street, she could see Mrs. Morley watching her from her living room window. Extending her middle finger, she held it up at the woman, giving her a venomous glare as she did. Mrs. Morley quickly closed the curtains, and Harper assumed her next move would be to pick up her phone. But she couldn't care less at that moment. She had just had her heart torn to shreds. Finally getting all of her things to her dad's steps, she rooted around in her purse for her keys, stopping when her dad quietly opened the door for her.

"Need a hand?" he asked, leaning on his cane and holding open the door.

Harper nodded, tears streaming down her face. Shoving her things into the front entry, she let a loud sob escape her. Her dad slid her bags out of the way, making room for more. When she finally had everything inside and had closed the door behind her, Roy pulled her in for a long hug, patting her on the back and making shushing sounds. "It's okay, Harper. It's all going to be okay."

"No, it won't. He just broke up with me." Humiliation and the pain of rejection mixed around in her empty stomach, making her feel completely nauseous. This was the worst feeling she'd experienced in her adult life. Harper buried her face in her dad's shoulder, feeling like a little girl again. He was here for her in her darkest moment, just like he always had been, and she knew that he would see her through this.

After a few minutes, she straightened up, drawing a long, deep breath before giving her dad a big nod. "I'm going to be fine, Dad. I actually have to get to work. I'm in the middle of a huge crisis at the magazine."

"When it rains, it pours, huh?" he replied. "Anything I can do?"

"No thanks. If you don't mind, I'm going to get set up at the kitchen table and get back to work."

"Of course," he answered. "I'll try to stay out of your way."

An hour later, Harper was still working, in spite of the occasional stream of tears that escaped her eyes. She wiped them away and continued on, telling herself there would be plenty of time to cry later. She didn't notice her dad making a pot of tea and some toast, but she did notice when a small plate and a mug were placed in front of her. Patting her shoulder with his large hand, he quietly told her to have something to eat.

"Thanks, Dad. I will," Harper said.

"Good. I could hear your stomach growling from the living room. I could hardly hear the game over it," he said with a little wink in her direction.

An hour later she finished up, closing her laptop with a heavy sigh. Her head pounded and her eyes burned with strain. Standing up slowly, she rolled her head from side to side, trying to work out the stiffness in her neck before making her way to the front entry to gather up her things. Her bags were gone. She looked over at her dad, who was watching her from his recliner.

"I put your things in your room for you."

"Dad, you didn't have to—" Her words were stopped by his raised hand.

"I wanted to. Now go get some rest. You look like hell."

Harper nodded, her eyes welling up again. "I've been hearing that a lot this weekend," she answered sadly. "Thanks for everything, Dad."

*　*　*

At that moment, Evan sat on the edge of his bed, staring at the diamond ring he'd bought Harper a few weeks earlier. His heart felt like someone was squeezing it from the inside. He'd never felt such a profound sense of loss in his life. For the past two hours, his mind had been going over what had just happened. The ugly scene repeated itself on a loop, as though some part of his brain was trying to give him a clue as to what he should do next. He refused to listen, though. He had made the right decision by ending things. Harper belonged back in her old life and he would never stand in the way of that. She needed to go live her dreams, and if he hadn't ended it, she might just have sacrificed everything she'd ever wanted and end up hating him for it later. Better to have her hate him now than when it would be too late for her to step back into her life in New York. So he had pushed her away with both hands.

He tried to convince himself that he'd been just fine before she came along and he'd be fine again without her. That he didn't need a self-involved, work-obsessed woman taking up space in his life. He wasn't going to curl up and die over her, either. Deep down, he knew these were all lies, but maybe if he repeated them to himself enough he'd start to believe them.

Sending her away was by far the worst thing he'd ever done. She was the love of his life and now she was gone. Even though things were as they had to be, he had no idea how he'd ever get over this. Get over her. For tonight, it would take every ounce of strength he had to stop himself from rushing next door and begging her to stay. He would have to keep telling himself over and over that this was for the best.

THIRTY-THREE

Harper's heart pounded in her chest when she saw the truck pull up. Evan was home. She'd been trying to concentrate on her work all day without any luck. She had made plans to move back to New York on Saturday, but she would need to survive five more days here until then. Five days with him right next door.

How was she supposed to go that long being so close to him and not make a complete ass of herself? In her mind, it was pretty much a foregone conclusion that she would drink too much wine on at least one of the next few nights and completely lose her inhibitions. That would lead to her either throwing herself at him or pounding on his door to scream in his face, depending on whether the wine brought out the sad, lonely Harper or the angry, hurt version. As she watched him from the safety of her darkened bedroom, her knees felt weak. He was so close that she could just open the window and call out to him. She wouldn't even have to yell. She could just say his name and he'd look up at her. But she couldn't. She wouldn't. And it almost killed her to be so close to the only man that she'd ever loved but not be able to do so much as call out his name.

Evan's shoulders slumped as he unloaded his duffel bag from the back seat of his truck. He glanced at Harper's bedroom window, causing her to duck out of sight. *Shit. He probably saw me.* If there was one thing that Harper couldn't afford right now, it was for him to think she was pining away over him. She needed to appear strong, breezy and carefree. There was no way she'd let him see that she had been completely crushed when he ended things. If he knew, he would pity her, maybe enough to be kind to her. And that was something she definitely couldn't have. If he was kind, she'd start hoping, and hope would lead to trying to get him back. And that was something her pride and sense of self-protection would never allow her to do. He sure as hell didn't want her and she would have to just keep reminding herself of that until she actually stopped wanting him.

But how long would that be, anyway? How could she stop needing someone she'd always needed? Especially after months of knowing the perfection that being with him could be. Months of sharing the same bed, sharing meals, sharing plans and hopes and dreams and disappointments. Maybe it wouldn't take that long. She was strong, after all, and she did have a new life to focus on. She would throw herself into her work until she had him out of her system. But for now, she had to keep a level head. That would mean absolutely no drinking. Well, maybe she'd just finish this last glass of wine in her hand. Then she would call it quits until she was sure she wouldn't throw herself at his feet and beg him to take her back.

Two hours later, Harper passed out on her bed, fully clothed and full of wine. Her last thought as she drifted off was that she had done it. She had made it through one evening next door to him without making a fool of herself. Only three more to go.

* * *

Evan lay awake in his bed for hours, even though he was tired from work. He tossed and turned, trying in vain to find a comfortable position. Suddenly it occurred to him that he could smell Harper's perfume, and the memories it brought were making him ache. Stupid perfume. Who the hell invented that, anyway? Was it for the sole purpose of torturing men? Getting up, he turned the light on and tugged the sheets off the bed, replacing them, along with the pillowcases, with fresh linens. That ought to do it, he thought as he balled up the sheets and tossed them into the laundry hamper.

Lying back down, he forced himself not to notice how empty the bed, the room, the house was without her. He would have to survive, knowing she was right next door, without going over to beg her to forgive him and to stay. As much as he knew that he was right about her wanting her old life back, he still wanted nothing more than to have her stay. For good. The thought of her going back to New York brought both relief and pain. She would be gone and she would move on.

In his estimation, it wouldn't take long for a woman as beautiful and fun and smart as her to find someone new. The thought gutted him. She was supposed to want to be with him. Wasn't that what people did when they found "the one"? They found a way to make things work, they made sacrifices and they stayed together.

He would need to just keep reminding himself over and over again that this was for the best. He was giving her what she needed. That would keep him from rushing to her, wrapping his arms around her, kissing her and asking her to stay. He had been right, and that meant he could keep his pride this time around. He might be brokenhearted but at least his dignity was intact.

* * *

Harper spent the next four days living outside her body. Every morning she woke and took extra care with her makeup, hair and clothing, just in case she ran into him. Her stomach flipped every time she walked out the front door or pulled up in front of her house. What if he was there? What would she say? Best to look amazing, say nothing and keep going.

She was going to have to keep going with or without him. Life wasn't about to stop just because Evan Donovan had stopped wanting her. She had to move on and start getting excited about the possibilities that life had for her. Her dad was doing so much better and they were closer than they had been in years. She was setting off to go live her dreams. She should be happy. Then why did she have no energy by suppertime, choosing to crawl into bed rather than eat? When had food lost its flavour? When would her passion for life return? Surely he couldn't have taken that with him.

On Friday morning Harper walked out the door on her way to Megan's. Her stomach lurched. Evan's truck was parked out front and he was just getting out, moving quickly as though he had forgotten something. He wasn't supposed to be there. She had planned carefully each morning so that she wouldn't leave the house until after his truck was gone. But there he was, looking so handsome that the very sight of him shattered what was left of her heart. She stood frozen on the step, hoping he wouldn't see her. Hoping he wouldn't think that she had been waiting for him. He glanced up at her, stopping in his tracks for a moment, his face impossible to read. Was that pain? Or anger? Or longing? *No, that can't be it, dummy. He doesn't want you anymore.*

Harper gave him a terse nod and made her way down the stairs, commanding her body to move gracefully. She had been at enough photo shoots to know how to carry herself in a way that exuded confidence with a slight edge of "you can't have this." She knew she looked her best, having put on tall brown leather boots, a cream-coloured knit dress and a luxurious cashmere crepe coat by Derek

Lam. She was doing a convincing job of it right up until her ankle buckled and her body did that quick, awkward tilt-to-the-side thing. Wincing with embarrassment and pain, she continued like nothing had happened. Out of the corner of her eye, she could see Evan standing on the road, watching her. She let out a rush of air as she slammed the door to her car and watched him jog up the steps and disappear into his house. Turning the key in the ignition, she wiped a tear from her eye, blinking quickly in an effort to stop the others that were waiting to fall. *No. I am not ruining my Dior mascara over that dick. He's not worth it. Get on with it.*

* * *

Evan leaned against the door, feeling like he had just had the wind knocked out of him. There she was, his beautiful Harper, looking so soft and touchable. Why the hell did she have to curl her hair like that? Where was she going looking like that? Why did she have to leave? Why couldn't she just be gone already?

He had seen her ankle give out, and instead of finding it even remotely amusing, it had made him want to rush over to see if she was okay. He knew she'd be feeling humiliated, and the thought of not doing anything to make her feel better was almost unbearable.

Propelling himself forward, he walked to the kitchen to grab the file he had forgotten to bring for the inspector on his way to work earlier. He needed to start forgetting her.

* * *

That night, Evan stood in the cold of his backyard waiting for the barbecue to heat up. He was already on his third beer and was grateful for the buzz that dulled the pain. He threw two steaks onto the grill, along with some cut-up veggies in a foil container. It was a familiar ritual, one that he used to relish but it had been ruined, along with everything else, by Harper. He couldn't enjoy it because it had been so much better with her. She was everywhere he went in his house: the pool table, the bed, the shower, the kitchen and even this spot on the deck where he was standing right now. She had ruined it all for him. And he hated her for it. She was like a tsunami that had washed over everything in his life, and now that she had pulled back, nothing would be the same again.

Just as he was about to go inside, he saw Roy walking out to his truck, using only a cane to steady himself. Draining his beer as he watched, he knew Harper was in the house alone now. Carrying his food inside, he set it down on the table and cracked open another bottle of beer. He then sat down to his meal, feeling every bit as alone as he was. He spotted the camera on the counter, still in the box, where she'd left it on Sunday night. Anger and pain stole his appetite for his favourite meal. Screw her. She couldn't do this to him. Grabbing the camera, he stormed out of his house, crossed the lawn and banged on Harper's front door loudly and continuously until she opened it. And there she stood, in her robe, hair dripping, no makeup, just how he loved her best. This was the real her and it was someone she'd let only him see. This wasn't savvy, career-woman Harper. This was Harper, the woman who loved deeply and laughed loudly and cared so much. For an instant, he felt his love for her surge through him as he stared into her blue eyes. And then he remembered that she was all but gone, never to come back to him again. The pain that seared through him hardened his heart again, distorting his love into bitterness.

"You left this and I don't want it," he barked, shoving the camera into her hands, then turning away. He stopped suddenly and pivoted back around. "You know what? I was dead wrong. I thought I'd never regret being with you, but that's all I've been doing this week. Being with you was a huge mistake. I wish you'd never come home!"

His words were weapons, each a grenade thrown with deadly accuracy. He could see in her face that he had aimed perfectly. His triumph dissolved almost instantly at the pained expression on her face as she opened her mouth to say something, then closed it, blinking back tears.

"No, don't you dare cry. I am not going to feel sorry for you when this is all your fault. You don't get to make me feel bad when you're the one leaving." He pointed at her as he ranted. "So off you go, Harper. I'm glad that you're moving, actually. I should probably thank you, because you showed me your true colours before I did something really stupid, like—You know what? Forget it!"

He turned, jogged down a couple of steps, then turned and came back up. "You know what I just realized? You're exactly like your mother! No, you're worse than your mother. You're a combination of her and Avery. Uppity, selfish and self-absorbed! You don't give a shit who you hurt as long as you get what you want!"

They stared at each other, both wide-eyed with shock at his words. He'd gone too far and he knew it. He regretted the words as soon as they had left his mouth. He watched as she sucked in some air; he saw the pain in her eyes and how her body went rigid. Then she slowly shut the door, saving him from seeing any more. He stood for a moment, his legs cemented to the step, reeling from what he'd just done.

He had wanted a fight. He wanted her to say horrible things back, to give him a solid reason to hate her. If he could hate her, he could forget that he had ever loved her. But she hadn't taken the bait. She hadn't given him a fight, and that was nothing like her. Harper was a fighter. She'd always been a fighter, from the time he'd first seen her over twenty years ago. He could remember a moving truck parked in front of the house next door, and Harper and her brothers spilling out of a station wagon behind it and onto the sidewalk in a full-out brawl. He had watched from his living room window as she delivered a blow to Craig's chin and another quickly to his crotch, bringing her much bigger brother to his knees. In all the years he had known her, Harper had never backed down from a fight like she had just done now. And that all but broke his heart to see.

Beyond wanting a fight, deep down in a place he would never admit existed, he wanted her to tell him she had changed her mind about New York, that she could never leave him, no matter what opportunity came along. He wanted her to beg him to take her back, to tell him she wasn't going. And if she had just done that, if she had promised to stay, he would have asked her to stay forever. He would have told her how sorry he was for every unkind word, every lie about wanting to be rid of her. And he would have picked her up and carried her back to his place so they could make love all night and go right back to where they were before her Manhattan magazine had come calling for her again. But she hadn't done that either. No fight. No begging to be taken back. She had just stood there staring at him as though she didn't know him at all. And this confused him more than anything else she could have done. Was she too devastated to fight, or had she never really cared at all?

* * *

Harper shut the door quietly and locked it before sliding to the floor and dissolving into tears, praying he couldn't hear her sobs. How could he say such horrible things to her? He'd said she was worse than her mother. Maybe it was true. She didn't know how to love. She had chosen her comfortable old life because it was what she wanted. Because it was safe.

She didn't hear the back door open or her father come in. She was still a crumpled mess on the floor when she saw his feet in front of her and his cane next to his left foot. Wiping her tears, she watched as he rested his cane against the wall before leaning forward and reaching out for her. Placing her hands in his, she felt her dad's firm grip as he hoisted her up to him and pulled her in for a long hug. Patting her on the back, Roy made gentle shushing sounds as she sobbed.

"I take it Dickhead just came by?"

Laughing a little at her dad's foul language, she nodded.

"Come on," he said, taking one hand from behind her back and grabbing his cane. Turning them both toward the kitchen, he kept his other arm wrapped around her shoulder as he started walking. "I bought you some ice cream at the store. Mint chocolate chip—your favourite when you were a little girl. You looked like you could use some today."

"Thanks, Dad," she whispered, resting her head on his shoulder for a moment.

That night, as she finally drifted off to sleep, she thought of how her dad had taken care of her. He knew what it was like to have your heart stomped on, and he had genuinely seemed content to help her through it. Tonight, through her tears and some ice cream, Harper realized that even if Evan didn't love her, at least she'd always have the love and support of her father. That alone was reason enough for her to have come home.

THIRTY-FOUR

Manhattan, New York

"Harper, you're finally here!" Blaire stood up behind the enormous glass desk in her office. "Did you get settled in at your apartment?"

Harper nodded, pasting a smile onto her face, hoping it would eventually cause her to actually feel happy. Or, at the very least, no longer devastated.

"Oh, it's so wonderful to have you back!" Blaire swept across the room and gave her a big hug. "Did you see your new office?"

"I did," Harper answered. "It's terrific."

"Well, it's important that you like it. You'll be spending the next decade or so in it." Blaire's enthusiasm was overflowing. "I made sure Jasmine set things up for you just the way you like. Go ahead and take an hour to get your bearings, then come find me so we can have a planning session, okay?"

"Actually, I'd like to get started. I'm ready."

"Even better!" Blaire said, grinning.

* * *

That evening, Harper and Blaire were the last two people in the building. Harper arched her back and rolled her neck, trying to work out some kinks. Her eyes hurt from staring at a screen for so long, but she and Blaire weren't going to be finished for a few more hours.

Blaire glanced over at her. "Tired?"

"A little, yeah," Harper answered.

"You've gotten out of pace since you left. You'll get back into it soon enough, though. It just takes a while to get used to."

"I'm sure you're right." Harper rubbed her eyes with her fingertips. "Blaire, do you ever think it might not be worth it? Working like this?"

Blaire gave her a blank look.

"I mean, this pace. This lifestyle. Two weeks of every month are really quite insane, when you think about it. We're here almost fourteen hours a day."

"Yes, but we're at the top, Harper. We're leading the fashion industry. Isn't having that kind of power worth putting in some long hours?" Her eyes glowed with enthusiasm.

Harper glanced to the ceiling, trying to decide. "I don't know anymore. I used to think that, but now I'm not so sure. Now I can't help wondering if someday I'll look back and regret giving my life to a magazine."

"Uh-oh, don't tell me you're hearing the ticking of your biological clock, because I don't think I could handle that right now."

"No. It's not that. It's just that when I was in Boulder, I did creative work that felt important too, but I still had time for a life outside my job. You don't ever feel like you're missing out?"

"Not for a minute. You know what all those bored housewives wish they were doing? Jet-setting around the world for photo shoots, dining with celebrities and living the life of glamour that you and I have. I bet there isn't one of them out there scrubbing macaroni and cheese off the bottom of a pot who doesn't wish she were here doing exactly what we're doing right now."

Harper nodded. "Maybe you're right."

Blaire put down her pen. "I know I am. You're just missing that ex of yours, that's all. Wait until Fashion Week. Once you surround yourself with all the glamour and delicious men again, you'll forget all about your house builder from Boulder."

* * *

Boulder, Colorado

The sun was setting, giving way to cold winter air as Evan shut off the heater and put the last of his tools into his tote. The house he had been working on that day had just reached lock-up stage and he was pleased with how it was coming along. The windows and doors had been installed earlier that week, which was always a relief to him as well as to the homeowners. The sound of a car door slamming caught his attention and he peered around the corner and out the front room window. His heart skipped a beat as his ex-wife made her way gingerly over the snow-covered yard, smoothing her hair with one hand. In the other was a large yellow envelope. After the shock of seeing her wore off, it was the envelope that held his attention. What could she possibly want after all this time? The divorce had been final for over two years already. Swearing under his breath, he made his way over to the front door.

"Hello, Avery." He kept his tone flat, doing his best to make his face expressionless.

She stared at him a moment before answering. "Hi, Evan. You look good."

"Thanks." He knew she'd be expecting a compliment in return, but he was in no mood to offer one.

She waited a moment, looking very uncomfortable, before speaking again. "I guess you're wondering what I'm doing here."

He gave a nod. "I'm especially curious about that envelope in your hand."

A look of understanding crossed Avery's face as she glanced down at it. "Oh, right. Of course. I imagine seeing your ex-wife with one of these could make a guy break out in a cold sweat. Nothing legal, I promise. I was going through a box of old things, and somehow I still had the original copy of your birth certificate and a few old photos."

"You could have mailed them," he said, hoping to draw out her real reason for being there.

She shifted uncomfortably in her high-heeled boots. "I'm getting remarried. I didn't want you to hear it from someone else."

"Oh." His head jerked back a little in surprise. "Congratulations," he said, his voice quiet. He reached for the envelope.

"You remember Trent?"

"Trent Baxter? Your divorce attorney?"

Avery gave him a sheepish look. "I know. But we're really good together."

"Well, that's important," he said, wishing she'd leave so this awkward moment would be over.

"That it is." There was a sadness in her eyes. It was a very familiar look; it was the expression she had worn during the last several months of their marriage.

"I know you blame me," Avery said suddenly. "You think I left you because the money was running out, but that's not true. I keep thinking of what you said to me, about how I had my fingers crossed behind my back when I said the 'for poorer' part. And it really kills me that you think that."

Evan's eyes hardened on her. "That's exactly why you left, Avery."

"Not it wasn't, and it hurts that you think that about me." Avery's eyes glistened.

"Should it really matter what I think?"

"It shouldn't, but somehow it does. I left because you kept pushing me away. You never let me in, Evan. When things started falling apart, you just wouldn't talk about it. You refused to lean on me. And that's all I needed. For you to lean on me sometimes."

"So now it's my fault that you were so angry about losing everything?" Evan scoffed.

"I wasn't angry about the house. I was angry that you wouldn't let me help. You shut me out, month after month, leaving me to wonder what was happening, telling me you'd figure it out. You'd go into your office when you got home from work every night and shut the door, and I sat there worrying and waiting for you to just come out and tell me the truth. That things weren't going well and we were in trouble. That's what married people do. They talk to each other and they fight and they figure it out together when a crisis hits. But you just started making decisions for both of us without even consulting me. And it hurt, Evan, it really hurt. I wanted to be your partner, not just some arm candy you married."

"Is that what you thought?" Evan's eyes softened a little. "I never thought of you as arm candy. I didn't talk to you about it because I didn't want you to be as stressed as I was. I was trying to protect you from all of it. I knew I could handle it on my own, but you didn't give me time. If you had just trusted me, we would have been fine."

"It had nothing to do with trust." Avery shook her head and stared down at the wooden floor for a moment. "I married you because of you. You were confident and fun and easygoing and thoughtful, and

I fell in love with you. Not your bank account. But then you stopped being you and you stopped loving me. You kept pushing me away, no matter what I tried."

"That's not true. You were furious that we were going to lose everything and you know it, so don't try to rewrite history just because the truth makes you look bad. You were so desperate to keep the house you got your father involved, even knowing how I'd feel about that."

"You know I asked for his help because we were drowning! It would have killed my parents if we had gone bankrupt without even asking for a hand. You didn't cause the recession. They knew that."

"How could you possibly think—You know what? It doesn't matter. We've had this fight a thousand times. Nothing's going to change the past now."

Avery looked up at the ceiling, rubbing her hands from her neck to her cheeks in frustration. Swallowing hard, she looked back at him. "I didn't come here to fight, Evan. I just wanted you to know it wasn't about the money. I hate that you think I'm just some spoiled brat who couldn't handle the fall when, really, what I couldn't handle was the loneliness."

"Well, thanks for sharing that. I feel much better knowing that you blame it all on me," Evan answered, his words laced with sarcasm.

"I'm not telling you this to make you feel bad, Evan. I'm telling you so you don't make the same mistake again if you ever find the right woman. I hope you'll be able to pull her in to you when you feel like pushing her away. I want you to be happy."

"I can tell." He folded his arms across his chest and set his jaw.

Avery reached up and placed her delicate fingers on his forearm. "I really do want you to be happy."

Evan let his body relax a little. "Okay, Avery. Okay. I know, in your own way, you're trying to help. I hope you and Trent do better than you and I did."

"Thanks." Taking a step forward, she stood on her tiptoes and gave him a kiss on the cheek. "I hope you find happiness."

Avery walked down the front steps of the house before turning back to him. "Congratulations on making it back to the top. I knew you would."

* * *

That night, as Evan sat watching sports highlights, he couldn't get the conversation with Avery off his mind. Why the hell was it bothering him so much? Shutting off the TV, he made his way to the pool table and racked up the balls. He selected his favourite cue, lined up the white ball and starting taking shots. The sounds and the sight of the balls rolling over the smooth felt were somehow soothing to his ragged nerves. Then it hit him. Avery's words upset him because he'd already blown it. He'd already pushed Harper away when he should have pulled her toward him. And now that she was gone, it was too late.

THIRTY-FIVE

Manhattan, New York

"Next!" Harper called as she finished dressing the second model for the shoot. The young man who appeared was so confident he was almost sneering. Harper looked at him for a moment before recognizing him. "Dustin. I haven't seen you since that first shoot you did for us. How are you?"

"Great. I've hit my stride this year. I told my agent I'd fit you in because you helped me out last spring." He gave her an approving nod.

Harper bit back a laugh. "Well, thank you for remembering." Her cell buzzed in her pocket. She took it out and saw that it was her dad calling. Turning to Jasmine, she said, "I have to take this. Can you finish getting the models prepped?"

Harper strode to the hall as she answered. "Dad, what's up? Everything okay?"

"Fine, Harper. I'm good. Did I catch you at a bad time?"

"I always have a few minutes for you."

"You let me know if I'm interrupting. I just wanted to tell you that some of those plants are starting to come up. The ones at the front of the flower bed. I'm just outside looking at them now."

"Really? That must be the daffodils. I wish I was there to see them."

"Me too. They're really nice. It's like you brought spring to the yard early."

Harper smiled even though her dad couldn't see her. "Thanks for letting me know."

"Of course. Well, I don't want to keep you. I just wanted to say hi. And thank you for everything you did when you were here."

"You can stop thanking me. But don't stop calling to say hi."

"Deal. You doing okay? You happy there?"

"Um, it's taking me a bit to settle in but I'll get there."

"I'm sure you will. Listen, don't be afraid to come home if you get sick of it."

"I'm not a quitter, Dad."

"It's only quitting if you leave because it's too hard. If you leave because you belong somewhere else, it's called living the life you're meant to."

Harper chuckled. "Have you been watching reruns of *Oprah*, by any chance?"

"No, I'm just growing very wise in my old age. I should let you go. Call me in a couple of days."

"Count on it."

Boulder, Colorado

Evan lay in bed that night, staring out the window at the moon and wondering if Harper might be doing the same at that moment. When he'd left work he forced himself to go to the gym to do some climbing. It seemed like the best way to work off some of the frustration and pain he was feeling. Now, as he lay there, he could feel every fibre of every muscle in his body aching along with his heart. She was gone. His Harper. The woman he'd been hoping to grow old with was really gone. And he'd done nothing to stop her. He hadn't even had the guts to tell her the truth—that he needed her to stay. That he loved her and he always would. What kind of man did that make him? A shit-poor excuse for one, in his book. But he would have to live with that. And he would have to do his level best to forget she'd ever existed. It wouldn't have mattered even if he had told her. She'd have gone anyway.

Manhattan, New York

Harper got home after nine for the fourth evening in a row. So much for the fun and excitement of New York. She'd done nothing but work since she got here, and from the looks of things, there was no end in sight. She stood in the entrance to her tiny apartment, suddenly feeling very confined. She'd gone from one box to another. The rain pattered at the window, calling Harper to open it and let in the air. The fresh smell was accompanied by the jarring sound of the traffic below. Harper longed for the quiet stillness of Maplewood Drive. She thought of how hectic the week had been, barely giving her time to breathe. Instead of the thrill she had expected to feel at being back, she felt hemmed in and irritated by it all. She had a sinking feeling that she'd made the wrong choice. Maybe this life wasn't meant for her after all.

Her stomach growled, reminding her that she'd missed dinner. Too tired to cook and too hungry to wait, she poured herself a bowl of cereal and plunked herself down at the table to eat. An old ritual, but not one that she relished.

She'd spent the weekend putting everything back in its place. It was all so familiar to her. And yet, different. She was different. She had tried on a completely new life and it had started to fit her. But she couldn't go back. Not after the way she'd left things with Evan. She couldn't live in a place where she'd run the risk of seeing him everywhere she went. Maybe what she was really feeling was the sense of having lost the man she loved.

Her mind wandered back to the moment the previous June when she had stood in this kitchen hearing about her dad's accident for the first time. That had been the moment that changed everything, setting her life on a new path. And it had changed her in ways she had never expected. Her priorities just weren't the same anymore.

Her cellphone rang, interrupting her thoughts.

"Hey, Megs," she answered.

"Hello, my friend. I'm calling to check on you."

"Oh, thanks. I'm fine. I'm all settled in. Crazy busy." Harper's voice was flat. "Do you mind if I crunch granola in your ear? I'm starving."

"Go for it. No time to eat?"

"None." Her mouth was full as she spoke. Chewing quickly, she swallowed. "Sorry."

"You okay?"

"You mean because of Evan?"

"Yes."

"Not so much." Harper's voice broke. The lump in her throat made swallowing impossible. Dropping her spoon into the bowl, she pushed her dinner away. "Stupid. Why the fuck did I think I could be with him for months without falling for him?"

"Humans are incredibly good at denial. I know you hate to admit it, but you are one of us."

"God. Don't say that. I need you tell me that I'll get over him soon. That I'll start to enjoy my life again, because right now I have a sinking feeling that I've just fucked everything up and I'll never be happy again." Harper's voice broke again. "And I'm just so tired, Megan. So tired that I don't know what to think or do."

"I know. You've been burning the candle at both ends for a long time now. And you've been through so much. It's bound to take its toll on you."

Tears streamed down Harper's cheeks. "I don't think I want this anymore. I think I might hate it here. I miss you and the kids and Luc and my dad and . . . and I can't just quit. I don't know what to do." Her voice was strained, her makeup now ruined.

"Oh, honey, don't decide anything right now. For now, crawl into bed and get some sleep. Call me as soon as you wake up, before you do anything."

"But it'll be early for you . . ."

"As soon as you wake up. Immediately. Don't even get out of bed to go pee," Megan ordered.

"Okay, Bossy. I will."

* * *

The next morning Harper lay in bed, numb. She'd had a big cry after she hung up the phone, then had fallen asleep as soon as her head hit the pillow. Now, ten hours later, she woke, feeling anything but refreshed. Her entire body ached, from her head to her toes, and there was a horrible emptiness in her heart where Evan had once resided.

She picked up her cell and called Megan. "I'm up."

"How are you feeling?"

"Shitty," Harper whispered, losing her voice.

"I know. What's the first thing you wanted to do when you woke up today?"

"Come home."

"Then come home."

"I can't. He's there. And I just can't be next door to him right now."

"So stay here until you get your own place. You need to be with people who love you right now."

"I can't. I just took my fucking dream job, remember? Maybe it'll turn out to be the best way to forget him."

"Your first instinct this morning was to come home, Harper. And you meant Boulder, not New York. You need to follow your instincts. If you want to be with Evan and make a life with him, do it. If the only thing that was standing in the way of you two making a life together was your job, then the answer is pretty simple."

"It's not. He doesn't want to make a life with me. He was really clear about that."

"You live on your terms, Harper. You said you wanted to come home. So come home. You've got a job and a really wonderful life waiting for you here even without him."

Harper let out a loud sob. "You're right. I don't want to be here anymore. I don't want the politics or the backstabbing or the working like a maniac all hours of the day and night. It's just not worth it for me anymore. I want to be with you guys and my family and have time to read and go for walks and think."

"Good for you, honey. You've figured out what you want from life. Now, go into the office and tell Blaire thank you, but no thank you. Get on a plane and come home. We've got a bedroom here for you until you find your own place."

"Oh God, I'm going to have to tell Blaire that I'm bailing on her. It's going to be so awful."

"Then do it this morning. Get it over with. Agree to stay on for a while until she can replace you. Then get the hell home."

THIRTY-SIX

Boulder, Colorado

Evan sat at his desk, alone in the trailer. He'd just gotten off the phone with Lacey, who was home with her new baby boy, after calling to ask for her help finding a file. Of course, she knew exactly where it was and was happy to take his call. He could hear the baby cooing in the background as they spoke, and something about that sound brought him a profound sense of loss.

His mind wandered back to their conversation. "You okay, boss man? Chad said you haven't been yourself lately."

"I'm fine, really. Nothing to worry about. Harper moved back to New York a few weeks ago and it's just taking me a little time to readjust."

"She did? I'm sorry to hear that. You two were so perfect together. I thought maybe she'd change her mind."

"She didn't."

"Oh, Evan. Is there any way she'll come back?"

"No. I made sure of that."

"Well, if she knew you were in love with her and she left anyway, maybe it's for the best."

"Technically . . . Oh, nothing. Doesn't matter."

"Technically what?" Lacey asked. "You never told her, did you?"

"Not exactly. I knew the deal going in, so I thought it better if I didn't say anything. It was actually my weird way of protecting her."

"You idiot," Lacey said. "I'm sorry, but you men are dumber than a sack of hammers sometimes. Protecting her from being loved? What about that makes any sense?"

"It's complicated, and I really don't want to—"

"It's simple. You two are in love. You're meant to be together. Now get your cute butt on a plane and go get her."

"You *do* know I'm your boss, right?"

"I haven't slept since this baby came and I don't have any patience for anyone right now, even you."

"Or any filter, apparently."

"That either. Now get going. Sitting at that desk moping isn't going to get the love of your life back."

After he hung up, he stared out the window, watching the rain streak down in thin rivers, feeling the empty fog that had settled over him. It had been weeks since Harper left and things weren't getting any easier. So much for no regrets. He'd been dead wrong about that.

But what was done was done. He couldn't change it now. Lacey was wrong. She didn't understand. He'd promised never to ask for more than Harper could give and he wasn't about to go back on his word. Suddenly, it occurred to him that he'd never promised not to tell her how he felt about her. That had been on the table the entire time, but he'd been too blind to see it. What if he had told her he was in love with her? That he always would be? Would that have changed everything? Could it still?

* * *

Harper sat in the cab of the Rent-Haul truck, freezing. Banging on the dashboard, she willed the heat to come on, but of course it didn't. She glanced up at the sky, hoping the sun would peek out from behind the clouds. One more day and she'd be home. She blew warm air onto her fingers and turned on the radio. The Clash posed the question, *Should I stay or should I go?*

"I'm going. And when I get there, I'm staying," she answered.

Megan and Luc would put her up until the possession date on her new condo arrived. Boulder was big enough that she could avoid Evan, but not if she was next door. She and Megan had agreed to make their partnership permanent, and Harper would call Monica and go back to work at Fashion Forward. She knew when to visit her dad so she wouldn't have to see Evan. She was going to have a rich and beautiful life, surrounded by friends and family and important work to fill her days. And even though it hurt to think of him, at least she was free from the fear of losing him that she'd felt when they were together. That had already happened and she was surviving it.

Her phone rang. It was Megan. "Where are you? I'm getting too excited to wait any longer!"

"I'll be there tomorrow night," Harper answered.

"Yay! I have your bedroom all ready. How are you feeling?"

"Good. Except when I think about Blaire. Then I feel pretty guilty."

"I know. It'll take a while, but she'll get over it. You couldn't live the rest of your life working at a job you don't want just because you didn't want to disappoint her."

"No, but she was right. I should have damn well decided before I came back."

"Sometimes it's impossible to know until you're in a situation," Megan said.

"At least now my mind is made up. There's no way I can go back to *Style* after leaving this time."

"Our gain, totally," Megan said. "You feel okay with it?"

"I really do. Right now my biggest complaint, other than what's-his-name, is that I'm fucking freezing. This truck has no heat."

Megan laughed. "Oh God, how about you make this your last cross-country move?"

"Deal."

A few minutes later, Harper called Monica. "Do you have room for a retired fashion insider?"

Manhattan, New York

"Thank you for flying with Jet Away. The weather in New York today is rainy and forty-eight degrees, but we hope you'll enjoy taking a bite out of the Big Apple anyway."

Evan's knee bounced restlessly as he waited for the plane to land. Once he had made the decision to go find Harper, he could think of nothing else. His heart pounded as the wheels touched the ground, bringing him closer to her than he'd been in weeks. He unbuckled quickly and grabbed his overnight bag.

Forty-five minutes later, he paid the cab driver and stepped out in front of *Style*'s head office. She was here. His Harper was here. And he was going to go find her. Taking a deep breath, he walked through the doors to a large reception desk. A young woman in a fitted red-and-black dress smiled up at him. "Third floor. Ask for Billie. But you're not going to get it. You're too young."

"Pardon me?" Evan asked.

"Your agent sent you for the silver-fox photo shoot, right? She wasted your time. You don't even have grey hair, but you might as well go up anyway. They're doing a rugged-mountain-man thing in a few weeks. Maybe they'll like you for that. Third floor. Ask for Billie."

"I'm not here for a photo shoot. I'm here to see Harper Young," Evan said.

The woman gave him a skeptical look. "Do you have an appointment?"

"No, but I'll wait."

"Okay. Have a seat over there and I'll see if I can find her."

Evan walked over to the window and stood, waiting. A few minutes later, he heard the sound of high heels clicking across the marble floor. He turned with a hopeful expression, but his face fell when he saw it was the woman from the front desk approaching him. "I can't seem to get a hold of her assistant. She must be in the photo shoot. Can I take a message?"

Evan nodded. "Sure. I think she must have changed her cell number when she moved back here, so I don't have it."

"I can email or put you through to her line so you can leave a voice mail."

"Voice mail would be great."

"Voice mail. Maybe you are old enough for the silver-fox shoot," she said wryly. She walked briskly to the front desk, dialed Harper's extension and handed the receiver to Evan.

Evan turned his back on her, hoping for a little privacy as he waited for the beep. "Harper, it's me. I'll be in New York for the next two days. I'm staying at the Radisson down the block from your office. Please text me or call when you get this. I need to see you right away."

* * *

The next day, Evan returned to the office early in the morning. A different well-dressed young woman was at the front desk; she blinked at him as he approached. "Can I help you?"

"Yes. I need to see Harper Young."

"Of course. Let me ring her assistant. Your name?"

"Evan Donovan."

She pressed a few buttons on her phone. "Jasmine, there's a Mr. Evan Donovan here to see Ms. Young." The woman's eyes grew wide for a moment. Then she turned her back. He had to strain to hear her. "Well, what do you want me to tell him?" There was a long pause. "Okay."

"I'm sorry. She's not in the office today. Her assistant said she'll pass along the message."

Evan's face was determined. "I'll wait."

"Pardon me?"

"I'll wait. She'll be back eventually." He walked over to the seating area and made himself comfortable.

The receptionist called Jasmine back once he was out of earshot. "That man, he says he'll wait for her. I can't just let him sit here all day. I have to tell him she's gone."

"You're going to lose your job if you do," Jasmine advised her. "Blaire said no one can know she's gone until her replacement is well established. No one."

"So we're just going to let him sit there? What if he comes back tomorrow?"

"Tell him she's in Paris to get ready for Fashion Week. That'll get rid of him."

"Okay."

A moment later, the receptionist made her way over to Evan. "I

{288}

just heard back from her assistant. I'm afraid Ms. Young is in Paris right now for Fashion Week. I misunderstood earlier. I apologize."

"Really? That's what she told you to say?"

Her expression turned cold at the challenge. "I said it because that's where she is."

"I understand. Thank you."

Boulder, Colorado

Evan poured himself some water and made his way back to his desk in the trailer, heavy-hearted. He'd gone to get her but instead of seeing him, she'd chosen to have people lie to him on her behalf. She couldn't even be bothered to give him a minute of her time, but he couldn't really blame her after what he'd said to her. Now he had to face the fact that it was over. All hope was gone. He had reached the part where he would have to forget about her and everything they'd done together and said to each other. He would have to erase her face and her laugh and her smile from his memory. Boots got up from the dog bed next to Evan's desk and rested his thick head on his lap, staring up at him with sad eyes. "I know. You miss her too. We're just going to have to get used to life on our own again."

THIRTY-SEVEN

Harper sat on her new couch in her new living room, surrounded by boxes. It was late in the evening and she was alone in her condo for the first time. Her father, Craig, Megan and Luc had spent most of the day helping her move. Craig had lingered until a few minutes ago, more to make sure she was okay than for any other reason. She had learned in the past weeks not to use the word *fine* if she wanted him to believe she was actually doing well. Today, she had done her best to put on a convincing show of a woman who was happily starting a new chapter of her life. As she sat in the silence now, she doubted that anyone had believed it.

Checking her watch, she saw that it was already after ten, and just the thought of making her bed seemed like too much for her. Wandering into the kitchen, she washed out her new kettle, then filled it with enough water for one mug of tea and set in on the stove to boil. Megan had brought Harper a gift basket of teas, chocolates and a couple of bottles of wine. Selecting a bag of camomile, she picked up her cell and sent Megan a quick thank-you text, thinking about how full her life really was.

As Harper poured boiling water into a mug, her mind took its normal detour down Evan Lane, as it did at least a hundred times a day. He'd be at home by now, maybe at his desk working or, if he was tired, in bed reading. She could picture him that way, propped up on two pillows, under the covers, no shirt to hide that hard body of his. She missed that body, even if the person in it had turned out to be so disappointing.

Bringing her tea along, she made her way down the hall to get her bed ready for its first night of service. She set the mug on the counter in her ensuite, glancing at herself in the mirror as she did. She looked tired. And, to her eyes, old. Standing a few feet back from the mirror, she could pick out every line and see those three grey hairs that had started to emerge again along her part. Normally those hairs would garner a swift reaction from her. She glanced at her make up bag for a second before deciding to leave the dreaded hairs in place. She didn't have the energy tonight to tweeze them. And what was the point, really? She wasn't trying to impress anyone these days. She really couldn't care less if she looked thirty or fifty at the moment. For the first time in her life, she didn't mind the thought of waking up at age fifty. By then she would have fifteen years between her and the pain she had been feeling since Evan ended their relationship. But she couldn't speed up time now any more than she could have stopped it when they were first together and everything had seemed so perfect.

Half an hour later, she turned off the light in the bedroom and found her way to bed in the dark, making a mental note to buy bedside lamps. Snuggling under the covers, she moved her pillow to the centre of the bed, stretching out her arms and legs, feeling the cool sheets and the soft mattress under her. This was okay. She could do this. She would take the next few days to get settled in and then find a routine of working, volunteering, going for long walks and reading. Through the window next to her bed, she could see clouds floating slowly past the almost-full moon. She watched them move, willing herself not to cry. This was her fresh start. Right here in her new bed in her new bedroom in her wonderful new condo. She wouldn't cry. Knowing that Evan wouldn't be crying himself to sleep helped her set the pain aside. He wasn't lying in bed heartbroken. He was relieved. And because of that, he didn't deserve another one of her thoughts.

* * *

"That's beautiful. Just like that," Harper said from behind the camera lens. "You two are an absolutely gorgeous couple. I can't wait to see how you'll look on your wedding day."

Patricia, the bride-to-be, beamed at Harper. "Thank you. I just love this location. How did you think of it?"

"Oh, my partner, Megan, knows all the best places in town. This must be the best staircase in the state though, right?"

"It is. I had no idea that the university had such great old buildings," the groom, Will, remarked.

The bride-to-be rolled her eyes, but her expression revealed pride rather than annoyance. "That's his subtle way of getting you to ask where he went to school so he can say 'Harvard.'"

"What? No. You thought I was . . . ?" He shook his head and then turned to Harper. "Harvard Law, actually. Graduated summa cum laude. No big deal."

Harper laughed at their adorable exchange. They were a fun couple and the wedding itself was going to be spectacular. It would be held in one week at the Boulder Country Club in front of three hundred guests. They were doing a last-minute engagement shoot on the insistence of the mother of the bride. Harper was looking forward to the entire event, from the rehearsal dinner on the Friday night to the gift-opening on the Sunday. She would know them very well by then, and it thrilled her to be a part of this special time in their life together. As she said her goodbyes and packed up her camera, she smiled to herself, thinking of them. They were both in their early thirties, well-established in their respective careers, he a lawyer and she a physical therapist. They were old enough and had been together long enough that there wasn't likely to be a lot of drama to the event.

She thought of the happy couple, wondering what that would feel like—to be in the middle of planning your wedding, getting ready to commit your life to the man you loved and knowing that he was going to promise his life to you in return. What would it be like to have the confidence in each other that she saw in them? A heavy sigh accompanied the click of her seat belt as she started the car and drove toward her condo. She would spend the evening with a pot of chai tea and her computer, carefully selecting the best shots to edit. She dialed Megan's number when she was stopped at a red light.

"How'd it go?" Megan asked excitedly.

"Really well. They're both such sweethearts. I think I managed to really capture who they are."

"I know you did. I've just finished the edits on the Parker baby shots you did. Gorgeous work! I'm going to add them to Dropbox so you can give them a look before I make prints. I should have the album finished and wrapped by Wednesday for them to pick up."

"That's great, Megan. I can't believe you got through them so fast."

"Well, Amelie has been particularly cooperative today. She had a long nap this afternoon," Megan answered. "Say, what are you doing tonight? Do you want to come by for dinner?"

"I thought I'd tuck in and get to work on these photos."

"You sure? You've done nothing for weeks but work. I think you're overdoing it. I saw that you edited over forty of the Anderson family photos on the weekend, which is a little bit—"

"Enthusiastic?"

"Obsessive. They only paid for ten edited shots, Harper. That must have taken you all weekend. Did you even sleep?"

"I slept as much as I needed to. I just don't need to sleep as much as you humans. I'm fine, seriously. Experience is the only way to improve."

"Hmm."

"Hmm what? You're not going to bring up Evan-Not-From-Heaven again are you?"

"It's just that I'm worried about you. You haven't been letting yourself have any fun, you're spending most of your time alone and you do need sleep, in spite of what you think."

"Honestly, there's no need to worry. I'm totally over what's-his-name."

"Really? Well then, how about a date with a nice guy?"

"Are you trying to set me up?"

"I met someone I think you'd really like. Handsome. Smart. Funny. Single."

"No thank you."

"Don't you even want to know a little about him?"

"I wish I did, but I can't imagine anything less appealing right now. And my cellphone is about to die. Talk to you tomorrow," Harper replied.

"Call me if you change your mind."

"About what?"

"Both. Dinner and the guy."

"I won't. Talk to you tomorrow."

"Bye."

"Bye."

* * *

The following Saturday morning was unusually relaxed for a wedding. The ceremony wasn't until late in the afternoon, meaning hair and makeup and family photos wouldn't start at the crack of dawn for a change. Harper was out the door at ten to pick up Megan and then meet the bridal party at the salon. She saw her friend waiting at the door when she arrived. Getting out of the car, Harper waved enthusiastically to Megan as she descended the steps.

"Good morning, Mrs. Chevalier!" she called.

"Good morning! Someone's chipper this morning!" Megan returned.

"I am. I'm excited about the possibilities today. We've got a great couple to work with, great weather and, as you saw last night from the photos, we're off to a pretty decent start in documenting their big day."

"I did! Nicely done, by the way. I took a quick peek at them right before bed last night. Have you got the address for the salon?"

"Already programmed into my GPS. We're off and running," Harper replied as they got into the car. "Coffee for two," she said, gesturing at the to-go cups in the console.

"Thank you! You're in such a great mood. I haven't seen you this happy in weeks. It's really nice." She sipped her drink. "What? Did you get laid last night or something?"

"No." Harper gently swatted at Megan's arm with the back of her hand. "I'm just ready to move on. It feels good."

* * *

The day flew by. Harper and Megan had gone from the salon to the groom's parents' house, then over to the parents of the bride's to catch shots of the bridal party getting dressed. Driving just ahead of the limo carrying the ladies, they made it to the country club at a few minutes past three, both quickly devouring protein bars and water along the way. The ceremony would be held at 4 p.m., followed immediately by cocktails and dinner in a large white tent on the grounds. There wouldn't be a moment to rest until late that night.

Megan accompanied the ladies to the dressing room while Harper went in search of the groomsmen. Walking along the wrap-around deck of the clubhouse, she stopped dead in her tracks. There stood Evan, looking out onto the grass below. Dressed in a light grey suit, he was devastatingly handsome. Harper stood rooted to the spot as she watched him take a sip of champagne. All thoughts of quickly doubling back were foiled when he turned, his gaze landing on her and his mouth falling open a little.

The sound of guests and light orchestral music became inaudible over the sound of her heartbeat pounding in her ears. She told herself to look away, turn and run, hurry past him, anything but just stand there like an idiot gawking at him. Shaking her head quickly, she brought herself back to reality and swallowed hard before setting her shoulders back and striding toward the stairs. She could avoid him if she went that way.

"Harper." Evan's voice was thick with emotion. "Harper, wait."

Pausing briefly, she continued on as though she hadn't heard him. It was not the time for this. She had an important job to do, a schedule to keep and she needed to keep a clear head. Moving quickly down the stairs, she was glad she had worn her red ballet flats instead of heels. She could put as much distance between them as possible. A hand on her shoulder stopped her progress.

"Harper, please," he said in a low voice.

"Never," she said, her voice determined. Against her better judgment, she allowed her eyes to settle on his. There they were, those ice-blue, gorgeous eyes that had haunted her. How could she still want him after he had tossed her aside so ruthlessly? *Where's your pride, Harper?* "Don't tell me you're one of the guests."

"Actually, I am. What are you doing here?"

"Obtaining photographic proof of the nuptials," she answered, her voice flat.

"I meant here in Boulder," he said gently.

"Living. Working—which I should get back to, actually, so if you'll excuse me."

He beamed at the revelation. "You're living here now?"

"Yes, but don't be too pleased. Now you have another ex to avoid in town."

He continued smiling as if he hadn't heard her, as if he couldn't help it. "God, you look really beautiful. I've missed you so much."

"Nope. You do not get to say that to me. Ever." Turning, she started toward the groomsmen, who were crowded around a cellphone, watching a video and laughing.

"Harper, I'm sorry . . ." Evan matched her pace.

"Nope. You don't get to apologize either," she replied, stopping and turning to him. Poking him in the chest, she went on. "And you do not get to be forgiven. You said some shitty, shitty things to me, Evan. You get to be alone. Or with someone else. I really don't give a rat's ass as long as you stay the fuck out of my way today so I can go back to pretending you don't exist."

Rubbing his chest where she had poked him, he watched her storm away, the fury that was Harper. She was all fired up, ready to do battle with him. Ready to win. An ache overtook him as he absorbed the sight of her in her dress. It was one he hadn't seen before, but it suited her, bringing out her curves in all the right places. The black flowing skirt, not so short as to be inappropriate, still managed to show off those legs. Those legs, long and lean and touchable, just the way they were in his memory. Those legs were carrying away the best thing that had ever happened to him.

But he wasn't going to let her scare him off. He would wait for the right moment and then he would make her hear him out. He was shocked that she was here, wondering how long she'd been back in town. The sudden realization hit him that she may have already been here when he went to find her in New York.

Grabbing a glass of champagne from a passing server, he downed it. He watched her as she gestured to the men to line up for a group shot. He could tell she had said something funny by their laughter and the way she was holding her hand on her hip, like she did when she was being sassy. He didn't like it. The way they were grinning at her. Yes, he knew it was for a picture, but still, he didn't like it. It was a group of good-looking guys in tuxedos, and he knew they'd enjoy the opportunity to pose for her, if only for the chance to stare in her direction. She smiled and laughed, charming them as she got the shots. The only time her face fell was when she glanced across the lawn and saw him staring. He knew she would have stuck her middle finger up if they were in any other situation.

After the dinner, speeches and first dance, Harper excused herself to run to the ladies' room in the clubhouse. She took off her shoes and sauntered back to the party through the cool, damp grass, needing to take a minute for herself. The band was doing a pretty reasonable version of "Not a Bad Thing" as Harper gazed up at the heavens. The clear sky gave a dazzling show of stars, and it occurred to her that this was exactly the type of wedding she would want, if she ever went down that road. Her thoughts turned to Evan. It was a good thing that she had seen him today. She hadn't crumbled into a million pieces like she thought she might. Sighing to herself, she wrapped her arms around her ribs, feeling slightly chilled suddenly.

"Here. Warm up." Evan's voice came from behind her as he draped his jacket over her shoulders.

Shrugging it off, she turned to him. "Don't. I'm not sure how I can be any more clear with you. I don't want to talk to you or see you. Please just leave me alone."

"I can't." He stated it as though he had no choice in the matter. "I just can't. I know I don't have the right to ask, but I'm going to anyway. I need to say something, so please hear me out.

"Every day when I wake up, you're the first thing I think about. And you're all I think about when I'm getting ready for work. And then your face pops into my head about a thousand times while I'm at work. And it's really distracting and, quite frankly, a little dangerous. And then when I go home to my empty house, I just stare at my phone, trying to think of a way to call you and tell you how sorry I am. And when I'm not watching my phone, I stare at the damn door, hoping that you'll knock on it. And if that wasn't pathetic enough, when I get into bed, I lie there and stare at your side of the bed, and I miss you so much it hurts physically. Some nights I go sleep on the couch to avoid the bedroom altogether.

"And then today, I finally see you. And I've spent the last three hours sitting here, trying to think of what to say to convince you to take me back. And this is what I came up with: Harper, the biggest mistake of my life by far was pushing you away. Because you were it for me, Harper. You are it. What we had was the best moment of my life. And I hurt you and ruined what we had, and I acted like an ass because I thought I was doing what was best for you. I thought that if I was any type of man, I would be strong enough to let you go live your dreams. But if you're here, I hope I could maybe be part of your dream. So please don't ask me to leave you alone. Because I just can't anymore. I just can't go on pretending that everything is fine or that I'm going to be okay without you, because I'm not. I need you, Harper. I'm in love with you. I've been in love with you since our first night together, when I saw you in your ball gown, eating fruit in your yard."

He paused. Waiting for her to say something. Trying to read her face. She seemed bewildered, as though he had been speaking another language.

"There you are!" The mother of the bride's voice came out of the darkness. "I'd like to do one more shot with our immediate family."

Harper turned to the woman. "Of course." She dropped her shoes and slid them on before following her back to the reception, leaving Evan with no clue as to what she had been about to say.

* * *

In the next hour, the bouquet was tossed and the garter removed and sent flying to the ceiling of the tent, only to get stuck on a cross brace. A ladder was hunted down so the least intoxicated groomsman could retrieve it for a do-over. Harper found herself capturing the last few moments of the day as well as fielding questions about her and Megan's services from a few of the guests. The entire time, she couldn't help but look for Evan. He was nowhere to be seen, so she assumed he must have gone home, leaving her with a lot to think about. And damn him for doing this now, just when she was starting to feel like she could move on without him.

As she and Megan strolled out to her car together, Harper started to tell her what Evan had said, continuing the story in full detail on the ride home.

"Oh wow, Harper. I can't believe he said all those things to you. What do you want to do about it?"

"I don't know. I just seriously do not know what to do. I think maybe the best thing would be to do nothing. Just leave it in the past. It's too confusing to be in love with him, and it just hurts too much. I mean, how he ended it, what he said to me. Besides, it would be better if I was with some nice, slightly boring guy who I could control my

{300}

feelings around. It could actually be just the key to a happy, steady, lasting relationship."

"Sorry, Harps, but that's not your style, I'm afraid. You've always been more of a 'grab life by the balls' kind of girl. What you just described might work for some, but not you."

Harper glanced over at her with an irritated look as she pulled up in front of Megan and Luc's. "Damn it, Megan. Why do you have to be right when I'm trying to be sensible?"

"Because I'm your best friend. And I want nothing less than the deepest of passions for you. I think you should consider this whole thing with Evan. He's had a good long time to miss you and think about what he really wants. Maybe he could be your happy, steady, lasting relationship, but with all that heat to go along with it."

Harper opened her mouth to protest, but Megan held up one finger to stop her. "If Luc had given up on me when I was terrified of being with him and chased him away, I'd be on my own right now instead of being incredibly happy. Being cautious with your heart doesn't make you a bad person."

"He wasn't just cautious, he was cruel."

"As was I when I was terrified of falling for Luc. Promise me you'll at least think about it."

"I've done nothing but think about him for months now. I need to move on."

* * *

Crawling into bed later, Harper felt completely worn out. It had been a long day on an emotional roller coaster. How was she supposed to sleep after everything Evan had said? She went over his words for the twentieth time since they had stood together outside under the stars. How could someone so perfect, so romantic, also be so hard to love?

Flipping on her bedside lamp, she texted Megan. *Are you still up?*

A moment later her phone rang. "Hey. Sorry to bug you so late," Harper said when she picked up.

"It's okay, my dear. I was still up," Megan answered.

"I think I might have made the worst mistake of my life today. What if he means it all? What if he would actually love me for the rest of my life and I just basically told him to fuck off?"

"Oh, Harper, I think he does mean it. Every word of it. And it's not too late yet, but if you want him back, you need to make up your mind. He laid his heart at your feet and you stepped over it and kept going. Now, I'm not saying you didn't have reason to, because you did. But the truth is that you're doing pretty much what he did. You're pushing him away because you've been hurt and you don't want to get hurt again."

"Crap." Harper sighed, more to herself than to her friend.

"You're kind of made for each other."

"Really? So you think I should say yes to him?"

"There isn't a shadow of a doubt that you're meant to be together, Harper. You've been in love with the guy for over twenty years. And he is absolutely in love with you," Megan said.

Harper could hear Luc's voice in the background. Megan spoke into the phone. "Just a second. Luc wants to say something." She put the phone on speaker.

"Harper. It's Luc," he said.

"I figured it was you."

"You clearly need some advice from a romance expert."

"Would you be said expert?"

"Yes, of course. Listen, you need to go to him and tell him that you want him back. I had a long talk with him on New Year's Eve, and it was pretty clear that he wants to spend the rest of his life with you, and have gorgeous babies with you, and grow old with you."

"Did he say that?"

"No, but when I was talking about why I wanted to marry Megan, he had a look on his face that is only seen on a man who is so over-taken by love that he wants it all, every glorious moment of it."

"Christ, Luc, I thought you had some viable information to give me. There's no proof in what you're saying. I need proof."

"The proof was in his face. Don't you remember when you came back into the kitchen and he was just staring at you with that look in his eyes? That was the look of a man who was seeing his entire life fall into place before him while he watched you cross the room. It happens in an instant and it's easy for the untrained eye to miss it. But I caught it, Harper. That man loves you, and if you let him, he'll be the best thing that's ever happened to you. Now, we're going to hang up so you can think it over while we have sex. The kids are asleep and we both have a little energy left tonight."

Harper laughed a little as she heard Megan start to scold him before he ended the call. She sat on her bed, stunned. Luc was right. She had seen it too. The look on Evan's face that night. She'd felt something shift. But that was before he broke it off with her. Her mind swirling, Harper finally drifted off to sleep, unsure of what to do.

THIRTY-EIGHT

The next morning, Evan's first thoughts were of Harper. She had looked so beautiful the day before it made him ache. Now that he knew she was so close, not being able to be with her, and touch her, and make her laugh was torture. Checking his cellphone, he saw he had a text message. His heart skipped a beat at the thought that Harper might have sent it. It was from Luc.

> You're close but she needs proof. She may be here this afternoon for dinner. I can't say for sure. Delete this message immediately. If questioned, I will deny everything.

"Proof?" He muttered, "How the fuck do I . . ." And suddenly it all came together for him.

* * *

Harper pulled up in front of the Chevaliers', having spent the morning trying in vain not to think about Evan. It was Sunday, and Luc was preparing something extra special to celebrate their success at the wedding. The delicious food along with the fun distraction of the kids would be a welcome way to spend the afternoon.

When she arrived, she was greeted by Elliott, who ran to the door with two Nerf guns in hand. "Come on, Auntie Harper! Let's play!"

Harper grinned at him. "You sure you want to battle me? I used to be with the Navy SEALs. I'm an excellent shot."

"You were a Navy SEAL?" Elliott asked, letting his arms flop to his sides in shock.

"No, I used to be with the Navy SEALs, as in I dated two of them back to back a few years ago. They taught me some cool stuff." Harper walked into the kitchen with Elliott in tow. "Let me give this wine to the chef, so I can school you in proper Nerf-warfare techniques."

Luc greeted her with a kiss on both cheeks. "Bonjour, Harper. Megan is just upstairs changing Amelie. I assume you brought your appetite."

"You know me so well. Smells delicious in here. Now, if you'll excuse me, I need to open a can of whoop-butt on your stepson over here." Harper looked at Elliott with crazy eyes, causing him to laugh excitedly.

Ten minutes later, their game was interrupted by the doorbell. Elliott ran to the door calling for a truce while Harper reloaded from her position behind the couch. Her heart skipped a beat when she heard Evan's voice at the door.

"Hey, Elliott. How are you?"

"Good. Auntie Harper and I are having a Nerf-gun war, but you can join! I just have to find my other gun." He waved Evan in enthusiastically.

"No, I can't stay, buddy. I'm just here to talk with your auntie for a few minutes." He walked in, his eyes fixing directly on Harper as she stood up from behind the couch, her fingers gripped around the bright green gun.

She smoothed her now-wild hair with one hand while giving him a serious look. Her heart thumped with fear and longing as she stared at him. Luc and Megan, who had come into the living room to see who was at the door, waved to Evan. Megan, knowing he and Harper needed some time alone, called for Elliott to have some appetizers in the kitchen with them. The expression on her face told her son not to argue.

"Hi. Can we talk for a minute?" Evan asked in a low voice. He had on a blue dress shirt with the sleeves rolled up. His hands were jammed into the front pockets of his jeans and he looked uncomfortable. And gorgeous. Why did he have to be so damn hot? That would definitely make it harder for her to be logical about what her next move should be.

"If you wanted to talk, you probably should have called."

"I'm sorry. It's just that I don't know where you live now, and I really need to do this in person." He paused, giving her a hopeful look. "Would you be willing to come sit outside with me for a few minutes? I was hoping we could finish our conversation from last night."

She put the Nerf gun on the coffee table. "Alright."

Evan nodded and held open the door for her. When Harper walked past him, she caught a whiff of his aftershave. Why did he have to smell so damn good? Fear gripped her again, reminding her that what she had with him would only end in pain. She should say no.

She plunked herself down on the front step, straightening her black jersey-knit top. She would have to be very strong to reject any attempts he was about to make now. That would be her only chance of getting out of this unscathed. She waited until he had settled himself next to her before speaking.

"Look, I only came out here so you don't embarrass yourself in front of my friends. The answer is no. I'm sorry, but I just can't do this." Harper stared straight ahead, letting her gaze fall on a bird that was pecking at something in the grass. It would be dangerous to look at him. Tempting. And she couldn't let herself be tempted.

"I was worried that you might say that. So there's nothing I can say that would change your mind?"

"Nothing. We need to leave this in the past. There's nothing left." She glanced at him quickly, hoping to gauge his reaction in the split second she would allow herself to look at him.

She wanted to turn away again but his fingers gently touched her cheek, causing her to freeze in place long enough for him to lower his mouth over hers and kiss her. It was that same kiss he had given her the first time. Urgent, passionate, full of longing. She gasped a little and he took advantage, sliding his tongue between her parted lips, searching her mouth for some sign that she might be willing to give him another chance. Getting caught up in him, she kissed him back, matching his passion and desire. When he finally pulled away, Harper was left little more than a puddle. Her eyes stayed closed longer than she intended. Shaking her head a little, she tried desperately to summon her sense of logic.

Evan spoke before she had a chance to refuse him again. "You still so sure that there's nothing left here? Because it feels like there is." He challenged her with his words, with his eyes.

"No. You're wrong. There's nothing left. You only want what you can't have. You wanted Avery because you didn't think you could have her. Then you wanted me because you shouldn't have me, and once you had me, it didn't take that long before you were pushing me away. And you know, Evan, I just can't go down this road with you again, no matter how much I think I want to. I can't go through that kind of pain twice. So just go. Okay? Please? Take pity on me and just leave me alone so I can get back to forgetting you."

"I can't. I'm fully, completely in love with you, Harper. I want to spend the rest of my life with you. I want us to grow old together. I want a life with you so badly that it hurts to think about it. I need you so much that I would leave everything behind and move to New York or Paris or . . . or Antarctica just to be near you. I want you so badly that I would stand up with the whole world watching and promise that I'll love you forever. And I would mean it, and I know I could do it, too. If you'd let me, I'd do it."

Moving onto the steps below her, he was on his knees now in front of her. Gently touching her chin, he guided her face so that she was looking at him directly in the eyes again. "I won't ever hurt you again, Harper. When you got the job at the magazine, I pushed you away when I should have pulled you close. But I won't do it again. I was worried that you'd stay for my sake, and I didn't want to cage you in like that. But I should have told you the truth. That I've been in love with you since I saw you sitting in your backyard in a ball gown."

Harper sat quietly, staring into his eyes for a long moment. He was on his knees, making all the promises she'd been too terrified to let herself want to hear. He was saying all the things she had imagined a thousand times in the weeks since they'd parted ways. He was still the same perfectly imperfect man she had always loved, and he had come to find her so that he could declare his undying love. But she just couldn't accept. This was still too terrifying. He was also still the man who was going to hurt her again if she gave him the chance.

Shaking her head, she said, "You're just lonely, Evan, and that's not my problem." Turning her head from him, she looked down, trying to regain her strength. "The answer is no, Evan. Please go now."

"So you need proof."

Proof. Damn it, Luc. She gave him a doubtful look. "This is something you can't prove."

"I can. Come with me. I need to show you something. If it doesn't prove to you that I want to build a life with you, I'll accept *no* and leave you alone forever. I promise."

Harper bit her bottom lip, considering his words. "I can't just leave. I'm here for supper."

"They'll understand."

Harper struggled with the decision a minute before giving in. "Okay, show me. I doubt it will help, but I'll see it."

A wave of relief crossed Evan's face. "Thank you." He jumped to his feet, ran up the steps and opened the front door, calling, "I'll have her back in a bit. Or maybe tomorrow, if she says *yes*."

Harper glanced back, seeing Luc and Megan standing in the window, arms wrapped around each other, smiling at her.

As she and Evan drove along the road leading out of town and up into the hills, they were both silent. They kept stealing glances at each other, but small talk was impossible.

"I really miss you," he said finally.

Harper just nodded. She wasn't going to admit anything. Not yet. When they arrived at Evan's property, he pulled over by the metal gate. There was a FOR SALE sign hanging on it. Staring out the window, nothing she saw gave her any explanation as to what was going on. He hopped out of the truck and strode around to open her door. He held out his hand as his eyes bored into hers. "I can prove it, Harper. Come with me."

She took his hand and climbed out of the truck. He pushed the gate open and they walked through the trees.

"I don't understand. How is you selling this place proof of anything?"

"For a long time, this place was my dream, but before I knew it, it became my dream with you. The house was going to go right where we're standing, with big windows in every room so we could enjoy that view, and a long, wraparound porch so you could sit out in the rain and just breathe in the scent of it. And there would be no one here to pry or bother us. Just you and me. This was going to be our hideaway from the world. I thought it would be the perfect place to raise a couple of kids, but only if you wanted that too. I thought it would be the perfect place to grow old together. The last time I was up here was the day Blaire called to offer you your job back. I stood here, trying to figure out my life, then I went to the store and bought you this." Turning to her, he pulled a small black box out of his pocket, placing it carefully in her hand.

"I was all set to bring you here that night and ask you to marry me, but then you got the offer and I figured I should hold off. I couldn't stand the thought of getting in the way of your dreams, Harper, so I put mine on ice while I waited to see how things would turn out. It was a mistake. I should have told you the truth, but I thought I was doing the right thing. And so I pushed you away. This is my dream for us and without you, I don't want any of it. A few weeks ago, I finally gave up and I put it up for sale."

He paused for a moment, seeing her eyes glisten and her face twist up as she fought back tears.

Harper stared at the box she had yet to open. "But you said you'd never get married again."

"I know, but I was wrong. It was something Luc said on New Year's Eve that changed my mind. He said that when you find that one person you will always love no matter what, you want the world to know she is yours and that you would do anything for her. For the rest of your life. And more importantly, you want her to know. And then you walked back into the kitchen and I knew in my heart that I'd never be the same again. And I didn't want to go back to the way things were. I wanted to start my life with you. And I still do, Harper. I'll always want a life with you. But if you really don't, I'll understand and I'll leave you alone."

"I want this, Evan," she whispered through her tears. "I want all of it exactly the way you've dreamed it. I'm just so scared of it all."

Evan wrapped her in his arms and pulled her close. "I know,

but there's nothing to fear anymore. Because this is real and I'm not going anywhere. Ever. When you start feeling scared, you tell me. We'll figure it out together, okay? I'll always pull you in. I promise."

Lifting his hands to her face, he lowered his mouth to hers. Kissing her gently, carefully. His kiss was a question. Would she marry him? Would she spend the rest of her life with him? And her kiss was the answer. Yes. She would stay. She would stay forever.

Wrapping her in his arms, he lifted her up and spun her around as they smiled and laughed, their lips meeting again. Their embrace contained all of the passion and yearning and love and lust that was them together. It stopped time for a moment and then started it back up again, so that they could begin their life together. The life they would share that wasn't going to end.

"I'm going to love you forever, Harper."

"I'm so glad, because I'm going to love you forever too, Evan."

"Wait, I have one more thing for you." He pulled a small gift out of his jacket pocket. "I thought I should have one more piece of proof in case you needed it."

Harper took it and unwrapped it carefully. It was her diary from when she was a teenager, the one that had *Harper Donovan* and *Evan-from-Heaven* written on every page.

"Your dad helped me find it. It was in a box in his basement. Open it to the back page."

Inside he had written:

Harper,
I know I'm late, but sometimes saving the best for last is the only way to know it when you see it. You are my best. You are my everything.
I promise I will love you forever,
Evan

Harper threw her arms around his neck, kissing him with abandon as tears streamed down her face. They stayed like that for a long time under the warmth of the late spring sun.

For the first time, Harper was absolutely certain that she could be herself anywhere, even in a place where everyone knew about her past. She could be the successful, passionate, creative woman she was, here. She was surrounded by the truth as much as she was blanketed by the love and acceptance of her family. And the past wouldn't control her fate ever again. She would. She would live a life rich in dreams of her own making, and best of all, rich in love.

Her heart belonged here with Evan. He would shelter it from the world if she ever needed him to. He would build a solid, true home for her heart in his. And she would do the same for him.

Evan pulled back a little and smiled at her, his face full of adoration. "Should we go home?"

"We are home."

Breaking Clear

SECRET SCENES GIVEAWAY!

Need *MORE* Evan? Here's your chance!

I have put together a booklet that includes two steamy scenes that didn't end up in the novel. They are melt-your-tablet hot! Anyone who posts an honest review of the book will get a copy of the booklet—for free, of course! Here's how to get yours:

1. Post your review of *Breaking Clear* on Amazon, Goodreads, Google play, iBooks, and/or Kobo.

2. Go to my website, www.mjsummersbooks.com, to get your booklet!

Happy reading, everyone!

—MJ

Break in Two

Book 1 of the Full Hearts Series
Romantic. Witty. Sexy as hell.

A story as satisfying as the perfect man—long and thick, with all the right moves at just the right pace . . .

Thirty-one year old Claire Hatley is running from Seattle after discovering that her live-in boyfriend has traded her in for a twenty-two-year-old hostess. Devastated and alone, Claire must make a fresh start. She answers an ad to be the chef at a guest ranch just outside Colorado Springs and finds herself face to face with Cole Mitchell, quite possibly the hottest man to ever ride a horse. Common sense tells them to stay away from each other, but their attraction is not to be denied. Cole gives Claire a glimpse of what love should be, but just as she starts to trust him, the past comes back to tear them apart.

Join Claire and Cole as they embark on the stormy love affair of a lifetime.

(Oh, and for those of you with husbands or boyfriends, please tell them MJ says, "You're welcome.")

Don't Let Go

A Full Hearts Series Novella
A sweet and sexy short read

Readers fell in love with Ben and Alicia's picture-perfect marriage in *Break in Two*, but for these two, the road to a happy ending wasn't always smooth.

Alicia Williams has been in love with Ben Mitchell since he picked her up out of the mud in elementary school. But baseball-obsessed Ben has dreams to make it to the majors and see the world, and those dreams don't include the girl next door, no matter how perfect she is. Ben is forced to choose and he leaves Alicia behind—but dreams can change and regrets can grow. When Ben returns home to the ranch in Colorado Springs, trying to rediscover the man he was meant to be, will the girl he can't get off his mind still be waiting?

Join Ben and Alicia in *Don't Let Go* as they fall in love and discover that sometimes life's greatest adventure is the one you find at home.

(Best read after *Break in Two* and before *Breaking Love*)

Breaking Love

(Book 2 in the Full Hearts Series)
Seductive. Heartwarming. Passionate.

Luc Chevalier is a satisfied man—or so he thinks. His businesses are thriving, he has all the excitement, money and beautiful women any man could want. He dines at the best restaurants and stays at the most luxurious hotels as he makes his way around the globe. So why does he suddenly find himself so restless?

Megan Sullivan is a single mom with a rather ordinary life. She is comfortable with things just the way they are. She has a six-year-old son, Elliott, a cozy house in Boulder, Colorado, and a photography business that puts food on the table. Megan is on her own and she intends to keep it that way. Her ex lives hours away in Florida, providing enough space for him to feed his drug addiction without exposing Elliott to his illness.

Megan's best friend convinces her to go to Paris for a few days. Little does she know she is about to be thrust into the arms of Luc, the sexiest man ever to set foot on the Eiffel Tower. They agree to one night together and no more. In those few short hours he manages to draw out the passionate woman that Megan has carefully hidden way for years. Once she has a taste of what she's been missing, she finds it almost impossible to go back to her life as it was.

Will two people who don't believe in happily-ever-after manage to put aside their doubts and find their forever?

Join Luc and Megan as they discover that everything they never wanted is the only thing they will ever need.

COMING NOVEMBER 2015 . . .

Breaking Hearts

(Book 4 of the Full Hearts Series)
Captivating. Enticing. Charming.

Three years have passed since Trey Johnson left his family's ranch in Colorado after having betrayed his cousin by sleeping with his sexy but treacherous Brazilian girlfriend. Guilt-ridden, Trey has kept his nose to the grindstone, finishing university a year early. As he jogs down the steps after his last exam, he is shocked to discover that he is about to become a full-time father to his son, a child he barely knows.

Travelling to Brazil, Trey suddenly learns that he is about to embark on the fight of his life in order to bring his son home. Settling in for the battle, Trey finds himself unexpectedly falling for Alessandra Santos, his son's beautiful young nanny.

Alessandra, an obedient daughter and excellent student, always does what others expect. Whether it's her demanding mother or her unreasonable employer, Alessandra finds it almost impossible to say no. Now that Trey, a young, handsome American, has sauntered into her life, she will have to find her true voice or lose him forever.

Join Trey as he becomes the man and the father that he was meant to be.

Get swept away by a love story so powerful it will make your heart ache, it will make you dream, it will make you believe.

Do you love historical fiction?

Want the chance to hear news about your favourite authors (and the chance to win free books)?

Mary Balogh
Charlotte Betts
Jessica Blair
Frances Brody
Gaelen Foley
Elizabeth Hoyt
Eloisa James
Lisa Kleypas
Stephanie Laurens
Claire Lorrimer
Amanda Quick
Julia Quinn

Then visit the Piatkus website and blog
www.piatkus.co.uk | www.piatkusbooks.net

And follow us on Facebook and Twitter
www.facebook.com/piatkusfiction | www.twitter.com/piatkusbooks

piatkus